I0656761

Richard Hooker Wilmer, Frederick Augustus Mitchel

Chickamauga

A Romance of the American Civil War

Richard Hooker Wilmer, Frederick Augustus Mitchel

Chickamauga
A Romance of the American Civil War

ISBN/EAN: 9783337347901

Printed in Europe, USA, Canada, Australia, Japan

Cover: Foto ©Andreas Hilbeck / pixelio.de

More available books at **www.hansebooks.com**

CHICKAMAUGA

A ROMANCE

OF THE

AMERICAN CIVIL WAR

BY

F. A. MITCHEL

LATE U. S. A.

AUTHOR OF "CHATTANOOGA"

NEW YORK

THE STAR BOOK COMPANY

202 BROADWAY

THE MERSHON COMPANY PRESS,
RAHWAY, N. J.

N. B.—As in " Chattanooga," while the present story is purely one of love and adventure, the dates, topography, location and movements of troops referred to are given correctly. The events pertaining to the battle of Chickamauga are as nearly correct as a careful study of different records has enabled me to judge of them.

F. A. M.

CONTENTS.

v

CHICKAMAUGA.

I.

THE Army of the Cumberland is awakening. For months its thirty miles of torpid length have been marked by clusters of white tents like the rings of a gigantic anaconda. But now there is an arousing from its long period of lethargy. The tents are being struck, the men are stuffing knapsacks, rolling blankets, or swallowing from tin cups a last draught of invigorating coffee. Wagons are being loaded with all kinds of camp equipage—tents, camp cots, cooking utensils, the pine tables and army desks of the staff departments. Here orderlies are holding horses, waiting their riders, and there men are strapping blankets or ponchos behind saddles, or cramming bacon and "hard tack" into haversacks, while strikers empty the contents of the demijohn into canteens. Each regiment, as soon as formed, moves out into the road, the whole taking up the line of march by brigades and divisions.

It is the right, or head of the monster, that awakens

first. The main body of this wing moves diagonally toward the front and left, while cavalry pushes directly south to conceal the movement and produce a false impression on the enemy. All day the infantry and artillery work their way over dirt roads, the men marching at will, smoking, chatting, laughing; the Irish regiments cracking jokes, the Germans singing; all with that *esprit* which pervades an army just starting, after a long period of idleness, on a new campaign. A lashing of artillery horses, a cursing of mules, words of command, bugle calls, picket firing, the occasional boom of a gun, mingle confusedly, and in a country used only to the peaceful lowing of cattle or the songs of birds. '

So stream those men of the right, guns, caissons, horses, mules, wagons, all day long till the sun goes down. Then a halt is called, followed by the smell of burning wood from myriads of camp fires, the odor of coffee, the sizzle of bacon; while along the front is heard the cracking of rifles on the picket line.

At midnight the right is in bivouac; the center and left still slumber in long rows of tents on avenues bordered with evergreens, the accumulation of a long continued rest in one place. But this is not the midnight of headquarters. There, all is in motion. Before the house of the commanding general at Murfreesboro leaders of corps and divisions are mounting or dismounting, either having received or about to receive their dispositions. Staff officers are coming and going with verbal messages, while couriers are flying hither and thither with dispatches. Through a murky night the stream of comers and goers flows on incessantly. During the small hours a group of staff officers on duty, yet for the time being unemployed, gather about a piano while one of their number sings inspiriting songs.

At break of day many a soldier is still slumbering peacefully whose fitful sleep, for months to come, will be haunted by dreams of toilsome marches through mud and rain, of shrieking shells and pinging bullets, of Union cheers and "rebel yells"; all tinged with contrasting visions of home. At six o'clock on the center and left are heard the clear, sharp tones of a bugle. There is a movement in the army of sleepers. Masses of men pour from the tents, and swarm in the avenues. Successive bursts of cheering, like billows beating on an ocean coast, sweep the line of camps. The mist of canvas rocks unsteadily in the early shadows, then melts before the day. Throughout its whole length the Army of the Cumberland is in motion, advancing on that campaign which is to maneuver the Confederates out of Tennessee and lead up to the battle of Chickamauga.

On a road running parallel with the Cumberland Mountains, which flank the Union army on its left, a strange-looking vehicle is going at a breakneck pace toward the south. The horse is a rawboned animal with long legs and neck, while the vehicle—a buggy—is so bespattered with mud that what paint remains on it is invisible. The bottom is partly gone; the dashboard would let through a cannon ball without being injured; the springs are badly bent; the top, which is let down,—there are no props to hold it up,—is shriveled and torn, its tatters flying behind in the wind. A woman in a striped calico dress, a sunbonnet of the same material, a pair of colored spectacles on her nose, holds the reins and urges forward the horse. Yet strange looking as is the conveyance and its occupant, for that time and region there is nothing unusual in the appearance of either. The country people inhabiting that portion of Tennessee are not cultured, and uncouthness is rather the rule than the exception.

Coming to a place where she can get a full view for some distance ahead, the woman glances over the intervening space between her and the next rise in the undulating ground. Seeing nothing to deter, she drives her horse on as rapidly as she can force him to go. Her buggy careens till it is in danger of going over; she is bounced from her seat with a prospect of being sent over the dashboard; the mud flies, the horse wheezes, the buggy groans, but there is no slackening of pace.

"Go on, Bobby, go on!"

Turning a curve in the road partly hidden by trees, she sees a cavalry camp ahead. In the road an officer stands talking to a man in a farm wagon, beside whom on a board seat, its two ends resting on the wagon's sides, sits a boy of fourteen; while on a back seat, evidently borrowed from a more pretentious vehicle, is a young girl, perhaps three or four years the boy's senior.

The woman of the striped dress drove up to the

group and, drawing rein, listened to what they were saying.

"Cap," said the farmer—all officers in the Union army were called by the people of the country either Cap or Gineral or mister—"Cap, I want ter go through the lines powerful bad."

"Well, I'm thinkin', me good man," replied the officer with the brogue of an Irishman, "that's exactly what old Rosey wants to do; unless he prefers to get behind 'em and bag 'em from th' rear."

"Oh, I don't mean fightin'. I wants ter go hum peaceful."

"Can't pass ye, me good man. Oi've orders not to pass anyone south while the army is mooven. There's no need to be tellin' ye that all day. Once ought to be sufficient."

"What's thet?" cried a shrill voice from the buggy. "Y' don't mean fo' ter tell me I can't go hum?"

"I fear, me dear leddy, that ye can't, if ye live beyond our lines."

"H'm. And so you'uns hev kem down hyar ter make war on women."

"Well now, that depends on the kind of war. We've come down *vi et armis* as me old preceptor at the university used to say—God bless 'im. Like enough the *vi* is for the men and the *armis* for the women."

"I don't keer," replied the woman. "You'uns hain't got no business fo' ter come down hyar nohow. You're a mis'able set o' black abolishioners. I'm a gal 'thout nothin' ter fight with and you'uns——"

"Beauty and the beast," interrupted the officer, bowing.

"Now see hyar, Mr. Yank, I got ter go hum. Pop he's away, and mother she's sick in bed."

The officer scratched his head and thought. ,

"Well, me friends," he said presently, "Oi'm thinkin' O'll refer the case of all of yez to brigade headquarters. Would ye moind sittin' where ye are till I get an answer?"

"Reckon not," from the farmer.

"Hurry up," said the woman in the buggy. "Mother's waitin' fo' me."

The officer stepped into his tent near by and came out with a pencil and the back of an old letter. With these he proceeded to take down the information required. Approaching the buggy he said:

"Will ye plaze favor me with your patronymic"— he paused while he looked to see if she were young or old—"miss?"

"My what?"

"Your patronymic."

"Oh, talk Tennessee."

"Well, then, your cognomen."

"See hyar, Mr. Officer, ef y' want ter git anything outen me, y' want to talk squar."

"Please tell me your name."

"Betsy Baggs. 'N yours?"

"Major Burke, at your service. Are ye Union or——"

"*Rebel!*"

"Where do ye want to go?"

"Hum."

"And that is at——?"

"Dunlap."

"Why are ye here?"

"I been ter MacMinnville ter see mother's old doctor."

"There's a shorter road from MacMinnville than this; why didn't ye take it?"

The girl showed a slight confusion.

"Oh, I got a friend at Franklin College. She'uns 'n I'uns allus ben powerful thick."

After getting the data as to all the party the major called a mounted man and directed him to take it to headquarters and ask for instructions.

"Do ye know who to take it to?" he asked of the man as he was about to ride away.

"It's to the gineral I'm takin' it."

"The gineral? Man, would you get me court martialed for disregard of the regulations? Take it to the chafe o' staff, ye lunkhead, and from him ye'll get the answer. It's not the loikes o' you can approach the gineral. Moind now, and don't spind the time talkin' with the guard."

While the messenger was away the party listened to the voluble tongue of the young Confederate sympathizer in the buggy. She entered into the causes of the war, depicted the benefits of negro slavery, especially on the slave, spoke admiringly of all Confederate soldiers, and ransacked the dictionary to find words to express her loathing of Yankees.

"Come now, Miss Baggs," said the major good-naturedly. "There's a young fellow in me regiment who'll suit ye exactly. He is an Oirishman from the crown of his head to the sole of his fut. He only came over a few years ago. He is as smart as a whip. There was but one gurrel in County Cavan who could outtalk 'im. That's the reason he left Oirland."

"When I want a man I reckon I can find one right hyar outen the yarth o' Tennessee, 'thout goin' to *Oirland* ter find one. Is he red-headed?"

"Red as the linin' of an artillery officer's cape."

"What kind o' eyes?"

"Blue as a robin's egg."

"Wal, trot him out; I'll take a look at him."

"Oi'll call him meself," and the major went into one of the tents. There he found Corporal Ratigan, the man he sought.

"Corporal Rats," he said—everyone called the corporal "Rats"—"there's a gurrel out there that wants to go through the lines. Oi've sent to brigade head-quarters to find out if they'll give her a pass. I want you to make her acquaintance."

"At your service, major," said the corporal, salut-ing. And the two walked out to where the travelers were waiting.

"Miss Baggs," said the major, "allow me to pre-sint Corporal Ratigan, commonly called 'Rats' by his comrades, one of the most gallant men in the regi-ment."

Corporal Ratigan bowed and uncovered a head of hair fully up to the major's description of it. It sur-mounted one of the most honest of countenances.

There was an air of gentility about the man despite his private's uniform, and the smile with which he greeted the young woman could not have been more bewitching had he saluted a marchioness. Admiration for the strapping Irish-Yankee soldier stood big in Miss Bagg's eyes.

"How'de," she said, with something that was intended for a bow. "Yer a purty likely lookin' feller ef y' air playin' Yank. Y'd better a stayed in *Oirland* than come down hyar to make war on women."

"And have I overpainted the beautiful tint of his hair?" asked the major, laughing.

"It'd make good winter har; needn't hev no fire in th' house."

Horses' hoofs were heard down the road, and in a few minutes the messenger who had been sent to headquarters rode up.

"Where's the answer?" asked the major.

"Divil an answer did I get, major," said the man, saluting awkwardly.

"And what d'ye mean by that?"

"Well, I kem up to headquarthers and the gineral was gettin' off of his harse to go in his tint. 'Have ye anythin' for me, me man?' he asked. 'Niver a worrud, gineral,' I answered, salutin' respectful. 'What's the paper ye have in your belt?' 'It's for the chafe o' staff.' 'Well, give it to me.' 'Divil a bit, gineral; it's not for the loikes o' me to be givin' yez a paper. Oi'm instructed to give it to the chafe o' staff.' 'Give me the paper, you cussed Oirishman,' he said, 'or Oi'll sind ye to the guard tint.' 'Niver will

I be guilty of breakin' the Regulations or the Articles of War, gineral.' 'Corporal o' the guard!' yelled the gineral.

"The corporal kem and saluted the gineral, him red as Corporal Ratigan's head. 'Take that paper from that man,' he roared. Well, bein' surrounded by the guard who were at the corporal's call I surrendered."

"And thin?" gasped the major, glaring at the stupid messenger.

"And thin the gineral said, 'Go to your camp and tell Major Burke to put y' in the guard tint for twenty-four hours. And whin he sinds another orderly to me not to sind a recruit, or I'll put him in arrest.' "

"By the Howly—— Ye infernal, raw—— Did ye get no answer?"

" 'Oi'll sind an answer by a soldier who has been properly trained,' said the gineral. Didn't ye tell me right, major?"

"Corporal o' the guard!" cried the major, by way of reply.

"'Take that man," he said, when the corporal came, "to the guard tent."

As the messenger was marched away, protesting against the injustice of his treatment for obeying orders, a staff officer rode up. Taking the major apart, he instructed him to let the applicants go through, provided they would take an oath not to give any information concerning the Union troops to the enemy. With the passes he brought a suggestion from the general to send some person with one or the other of the two parties under pretense of an escort, but really with a view to discovering the proximity of the enemy. Now that the main army was moving it might be well to discover if the cavalry on its flank had fallen back. The ground was unfavorable for a reconnoissance, hence the suggestion to get the information by strategem.

The major hunted the camp for a Bible on which to administer the oath, and called on Corporal Ratigan to help him. He explained the general's request and told Ratigan that he wanted him to go with Miss Baggs. Having given the corporal a full understanding of what was required of him he went back to the party with a Bible, followed by Ratigan.

The farmer and his family were first sworn, and then the major offered to swear Miss Baggs.

"I hain't goin' t' do no swearin'," she said defiantly.

"Oi'm glad to hear that," remarked Corporal Ratigan.

"What fo', fire top?" she asked, surprised.

"I'd be breakin' me heart at partin' with ye."

"Y' hain't got no heart nohow, or y' wouldn't be in th' Yankee army."

"Don't ye believe it," exclaimed the major, "his heart's as warrum as the color of his hair. Come, young leddy, take the oath. I'd be sorry to be partin' ye from your mother, and she sufferin'."

"I won't."

"Won't ye take it for *moi sake?*" queried Ratigan with a mock appeal.

"Y'll hev ter git some 'un uglier'n you'uns ter move me. I hanker after ugly men, but you'uns ain't quite ugly enough fo' me."

"Now ye're talkin' with a seductive tongue," quoth Ratigan. "If the major will permit Oi've a mind to see ye through the line• meself without the oath."

The corporal looked slyly at the major and the major returned the corporal's sly glance.

"Very well," said Burke. "You go with her, and moind that she isn't keepin' her ois open to see things for Gineral Bragg's benefit. Miss Baggs, if ye'll just keep lookin' roit into the corporal's blue arbs ye'll get through all right, and if ye're tempted to look aside just fix 'em on his head and ye'll be blinded."

The corporal went for his horse, buckled on his revolver, and coming back started out to play diplomat; in other words to acquire knowledge by strategy.

II.

CORPORAL RATIGAN rode gallantly beside Miss Baggs, the two keeping up a constant picket firing which occasionally warmed to the dignity of a skirmish. Miss Baggs was in an excellent humor, and the corporal quite delighted at the rôle he was playing. He pretended to watch her carefully whenever anything belonging to the army was passed on the road, while he was secretly forming his plans for getting far enough on the way to determine the proximity of the enemy. He felt no suspicion as to Miss Baggs carrying information. Being on the flank of the army she would not be likely to have much information to carry. The country people were constantly passing between the lines, and considering their harrowing excuses no one except with a heart of stone could well prevent them.

"What's in the box ye have with ye?" asked Ratigan, looking at a square little box on the seat beside her. It had been covered with a shawl, which had fallen from over it, exposing it to view.

"Thet? Thet's a philosophy machine. Y' see my friend, Sal Glassick, she knows a heap o' things. She's tryen ter beat some on 'em inter my pore noddle. Reckon she won't hev no easy time."

"What branch does she teach ye with that?"

"Wal, ye see mother she's sufferin' with palsy, 'n this hyar box is a—wal, Sal, she calls it a gal—gal——"

"Galvanic battery?"

"Thet's it. Y' hit it right thar. A galvanic battery. We'uns 're goen ter try 't on mother. Lord-a-massy, what's thet?"

She directed his attention from the box to a cloud of smoke hanging over the gaps in the hills far to the west. They were crossing a mountain spur and could see it quite plainly.

"There's foightin' goen on there," remarked the corporal.

"'N you'uns air gitten licked," observed the rebellious Miss Baggs.

"How d'ye know that?" asked Ratigan, surprised that she should know anything about it.

"Oh, I reckon."

"It's a quare thing, the reckonen ov gurrels."

"Wal, ye see women hain't got the big heads men hev. Th' can't reason things out. They hev t' jump at 'em, mebbe, like ants. Ants is powerful small, but they're most times right when they reckon."

Ratigan made no reply. He was thinking that Miss Baggs did not appear to be so plain a personage as he at first thought her. He looked at her hands, encased in coarse gloves, and noticed that they were small for "poor white trash." Her attire was very cheap and her cowhide shoes did not betoken refinement; but somehow he began to gather a notion that Miss Baggs was not so dreadfully common as she appeared. The corporal came of an excellent family in his native land, and under ordinary circumstances could detect refinement. He looked for Miss Baggs to use some expression beyond the ken of a "poor white" girl, but she did not. So he dismissed the matter from his mind and began to wonder what excuse he could make to go on with her under flag of truce when she should pass the Union pickets.

"We'uns air goen slow enough ter worrit a snail," remarked Miss Baggs.

"And why should we be goen faster?"

"Whar'd y' steal thet critter?" she asked, instead of replying, looking sidewise at the corporal's mount. "It's likely 'nuff fo' Tennessee blood."

"Oh! That's United States; don't you see the 'U. S.' branded on him?"

"Can he trot?"

"He can beat anything in the brigade."

"D'ye think he can trot with this hyar critter o' mine."

Ratigan looked at her raw-boned brute and burst into a laugh.

"Wal, now, you needn't take on so. Reckon I c'd give y' a brush ef y' was minded."

"All right, me dear; here's a straight bit of road."

"Fo' what stakes?"

"A five-dollar greenback."

"Agin Confederate money?"

"With pleasure."

The corporal drew forth a crisp five-dollar bill.

And Miss Baggs put the thumb and finger of one hand
in the palm of the other under her glove, and drew
out a Confederate shinplaster.

"Who holds the stakes?" asked the corporal glee-
fully.

"You'uns."

"Divil a bit. The lady shall hold 'em."

She took the bill he handed her and gave the lines
a jerk with a "git along thar!"   "Remember, it's a
trottin' race."

Ratigan was at a disadvantage from the first.   He
did not dare to use his spurs lest his horse should
break from a trot.   Miss Baggs's animal began to reach
his lank legs out, triangulating in a lumbering fashion
that put him over the ground at no inconsiderable
speed.   The corporal did his best and kept pace
pretty well.

"Reckon my 'Bob Lee' kin knock the stuffin' outen
your critter, Mr. sojer.   Git up, Bob."

With that Bob increased the length of his triangula-
tions, increasing their frequency at the same time.
The result was that he carried the old buggy with
Betsy Baggs in it right away from the corporal.   Indeed, Ratigan fell behind steadily.   If he should
break from a trot he would lose the race, if he should
keep up his trot he would lose Miss Baggs.

Suddenly an officer appeared on the road and regarding him sternly ordered him to halt.

"Oi'm followin' the young lady, sir.   Oi'm on of-
cial business for the gineral, commandin' the ——th
cavalry brigade."

"Well, my man, you're a well-disciplined orderly; you keep the regulation forty paces to the rear. Give your horse the spur and catch up."

Ratigan, who could not well explain to an officer that he was running a race, and fearing to lose his charge, gave his horse the spur and dashed after her at a gallop. He reached her in a "blown" condition.

"Oi've lost," he cried, out of breath.

"Reckon y' have," was Miss Baggs's sole reply.

"The money's yours."

"Reckon it ar," repeated Miss Baggs.

"Yer always reckonen. Mebbe ye reckoned about the end of the race loike the ant ye were talkin' about."

At that moment they espied the outpost ahead.

"Wal, hyar we air," said Miss Baggs. "Don't want t' part from you'uns, Mr. sojer. I'm powerful bad struck hyar." And she put her hand on her heart.

"Like enough Oi can find some reason to go on with ye a bit. Oi'm all broken up meself, sure enough."

"I hopes y' kin."

"Lieutenant," said the corporal, saluting an officer who came out from the picket post. "Major Burke ordered me to see this young lady out of the lines. She has a pass to Dunlap."

The lieutenant read the pass and told Miss Baggs she might go through.

Ratigan was racking his brains to know what to do. He had been instructed to go through with Miss Baggs under some pretense, but his ingenuity when put to the test failed him.   Miss Baggs came to his relief.

"Mr. Corporal," she said, "I don't hanker ter part 'ith thet bloomen head o' har o' yourn.   Would y' mind seein' a pore lone woman ter th' Confederate lines?"

The corporal whispered a few words in the lieutenant's ear.   The result was that in five minutes four cavalry privates were placed under the corporal's orders, who held in his hand a pole cut from a tree at the side of the road, to which he had attached a white cotton handkerchief.

Then the old buggy, which rattled at every turn of the wheel and threatened to collapse at every mudhole, proceeded down the road.   Corporal Ratigan cantered alongside, while the   four   privates   followed directly in rear.

But a few miles had been traversed when a horseman—he proved to be the enemy's vedette—was seen standing in the road ahead.   As the party approached, they saw a dozen more advancing to his support.   But the Confederates evidently saw the white flag, for no other demonstration was made than the riding forward of an officer with half a dozen men to meet those who were advancing.

"What do you want?" asked the officer gruffly.

"Flag to see the lady to your lines."

"Under a commissioned officer?"

"Only meself, a corporal," said Ratigan.

"Well, you can turn about pretty quick, and get back to where you came from.   The next such flag sent out will be taken in and won't get out again."

"Captain, don't you know me?" said Miss Baggs, smiling at the officer.

"Well, upon my word. You don't mean——"

Miss Baggs put her finger on her lip.

"These men came at my request," she continued, "so I hope you will not find any fault."

The officer raised his hat, but said nothing.

"Good-morning, corporal," she said. "I'm much obliged for your trouble."

"You're quite welcome, miss."

Both parties moved away simultaneously. They had scarcely started before the corporal heard his name spoken in a woman's voice, but one with which he was not familiar.

"Rats!"

He turned and saw what must be Miss Baggs, for her dress was the same, though the head and neck were changed, standing in the buggy, her back to the horse, her face directly toward him. Her glasses were gone, her sunbonnet hung in one hand, while she held the reins in the other. Never had the corporal beheld so great a change in so brief a space of time. The jolting had disarranged a mass of dark hair which had partly fallen over her shoulders. Her eyes were black and lustrous, her complexion an olive relieved by a ruddiness on the cheek. Her superb head was set on her neck as if it had been placed there by an artist. The face was lighted by a smile of triumph — a smile so bewitching that it haunted the corporal to his dying day.

Ratigan had not recovered from his surprise before she spoke to him in a rich contralto voice, as little like that he had heard from her as a fife is like the mellow tones of an organ.

"Corporal, please present my compliments to Major Burke and thank him for me for his kindness, and tell him that when he sends another woman through the lines under pretense of keeping her eyes shut, when he has an especial purpose of his own in view, not to send an *Oirishman* for an escort." The smile on her lips broadened and showed a set of white teeth. "The *Oirish* race as diplomats are not usually successful. *Au revoir*, corporal."

There was a grin on the faces of the Confederate lookers-on, and astonishment on the honest countenance of Corporal Ratigan.

"And Rats," she continued, evidently enjoying bringing out the word with her rich voice, as one loves to roll old wine on the tongue, "when a woman desires to race, it is not always for the money up." She tossed the bill she had won toward him.

"And, Rats! don't race again with anyone with a raw-boned animal with long legs. 'Bobby Lee' is from the Blue Grass regions of Kentucky. There's something wrong about his breathing apparatus, but even with that disadvantage he can trot a mile over a good road in 2.50."

Had Miss Baggs appeared less bewitching as she stood there under the protection of half a dozen Confederate troopers, Ratigan would have turned away impatiently. As it was, she seemed to hold him by a spell.

"One thing more, my bonny cardinal flower. Tell the major that I like 'the young man from County Cavan' he has recommended to me, very much." Her eyes fairly danced. "When the war is over I hope you will look me up. Inquire for Betsy Baggs at the St. Cloud Hotel, Nashville."

With this she threw him a kiss from the tips of her fingers, which, now that her glove was removed, he noticed were white and round. There was really something sympathetic in the last glance she gave him. In it was a regret that it had been necessary for her to deceive so honest and manly a fellow. It was the final dart that pierced the Irishman's heart and completed his enthrallment.

Leaving the corporal and his men gaping in the road the party moved away. The last thing Ratigan heard was a hoarse laugh from one of the Confederates, which was rebuked by Miss Baggs and reprimanded by the officer.

The corporal led his party northward in no good humor. At the picket post he left the men he had taken with him, and rode on alone meditatively. In passing a part of the road where there was no one to hear he reined in his horse and exclaimed aloud:

"Damn it! I believe the witch is carrying important information."

The thought filled him with horror. Who was she? What was she? What was the box she called a galvanic battery? For more than an hour he had attended a rude country girl, who when under the protection of Confederate officers, bloomed into a handsome woman. He was as much chagrined at his own stupidity as he was bewildered by the cunning of Miss Baggs.

Entering camp he slunk away to his tent, and did not report the outcome of his mission to Major Burke till just before "taps." Then he only said: "Their pickets are three miles down the road beyond ours."

"Are ye shure?"

"Oi am. Oi left the young lady—Oi mean the counthry gurrel—among 'em. And the vixen blew me a kiss at parten."

"Ah, Rats, ye're a sly dog. Oi'm shure ye did your work well."

"Major," replied the corporal, "don't ye believe it. All the divils in hell if they be men are no match for a woman."

"And if they be women, Rats?"

"Then God save 'em both."

III.

ON the morning of the general advance of the Army of the Cumberland a drizzling rain set in which lasted, at intervals, during the whole campaign. Day after day the men tramped through the mire, often to lie down at night with no means of lifting themselves out of pools except by cutting the wet branches from the trees, and on these making a bed in drenched clothes. The artillery soon cut up the roads so that the guns sank to the hubs of the wheels. The right continued to march toward the left and in the direction of the base of the Cumberland plateau, where Miss Betsy Baggs and the others were passing between the lines. The Unionists were moving upon gaps in the foot hills held by the Confederates, and necessary to the latter to prevent their enemies getting on their right, and thus compelling them to leave their fortifications at Tullahoma and fight on open ground.

It was the day that the Union men attacked these gaps that Miss Baggs passed under Confederate protection, and the farmer and the two young people with him were also pursuing their route south. Fortunately for him, the farmer, being on the flank of the two armies, was not forced to pass over roads cut up by

either.   After Major Burke had administered the oath
not to divulge anything they had seen concerning the
Union forces to the farmer and the young girl in the
wagon with him (he considered the boy too young to
treat in the same way), the party were suffered to
depart and proceeded down the road.

"Jake," said the farmer, slapping the horses' backs
with the reins, "what hev y' larned at skule?"

"Larned how terp lay 'hop scotch' and 'shinny.' "

"I don't mean thet kind I mean real larnen."

"Jakey was at a great disadvantage, pa," remarked
the girl on the rear seat, "because he was obliged to
go in classes with little bits of boys.   You remember
he didn't know his letters when he went to school."

"No more did you," said the father.

"Oh, yes, I did.   I began to study them a month
before I went away, and I taught Jakey, so that he
knew something about them, too, when he got there."

"Air th' doen much talken 'bout th' war up no'th?"

"Well, it isn't at all like it is down hyar" (no South-
erner will ever change the pronunciation of this word).
"They take lots of interest in it 'n all that, but laws,
't's one thing to get up in th' morning 'n read the
papers 'bout battles 'n such things, 'n another to have
soldiers running all over y', specially taking the gar-
den truck 'n the horses outen th' barn—I mean *out of*
the barn.   Teacher, she had the hardest work to break
me from saying 'outen' for 'out of.'   It seems she
hasn't quite done it yet."   She spoke the last words
with a sigh.

"Lordy, Souri, y' talk like a fine lady compared

'ith what y' did afore y' went no'th.   Jake, would y'
like ter drive 'em?''

"Reckon.''

The father handed the reins to his son, who, considering that he had not driven a horse for a year, handled
them with considerable skill.

"How did y' leave ma?'' asked the daughter.

"Wal, yer maw she war a heap lonesome 'thout
you'uns, 'n she's been a worriten fo' fear ye'd git sick
up thar 'ith no one ter tend ter y', but sence th' time
fo' yer comen hum hez drawed nigh she's puckered
up pretty peart.''

The boom of a gun came faintly from far down on
the lower level and the cannonading heard by Corporal Ratigan and his charge began.   Taking up the
whip the countryman gave his horses a cut.

"I want ter make hum afore somep'n happens.
Thur's goen ter be a big fight 'bout Tullyhoomy.
Thur's forts all round the place 'n big guns on 'em.''

The horses trotted on briskly for a short distance,
when looking ahead the farmer could see the picket
post.   He got his pass ready and when they reached
the post an officer came out to examine it.

"Is your name Ezekiel Slack?'' he asked of the
farmer.

"Zeke Slack, yas, thet's my name.''

"And yours?'' to the girl, raising his forage cap
admiringly.

"Missouri Slack.''

"The other name on the pass refers to the boy, I
suppose.   You have a name, sonny, haven't you?''

he asked absently, while he was studying the pass. Though it is questionable if the inquiry was not intended to show some facetiousness before the pretty girl.

"Hev I got hr ?"

"O Jakey," said his sister, "don't fall back into that habit of asking questions, instead of answering them. You know how hard they tried to break you of it at school. And say 'hair,' not 'har.' "

"I got a name," said Jake. "D' y' reckon a boy, fourteen 's goen ter git on 'thout a name?"

"Well, what is it?" asked the officer, smiling.

"Jake."

"Jake what?"

"Slack," answered the farmer. "These two'uns is my children. Th' ben ter skule up in Ohio. Th' got lots o' larnen. Reckon they'll down th' old man."

"Union or Confederate sympathies?"

"Union."

"All right. Go ahead."

Leaving the picket, they came to an opening in the country which enabled them to get a view of the region lying to the west. The farmer, though desirous of getting on, could not resist a temptation to rein in his horses and watch the fighting, or the distant evidences of it, that morning going on at Hoover's Gap. Volleys of musketry were mingled with the deeper tones of cannon. Then the firing ceased for a while, when the booms began again, continued and rapid. A white smoke rose above a ridge on which Confederate cannons were shelling the advancing Union troops on the ground below. Souri Slack thought of the lives that were passing from under that smoke and covered her face with her hands.

When the sounds ceased Farmer Jack drove on, and soon reached the Confederate picket. The party were sent in charge of a trooper to the headquarters of an officer commanding a body of cavalry on the Confederate extreme left. His headquarters were in a house beside the road. It had once been in the center of a neat country place. The fences, the out-houses, the walks, had all been in excellent condition prior to the first passage of troops. Now, of the fences there was an occasional upright post left; the walks were overgrown with weeds and grass; the out-houses had nearly all been torn down. The place was a picture of desolation. Nevertheless, the general who temporarily resided there was making himself very comfortable.

The wagon drew up before the house and the con-ducting trooper sent in word to the general that a party, who had come in from the Union lines, were waiting outside, desiring permission to go on south. An order came to send the party all inside.

The three travelers entered the house to find a tall man with an iron-gray beard reclining in a rocking-chair with as much apparent unconcern as if war were simply a pastime.

"You have just come from the enemy's lines, I hear," he said to the farmer,

"Yas, sir."

"What force did you see in the region through which you passed?"

The farmer explained that he could not answer the question, inasmuch as he had been permitted to pass after taking an oath not to give any information.

"H'm. You are quite right not to answer under the circumstances," observed the general. "Did your daughter take the same oath?"

"Yas, general," said Souri.

"Surely they didn't administer an oath to a boy of your age?" he said, turning to Jakey.

"Reckon th' thought I war too little to swar," said Jakey. He thrust his hands in his pockets, a sure sign that he was steadying himself for a conflict of wits and words. But the general was not acquainted with the peculiar characteristics of Jakey Slack, and prepared to question him as unconcernedly as he would pump water from a well.

"What route did you come?" he asked of the farmer.

"I met the children at Galletin," replied Slack. "I driv 'em from thar through Lebanon and Liberty."

"Sonny," said the general, turning to Jakey, "did you pass any troops on the way?"

"Lots."

"Infantry?"

"What's thet?"

"Soldiers who walk and carry guns."

"Didn't see none o' them kind,'

"Did you see any artillery?"

"Don't know what them'uns air,"

"Men with great big guns—cannon."

"No, sir. Didn't see no 'tillery."

"Then what you saw must have been cavalry."

"Didn't see none o' them'uns nuther."

The general looked surprised.

"Then what *did* you see? That's all the arms of the service I ever heard of; and I am an old soldier."

"Critter companies."

"Oh, I see," exclaimed the general, remembering the mountain Tennesseans' name for cavalry. "How many soldiers belonging to the 'critter companies', as you call them, did you see?"

"Wal, I counted twenty, 'n thet's 's fur as I got at countin' in skule."

Souri was about to remind her brother that he had proved himself one of the best boys in the school at mental arithmetic, but desisted.

"H'm!" The general thought a moment and beat a reveille with his fingers on the arm of his chair.

"What were they doing within the Federal lines just before you left the outposts?"

"Wal, I only noticed one man, 'n he war doen somep'n very partickeler."

"What was it?"

"He war looken at the sky through a flat round thing what looked like a big squashed apple."

"Not a field glass, was it?"

"No, sir; reckon 'twasn't thet."

"Was the man of high rank?"

"Reckon he war; he had stripes on his arm."

"Tut, tut, he wore chevrons. He was only a non-

commissioned officer. Can't you describe more nearly
the object through which he was looking?''

"Wal, I think I hearn some'un call it a can—
can——''

"Not a canteen?"

"Yes, thet's it."

The general looked sharply at the boy, who looked
stolidly stupid. He determined to try another route
through which to lead Jakey's infantile mind.

"Were the troops you saw in camp, or on the
march, or in bivouac?''

"Don't know what thet ar last air; but th' trees 'n
brush war so thick I couldn' see plain.''

"Can't you tell me if you saw any infantry; soldiers who walk and carry guns, you know?''

"I never looks at them kind o' sojers," replied
Jakey contemptuously. "I only notices 'em when
they're on critters' backs."

"That will do," said the general. Then turning to
a staff officer near him, he said:

"Captain, you may pass these people South," and
added in an undertone: "Ride over to division headquarters and say that nothing has yet been obtained of
the enemy's movements in this vicinity by questioning
citizens. Only one party has come through, a farmer
with his son and daughter. The farmer and his
daughter took an oath not to give any information
concerning the dispositions of the enemy, and the boy
is profoundly stupid.''

There was a sound of hoofs without, mingled with
the rattle of wheels. Looking through an open win-

dow, an officer was seen to dismount and hand a woman from a mud-covered, paint-rubbed buggy. All recognized Miss Elizabeth Baggs. The general arose from his chair and went out to meet her at the front door. From there he conducted her into a room where they could confer together alone.

"What luck?" he inquired.

"I struck their wires within their lines midway between Murfreesboro and MacMinnville, at midnight, and no one was near. I threw my wire over the line and made my connections with my instrument. I waited till nearly daylight before any message of importance came along, though dispatches were passing all the while. At last one came in cipher. I took it down, but as we haven't the key, I fear it will avail us nothing."

"Let me see it," said the general.

Miss Baggs handed him a piece of paper on which was written:

MURFREESBORO, TENN.
June 28, '63.

Volunteers Garfield with circling between you possession turn an be cob Bumble at to get that possible by move Benjamin pony chief rapidity around that put of the hours ready shingle to notice enemy's Tullahoma your point the by of poliwog of plateau Niggard if desire and hope forward to haha move we right I command and mountain order staff.

The general read the dispatch over carefully and then, looking up at Miss Baggs, remarked:

"Balked."

"Can't it be interpreted, general?"

"I fear not without the key. It is doubtless an important dispatch, and I shall send it at once to general headquarters. If they can decipher it they are welcome to do so. I don't care to try it."

Calling an aid-de-camp the general bade him carry the message to the army telegraph station, a short distance to the rear, and repeat it to General Bragg.

"General," said Miss Baggs in an undertone, "if you will let me have the original or a copy, I will try to decipher it. I may find a clew that will aid me hereafter, though I fear it will be too late to take advantage of information contained in this one."

"Certainly. Lieutenant, return the dispatch I have given you to this lady, after it has been repeated."

The officer departed. The general turned again to Miss Baggs with a serious look.

"Do you know that you are engaged in a very hazardous service?"

"Perfectly."

"And do you understand the penalty, if caught?"

"Death, I suppose."

"There's no telling whether it would be death or a long imprisonment in the case of a woman; a man would hang."

Miss Baggs's countenance changed from an expression of indifference to one of those flashes of the superhuman attributes that lurk within the human soul.

"Am I to make anything of my life, when thousands of the South's defenders are giving theirs every day? Have I not seen our homes laid desolate? Have I not seen my brothers, my friends, those I have loved, those I have played with as children, cut down by either the bullet or disease? For months I devoted myself to the care of the sick in the hospitals. There I learned to dread a long continuance of this struggle. There I conceived the idea of doing something to win success for our armies by giving them an advantage not possessed by the enemy. I consulted one high in rank. 'How can I give my life to the best advantage?' I asked. 'In the secret service.' 'Point the way.' 'Do you know anything of telegraphy?' 'No, but I can learn.' 'Go and study a month, and then come to me.' For a month I studied night and day. I learned to read words from the clicking of the keys as readily as I can read letters. I returned to my adviser. You know the rest."

The general paced the floor with a clouded brow.

"I dread a catastrophe," he said, "in the case of one inspired by such noble sentiments. I dread to see a woman exposed to ignominy—perhaps death."

"If that time comes, general, God will give me strength to bear it."

The general was silent a moment, and then asked abruptly:

"Is your brother aware of what you are doing?"

"He is."

"And he consents?"

"He does not. We are individuals. He is one of the noblest of the South's legitimate defenders, but he is not responsible for my acts—one of its illegitimate machines."

"The pitcher that goes often to the well is at last broken."

"Then, someone else will spring up to carry on the work."

"God grant that the day may be far distant; that it may never come. I can hardly approve of it, though you are working in my cause."

"General," said the woman, her face again lighting as if inspired by some absorbing thought, "each side has an organized secret service. What general would dare report to his government that he had acquired information which would enable him to destroy his enemy, but it had been obtained by illegitimate means and he would not take advantage of it? Yet what general would care to be called a spy himself? We are engaged in a terrible struggle. Before its close any and all means will be used to conquer. Cities will be burned, vast districts will be laid waste. Must I cease to employ the most effective method of all, because I am doing illegitimate work? Is my work more illegitimate than trying to conquer a people fighting for their independence?"

The general made no reply for a time.

"Yours is a singular family," he said presently. "You are all alike, and yet you differ."

"We are united in the cause, we differ as to the means."

The interview was interrupted by the ringing of a dinner bell in the hall. The general called a negro and bade him show Miss Baggs to a room upstairs, to which she retired for a few minutes. The servant brought in her belongings from the buggy, together with the little box. When she came downstairs the party were waiting for her before going in to dinner. Souri, who had seen her covered by the sunbonnet and her eyes screened with glasses, was astonished. She saw a woman three or four years older than herself, the beauty of her head and neck contrasting with the homeliness of her costume. Miss Baggs noticed Souri's surprise, and going up to her took both her hands and kissed her cheek.

"You sweet child," she said feelingly, "you can't get over my appearance when you met me on the road this morning, can you? What a 'fright' I must have seemed to you! I don't care for those Yankee officers, but bless your innocent heart, I can't bear to have shocked you."

Souri did not reply in words, but she looked at Miss Baggs admiringly.

"Don't think hard of me," the latter went on, drawing Souri aside and motioning the rest to go on into the dining room, "I do only what I believe to be a duty, for you must suspect that I keep a secret. You could not play a part beneath you, child; you are too loving, too innocent, and you wonder how any other woman can."

"I did once."

"When?"

"Before I went to school."

"For your country?"

"No."

Miss Baggs looked into Souri's deep eyes, and asked softly:

"For love?"

Souri dropped her eyes to the floor, but her questioner, who by this time had put an arm around her, received no reply.

"Come," she said, "let us not torture each other. I see we both have our secrets."

She led the way to the dinner room, where the general and his staff were standing waiting for the two women. The party were joined by Farmer Slack and Jakey, and all sat down at a signal from the general.

It was a singular mixture of people about the board. All were Confederates except the Slacks, and their Union sentiments were soon discerned. In a moment the general and his staff grew reserved. Not so Miss Baggs. Seeing that Souri, with her natural sensitiveness, felt the change, she treated her with far more attention than before.

"Never mind, my dear," she said sympathetically, looking reproachfully at an officer who referred slightingly to the "Union ruffians" of East Tennessee. "We were all Federal once, and nobody knows but we may have to be again. The country is large enough for all. We are engaged in settling the matter, and have no time for recriminations. All we have to do is to keep our wits and strike hard. They say all's fair in love and in war."

"Which air Rats?" asked Jakey, looking up at her with a pair of little black eyes that glistened with— she could not tell what. If forced to express it she would have used some such paradoxical expression as "glistened with stupidity."

"What do you mean, you *enfant terrible?*" she asked, slightly coloring.

"Is Rats love or war?"

"Who's Rats?" asked the general.

"He means Corporal Ratigan, general, a splendid specimen of a young Irishman, whom I was obliged to hoodwink this morning in the Yankee camp. I admire the Irish; they are so ingenuous. But we all admire those unlike ourselves."

"What's hoodwinken?" asked Jakey.

"Well, I was obliged to appear pleased with him."

"Looken at him outen yer eyes that-a-way?"

"Come, come, you little fiend, if you say another word, I'll turn you over to the general to be dealt with summarily for interfering with Government agents." She laughed, but there was a lack of heartiness. Evidently Jakey had touched some chord that twanged discordantly.

IV.

A GUERRILLA'S HOME.

"A DISPATCH for you, general."
An aid-de-camp entered, followed by a tall,
bronzed Confederate cavalryman with very muddy
boots, and a Southern sombrero on his head. In his
hand he carried a sealed envelope, on the left-hand
corner of which was printed "OFFICIAL BUSINESS."

"Why not bring it yourself?" asked the general,
evidently put out at being interrupted at dinner.

"The messenger says that he was instructed to
deliver it to no one but yourself. It is from general
headquarters."

The man stalked in, his accouterments rattling as
he did so, and removing his hat, handed the general
the communication. He opened it, and seeing that it
was in cipher, handed it to a member of his staff who
possessed the key, and directed him to unravel it. It
read as follows:

HEADQUARTERS ARMY OF TENNESSEE,
June 27, 1862.
*To General ———, Commanding Cavalry on extreme
right.*
Mlr rrwec lrddrx mexrr lzi krxn m nbpy
mfsfhse ut tixwrax dari sm mirwc gb igjq

vvim kltvq gs ljssga mikkingmfy fc lvdzvkwvgc.
Egzi jwpxy tx bagw.*

BRAXTON BRAGG, Comd'g.

Scarcely had the·general given the dispatch over for interpretation when another from the same source, which had come by telegraph, was handed him also, evidently an inextricable jumble of letters. This too was taken up by the cipher officer. In the course of half an hour he handed interpretations of both to his chief. The first read as follows:

The enemy having taken the gaps I will abandon

---

* To decipher this dispatch take as key words "Tennessee River." Run the eye down the column at the top of which is the first letter of the key-term till the first letter of the dispatch to be deciphered is reached. To the left in the column will be found the first letter of the interpretation. Thus :

T e n	n e s s e	e r i v e r
m l r	r r w e c	l r d d r x

```
m under t at left of table is t
l    "    e   "      "      "   h
r    "    n   "      "      "   e

r    "    n   "      "      "   e
r    "    e   "      "      "   n
w    "    s   "      "      "   e
e    "    s   "      "      "   m
c    "    e   "      "      "   y

l    "    e   "      "      "   h
r    "    r   "      "      "   a
d    "    i   "      "      "   v
d    "    v   "      "      "   i
r    "    e   "      "      "   n
x    "    r   "      "      "   g
```

This process is repeated to the end of the dispatch. This code my present line. Be ready to form rear guard to troops retreating by University. Move south at once.

Here is the second:

Enemy's telegram in cipher received   Cannot Miss Baggs secure information of the enemy's intentions as to following this army across the Tennessee? Such information would enable us to be prepared if he attacks in concentrated form or cut him up in detail if he divides.

The general gave the two messages a few minutes'

---

was used by the Confederates during most of the period of the war.

KEY.

```
26 25 24 23 22 21 20 19 18 17 16 15 14 13 12 11 10  9  8  7  6  5  4  3  2  1
 1 a  b  c  d  e  f  g  h  i  j  k  l  m  n  o  p  q  r  s  t  u  v  w  x  y  z
 2 b  c  d  e  f  g  h  i  j  k  l  m  n  o  p  q  r  s  t  u  v  w  x  y  z  a
 3 c  d  e  f  g  h  i  j  k  l  m  n  o  p  q  r  s  t  u  v  w  x  y  z  a  b
 4 d  e  f  g  h  i  j  k  l  m  n  o  p  q  r  s  t  u  v  w  x  y  z  a  b  c
 5 e  f  g  h  i  j  k  l  m  n  o  p  q  r  s  t  u  v  w  x  y  z  a  b  c  d
 6 f  g  h  i  j  k  l  m  n  o  p  q  r  s  t  u  v  w  x  y  z  a  b  c  d  e
 7 g  h  i  j  k  l  m  n  o  p  q  r  s  t  u  v  w  x  y  z  a  b  c  d  e  f
 8 h  i  j  k  l  m  n  o  p  q  r  s  t  u  v  w  x  y  z  a  b  c  d  e  f  g
 9 i  j  k  l  m  n  o  p  q  r  s  t  u  v  w  x  y  z  a  b  c  d  e  f  g  h
10 j  k  l  m  n  o  p  q  r  s  t  u  v  w  x  y  z  a  b  c  d  e  f  g  h  i
11 k  l  m  n  o  p  q  r  s  t  u  v  w  x  y  z  a  b  c  d  e  f  g  h  i  j
12 l  m  n  o  p  q  r  s  t  u  v  w  x  y  z  a  b  c  d  e  f  g  h  i  j  k
13 m  n  o  p  q  r  s  t  u  v  w  x  y  z  a  b  c  d  e  f  g  h  i  j  k  l
14 n  o  p  q  r  s  t  u  v  w  x  y  z  a  b  c  d  e  f  g  h  i  j  k  l  m
15 o  p  q  r  s  t  u  v  w  x  y  z  a  b  c  d  e  f  g  h  i  j  k  l  m  n
16 p  q  r  s  t  u  v  w  x  y  z  a  b  c  d  e  f  g  h  i  j  k  l  m  n  o
17 q  r  s  t  u  v  w  x  y  z  a  b  c  d  e  f  g  h  i  j  k  l  m  n  o  p
18 r  s  t  u  v  w  x  y  z  a  b  c  d  e  f  g  h  i  j  k  l  m  n  o  p  q
19 s  t  u  v  w  x  y  z  a  b  c  d  e  f  g  h  i  j  k  l  m  n  o  p  q  r
20 t  u  v  w  x  y  z  a  b  c  d  e  f  g  h  i  j  k  l  m  n  o  p  q  r  s
21 u  v  w  x  y  z  a  b  c  d  e  f  g  h  i  j  k  l  m  n  o  p  q  r  s  t
22 v  w  x  y  z  a  b  c  d  e  f  g  h  i  j  k  l  m  n  o  p  q  r  s  t  u
23 w  x  y  z  a  b  c  d  e  f  g  h  i  j  k  l  m  n  o  p  q  r  s  t  u  v
24 x  y  z  a  b  c  d  e  f  g  h  i  j  k  l  m  n  o  p  q  r  s  t  u  v  w
25 y  z  a  b  c  d  e  f  g  h  i  j  k  l  m  n  o  p  q  r  s  t  u  v  w  x
26 z  a  b  c  d  e  f  g  h  i  j  k  l  m  n  o  p  q  r  s  t  u  v  w  x  y
```

consideration, and then dismissing the aid who had interpreted them, directed him to inform Miss Baggs that he would like to see her.

When she entered the general handed her the inter-preted copies of the two dispatches.

"Here is a more important work for you than any you have yet attempted," he said.

She read both the dispatches and then thought a few minutes.

"I am ready to undertake it, general," she said, "but without much hope of success. I must first suc-ceed in taking off a message in which the plan of the Yankees is given, or hinted at so clearly as to be inferred, and then it must be interpreted, for it will surely be in cipher."

"If you could succeed in both you would insure us victory in the west, and that would be half the battle to the cause."

"I will undertake it."

"You will be exposed to a frightful danger."

"You know, general, that I have devoted my life to this work. I consider that as already sacrificed."

"We move from here at once, as you see by the order just received."

"I will go with you a part of the way and watch an opportunity to slip back behind the Union lines."

With that Miss Baggs went out and the general began his preparations to cover the retreat of the right of the Confederate army.

No further attention was paid to Farmer Slack and

his family. Evidently there was business of greater importance on hand. They went out on to the door-step, where they stood wondering what was going on about them. Everyone was stirring. An orderly dashed up to the door leading an officer's horse saddled and bridled. An aid ran out of the house, and mounting in hot haste rode away. A man from an upper window called out to him:

"What's up?"

"They've secured the gaps."

"Which?"

"Liberty and Hoover's. All of 'em."

"Well, what of it?"

"What of it? It means retreat." And before the last word was spoken he was out of sight.

In a few minutes a bugle was heard. Its tones had scarcely died away before the camp was alive with men preparing to move.

The farmer determined to get his children into the wagon as soon as possible. He had been given his pass, which for the present at least was likely to be of little use, as he would simply follow the army. The party lost no time in getting to the wagon and into it, and drove down the road. But they were too late. The way was choked with horsemen and wagons and they were soon brought to a halt. The general dashed past with his staff, and who should be by his side, her striped dress covered with a gray riding skirt, a sombrero on her head, with a jaunty cock's feather encircling its crown, but Miss Baggs. Seeing the farmer's wagon waiting by the roadside, she reined in "Bobby Lee" beside Souri and took her hand.

"Good-by, my dear. I trust that your innocent heart will not have to suffer more than the rest of us during the continuance of this fearful struggle. You know we are all being tried in a fiery furnace. We'll meet again; I know it. If you ever need any help or protection when our army is near, hunt up Betsy Baggs."

"Whar's th' chicken coop?" called Jakey, as she rode away.

"What chicken coop?"

"Th' one on wheels."

"Oh! The buggy," she said, smiling. "I left that for the Yankees to pick up when they come along."

"Rats 'll be ridin' inter it, I reckon."

"If he can find it, he's welcome to it," and with a laugh she dashed after the rest.

Farmer Slack only succeeded in getting a few miles on the way before nightfall, then coming to a small village he made up his mind that it would be better to sleep there than attempt to go on through a country being abandoned by one force to be immediately occupied by another. He knew well the crowded condition of the roads, and the perils of night travel. So singling out a house beside the road, which was the main street of the place, and seeing a woman standing in the door, he asked if she would give him and his party a night's lodging.

"Reckon I kin keep you'uns, but hain't got no stablen fo' th' critters."

"Oh, I kin find a place fo' them'uns," said Slack, and handing out his daughter she went into the house with Jakey, while the farmer drove off to find shelter for the horses.   Jakey wished to go with him, but his father bade him stay with Souri.

The woman of the house was depressed.   She was not strong, and the continued successive occupation of the country, by Union and Confederate troops, for more than a year, had completely worn her out.

And now another shifting was at hand.   At first she had spoken her sentiments freely—they were with the Confederacy—but lately she had come to endeavoring to find out the sentiments of strangers before betraying her own.   Wondering whether she was harboring Unionists or Secessionists, she began to question Jakey.

"Reckon you'uns live nigh 'bout hyar, don't y', boy?"

"Nigh onter th' Sequach."

"Let me fill that kettle for you," said Souri, seeing the woman about to take up a wooden bucket she was scarcely able to lift.   The woman suffered her, and went on making inquiries of Jakey.

"Thur mixed over thar; some's Union 'n some's Secesh.   Which air yer paw?"

"Wal, I ben ter skule a year 'n paw he mought 'a* changed sence I went away."

"Don't say 'mought,' Jakey dear," said Souri.

The woman looked at Jakey inquiringly.

"Y' couldn't 'a' larned much at-skule, ef y' reckon a man's goen ter change sides in this hyar fight.   Th' git wusser 'n wusser. Still, ef ye'd a ben hyar, ye'd a larned thet. Reckon y' ben no'th to skule."

"We *have* been north, in Ohio," said Souri, as she put the kettle on the stove.

The mistress of the house was entirely alone save for her children, who were all small. She managed to get up a fair supper for her guests—though Souri did most of the work in preparing it. Notwithstanding the soldiers had drained everything visible in the house, the larder was by no means depleted. If people who live for a long time in a country overrun by troops don't learn to keep a bite for a hungry day concealed in a safe place, they are not remarkable for brightness. At any rate, the hostess suddenly appeared in the kitchen with a good bit of bacon, which seemed to come from the sky. In a few minutes it was frying in a skillet, and Souri took some coffee from her bag, which she began to grind. It was not long before all were around the table, the hostess drinking the first cup of real coffee she had drank in a year.

By dark the Southern troops had vanished from the place, and the inhabitants began to dread the coming of another army. At nine o'clock all was quiet and the denizens of the house in which the Slacks rested were in bed. There were four rooms. One was given to Souri, one to Farmer Slack and Jakey, a third being occupied by the woman and her children. The fourth was parlor and kitchen combined.

There is something dismal in a country place on the first night after the departure of an army, whether they be friends or foes. While it is present there is some feeling of protection. Officers are there to restrain lawlessness. But upon their departure the country is left in a rear more to be dreaded than the presence of soldiers. At the front there is no lawlessness, unless it be the lawlessness which exists between armed enemies. All is at the highest possible tension. Two thin lines of men hold all about them at the muzzles of gleaming rifles. Behind this line is the main force, in the midst of which the generals govern with autocratic military authority. But in the wake of an army comes a flow of refuse as in the channel of a river suddenly cleared in logging time. No one commands. There is either confusion or nothing; and in the South during the Civil War the rear was infested by the land pirates, the dreaded guerrillas, who respected neither man, woman, nor child, and whom no man respected.

It was midnight at the little frame house where slept the Slack family. Farmer Slack was awakened by a pounding at the front door. Then he heard the woman by whom they were sheltered get up, and going to the door let someone in. The partition was thin and every word that was said could be plainly heard.

"Lordy, Ben, whar did y' come from?" asked the woman.

"'Tullahomy."

"Whar y' goen ter?"

"Up inter the mountings."

"What fur?"

"Ter lay low till the armies move on south. Then we'uns 're goen ter hang in the tailens of the Yanks. Thur's better feedin' than thur is behind Confederates."

"O Ben, I wish you'd stop this business. Go 'n jine one o' the armies, I don't keer which; only stop this kind o' work."

"Polly, you know I've been driv to 't. What have they left us? Nothin' but this house. Ef I didn't rake among the refuse that the Yankees leave behind 'em whar w'd you 'n th' children be?"

"But why air y' leaven now, Ben? What does 't all mean, the men goen south? Hain't th' goen ter fight at Tullyhomy?"

"Ther gitten outen Tullyhomy this very minute."

"How d'ye know?"

"I kem from thar this afternoon. The trains were goen outen the place loaded with supplies. What's them things doen thar?"

He pointed to some of the belongings of the Slack family. The farmer could hear the woman caution her husband to speak low; but by that time Slack's ear was at a crack.

"Ther's a family hyar stayen all night," she whispered.

"Any critters?"

"Two; but I don't want y' ter take 'em, Ben. It's onnateral. Thur's a sweet young gal ez helped me git supper, 'n I wouldn't hev nothin' happen to her fur the world."

"I won't take thur critters tel after y' git me some-

p'n ter eat.   Come, be lively, my dear, I hevn't hed
a squar meal 'n two days.''

"Whar's the gang?''

"I left 'em a mile t'other side o' th' town.   We got
ter git inter th' mountings afore th' Federals come
along.   Whar air the young'uns?''

"In thar.''

The farmer could see the man go into a room into
which the candle from the one adjoining cast a dim
light.   The father bent over the sleeping little ones.
He said not a word, but Slack could see upon his face
what he would say:

"My home is broken up.   I am a vagabond—a
wreck.   If caught by either side, I would be sent out
under care of a file of soldiers, told to run for my life
and be shot down.   These innocent children must
suffer with the rest.   They will grow up to point to a
father who, from an honest man, became a guerrilla.
My wife is breaking down and will not last long.   If
I live to the close of the struggle I shall doubtless
come back to a heap of ashes where this house stands.
For when they learn to whom it belongs they will
burn it.''

The man put his lean face down beside the round,
warm cheek of a child and groaned.

"Jakey!'' whispered Farmer Slack.

Jakey awakened, but could not make it known,
because his father had clapped his hand over his
mouth.

"Be still, my boy, till I git yer clothes.   Don't yer
make no sound fo' yer life; thur's guerrillas in th'
house,''

The farmer got Jakey's clothes and his own. They put them on, using all the caution possible. Then the farmer took his son's hand and led him on tiptoe to the open window. Once there he took him up in his arms and, passing him through it, dropped him on the ground a few feet below. Then Slack got through himself and dropped beside Jakey.

"Now for the stable, my son."

Going across some vacant lots they reached the stable and took out both the horses.

"Jake," said the father, "I'm goen to the head-quarters of the Federals. I want yer to stay 'n take keer o' yer sister."

"Souri don't need no one ter take keer o' her."

The farmer went back into the stable, leaving Jakey to hold the horses, and brought out a saddle and bridle.

"Wal, Jake," he said presently, "she's a gal 'n may need y'."

"What yer goen fo'?"

"T' tell 'em the Southern men air gitten outen Tullyhomy. 'T may make a lot o' differ ter th' cause."

"Why can't *I* go 'n do thet?"

The farmer made no reply; he went on equipping the horse for a ride; but he was thinking. After all, wouldn't a boy have a better chance to get through than a man. He had great confidence in Jakey's abilities in this direction, for they had been tested long before, nearer the beginning of the war. Then he disliked to leave his daughter without protection in a lawless territory.

"Jake," he asked at last, "do y' think y' c'd do 't?''
"Reckon."

"I kin put y' on th' road 't Manchester. Thar or before y' git thar y'll find Yankees. But yer powerful little fo' sich a job." And the farmer looked at his son undecidedly.

"Do y' think I'm a babby ter be rocked in a cradle?"

"No, Jakey; yer a 'markable little chap. Thur's not 'nother boy o' your age livin' I'd trust to carry this message. I reckon I'll let y' try it."

Slack took Jakey up in his arms and sat him on the horse. Then he shortened the stirrups till all the holes in the straps were exhausted, when he cut new ones, making the length a proper one for Jakey's little legs.

"Now, Jake," said his father, in a tone that bespoke a desire to put resolution into himself and the boy at the same time, "tell th' Federal general that a guerrilla kem to the house whar we war sleepen, and tole his wife thet the Southern men air gitten outen Tully-homy. He kem from thar this afternoon. 'N, my boy, ez I ofen tole y' afore, remember yer a Unioner, 'n hain't afraid o' nothin'. Thar's th' road."

"Tom, you git."

V.

CARRYING THE NEWS.

HAD not Jakey Slack possessed a stout heart he would have quailed at pushing out in the middle of a dark night on a road of which he had no knowledge, and possessing the disadvantage of being occupied by neither Union nor Confederate troops. Between the rain and the artillery and the wagons, the roads were all cut to pieces. Water stood everywhere, and often where the way was over a depression in the ground, it was necessary to pass through small lagoons. This, in the daytime, when one might keep the road by observing the fences—when there were any—would not have been so difficult, but overshadowed by the great black wings of night there was absolutely no guide, save by feeling underfoot, or an occasional glimmer ahead indicating that the way lay through an opening in the forest.

Tom floundered along at a very slow pace. Jakey found it not only difficult to keep him in the road, but impossible to keep out of mudholes when on it. Now Tom's fore legs would sink into a soft spot and again would splash into a deep rut; or one leg would be in the rut while the other was on the higher ground. Then he would flounder, while Jakey held on to the saddle with all his strength, to keep from being thrown off by Tom's writhings. All the while a drizzling rain was slowly working its way through Jakey's jacket to get at the skin. The boy tried to guide his horse for a while, but finally concluded that Tom was far better qualified to find his way than he was himself, and dropping the reins on the pommel of the saddle, turned his undivided attention to keeping his seat. Every now and then Tom would stop, and look about him, as much as to say: "Jakey, I don't like the looks o' things at all." But if Jakey understood him he made no comment on the remark. He had placed Tom in command and did not propose to interfere.

Along the way there were signs of an occasional camp fire, which Jakey assumed doubtless warmed guerrillas. But Jakey was not so much afraid of guerrillas as they were of him. At times when they would hear his horse's hoofs beating on the road or splashing through water, Jakey could see them trying to cover the embers, or kick out the fires with their boot heels. No one would ever suspect any save a troop of cavalry to be traveling that road at that time of night and through so much mud and water. Jakey paid no attention to these marks of life by the way, but suffered Tom to grope through the darkness. True, he did not know but at any moment some bushwhacker, supposing him to be alone, would put a bullet through him in order to discover if he had any valuables about him, or more likely with a hope of becoming possessed of a good pair of boots—a necessary luxury in the South in those days—but the thought was no more terrifying than a tree looming specter-like beside the road. It was too dark to distinguish the true character of any object, and all took on fantastic shapes, especially when touched by the tints laid on by Jakey's imagination.

Just before morning the darkness grew thicker. Tom had for several miles proved himself worthy of the confidence reposed in him and had kept the road, but all of a sudden he brought up against a snake fence.

Jakey was discouraged. He knew that Tom had lost the road, and as for himself, he did not feel competent to find it again. Bringing the horse sideways to the fence he slid off onto the top rail and then down onto the ground. Holding the reins and leading Tom,—for he dared not leave him lest he might not find him again,—the boy groped around for a while looking for the road. It was of no use. Go where he would there were only stumps and grass, every hollow being filled with water.

He thought of lying down in a fence corner to sleep till morning. But he did not like to do this, for fear that, once asleep, he would not wake up till late the next day; and then the Southern army might be away from Tullahoma with all its stores, and perhaps there were a great many other advantages they would gain that caused Jakey—being a good Union boy—to wince, though he could not name them. But there seemed no alternative; it could not be more than two hours before daylight would show him the road, and he reluctantly concluded to go into bivouac. As he was looking for a good, broad, flat rail to stretch himself on, Tom put his nose over his shoulder affectionately and rested it there.   Never before had Jakey felt so deeply any interchange of sympathy with a dumb brute.

"Tom, ole critter," he said, putting his arms about the horse's neck, "this air lonesome."

And Tom seemed to respond as plainly as if the words were spoken:

"Jakey, you bet."

Maybe Tom had an object in view more important than an offer of sympathy.   Maybe he had something to communicate.   At any rate, as Jakey stood with his arms around the lowered neck and looking over it, he espied a light.

"Golly, Tom!" he exclaimed, "I reckon y' sor 't."

In a moment he had climbed the fence and had regained his place in the saddle.   Then pointing the horse's head directly for the light with a "Git up, Tom," rider and horse were soon away in the direction of its appearance.

Suddenly there was an ominous click, which in the stillness of the night sounded with all the distinctness of the cocking of a gun.

"Who comt dare?"

"Mister, can y' put me onto the road?"

"Who you vas?"

"I'm a boy, I air."

"Vat you vant?"

"I want 't go to Manchester."

"Vat for?"

Jakey thought a moment before replying. The question occurred to him, was this surely a Union picket. No Confederate would be likely to challenge with a German accent.

"I've got some information for Mister Rose—Rose—what's his name."

"Sheneral Rosecrans?"

"Yes."

The picket being convinced from Jakey's voice that he was a child, called out: "Comt up here."

Jakey jogged Tom, and endeavored to find the man, but he was ensconced behind a little runnel in a clump of trees, and Jakey couldn't get at him.

"Vy you not comt nearer?" asked the picket sharply.

"Why hain't I got cat's eyes?" replied Jakey. "Oh, thar y' air, air y'? Nobody hain't goen ter shoot 'thout finden y', 'n nobody hain't goen ter find y' 'cept somebody what's used ter hunten in th' dark."

"Comt along mit me, young vellar."

The picket put Jakey on the road, which was not a hundred yards away, and led him to the light he had seen. It proved to be a smoldering fire of a picket post. A lieutenant was there and a dozen men, some sitting on the roots of trees, leaning against the trunks, or against stumps dozing, while others huddled about the fire, which was dying for want of fuel, since all the dead wood lying about had been consumed.

"Vat you haf dare?" asked the lieutenant, seeing the picket come in, followed by Jakey seated on Tom

"You vasn't trifen in py a poy like dot, vas you?" asked a man lying on his stomach by the fire.

"I want to go to headquarters," said Jakey.

"Vat for?"

Jakey went through the explanation he had made to the picket.

"Corporal," said the lieutenant, "take him to de guard tent and durn him ofer."

Jakey was not aware what being turned over meant, but he followed the corporal without question. Had he been familiar with soldiers' expressions he would have known that everything a soldier is responsible for must be turned over to someone else before his responsibility ceases. The boy was led for more than a mile to a cavalry camp. By this time there was a glimmer of coming day, and objects were gradually becoming visible. As they reached the camp the "officer of the day" was starting out to ride along the picket line. Seeing Jakey led in, he rode up to him and began a fire of questions. All these troops were Germans, and everyone spoke with the German pro-nunciation. Jakey waited till the officer and the sen-try had exhausted the vocabulary of German-English words, and then informed the former that he had some very important information of the enemy's move-ments, that he wished to deliver to the proper person.

"Vat is it?"

"I'll only give it t' th' general."

"Vat sheneral?"

"Any general what ought ter know 't."

"Vill a colonel vat acts as prigatier-sheneral do?"

"Reckon."

"All right. Corporal, dake him to prigade head-quarters."

And the officer rode off to perform his morning duty of a six or eight mile ride before breakfast.

Jakey was led over a stubble field which had not been planted since the previous season, and brought before a group of half a dozen tents, the headquarters of the colonel commanding the ——th cavalry brigade. The colonel had not yet risen. Jakey's conductor explained to the sentinel on post that the boy had important information, whereupon the sentinel shouted, loud enough to wake the whole army: "Corporal of the guard!" The summoned soldier came and it was explained to him that Jakey had important information. The corporal went off to fetch the officer of the guard.

"What you want, sonny?" asked that person when he arrived, buttoning a coat he had just put on.

"I don't want nothin'."

"Oh, you don't. I thought you did."

"Reckon I got somep'n you'uns want, but I'm gitten tired answeren questions 'bout 't."

"Well, what is it, my little man?"

"I ain't no little man. I'm a boy."

"Can't you tell me what you have for us?" asked the officer, smiling.

"Can't tell nobody but somebody big."

"I don't know anybody bigger than our chief of staff about here. I'll call him."

So the chief of staff was called up and informed that Jakey had information of the enemy.

By this time Jakey began to fear that by the time he could get in his information to the commander of the army, General Bragg would be across the Tennessee River, but he was doing his duty as best he could, so he waited, trusting that along this line of red tape he would at last find some end. He had reached that point. The chief of staff called up the colonel commanding, who suddenly appeared at the tent door in a pair of trousers and a woolen shirt.

It was evident from the moment the colonel espied Jakey sitting on old Tom in front of the tent, and Jakey espied the slender figure of the colonel with his blue eyes and light hair, that they had met before. Not only that they had met, but that they must have been united by some cord of great durability. There were two exclamations like pistol shots.

"Big brother!" from Jakey.

"Little brother!" from the colonel.

Colonel Mark Maynard strode up to the boy, took him in his arms, and Jakey might have as well been in the embrace of a bear for a time, while not a word was spoken. Then there was a fusillade of questions and answers, after which the colonel took Jakey into his tent and sat him on his own camp cot. Jakey lost no time in giving a brief account of his trip from school, how he had slept at the guerrilla's house, and how his father had heard of the evacuation of Tullahoma.

The colonel, throwing open the tent flap and seeing his chief of staff outside, called him in.

"Captain," he said, "ride over to corps headquarters, and say that a boy has just come in, who is sent by his father to say that he slept last night at the house of a guerrilla, who told his wife, not knowing that he was overheard, that they are getting out of Tullahoma. Say that the information is perfectly reliable, as it has been brought by a Union boy who went with me on my most important mission when I was a scout, and rendered me, on that occasion, the most valuable service a human being can render another. Ride at once. Never mind the division commander. There's no time to spare for army etiquette. Go."

The captain saluted, and without waiting for his own horse to be saddled, mounted the horse of an orderly and dashed away.

VI.

TULLAHOMA.

COLONEL MAYNARD was ordered to push forward down the road from Manchester toward Tullahoma in order to test the truth of Jakey Slack's information. Jakey begged permission to go with him, but the colonel told him that he had better go back to his father and sister. Jakey argued that he could as well return from Tullahoma, if they should reach it, and if not, from any point where they might halt. The colonel at last consented, and as they rode off he remarked to the members of his staff, using the conventional military phrase for announcing a staff officer in orders, "Gentlemen, this is Jacob Slack, volunteer aid-de-camp to the colonel commanding the ——th cavalry brigade, and will be obeyed and respected as such." The announcement, couched in these terms, so delighted Jakey that he came well-nigh losing his balance and falling off old Tom's back and getting himself trampled on by the rest of the staff. But after the first flurry he made a most efficient aid-de-camp; that is, if riding close beside the colonel, and being always ready for an order which was never given, constitutes a good staff officer.

And now began a ride in which the advancing force

was spurred on by a curiosity to know what they were going to find. Would the place be evacuated, or would they suddenly be checked by a volley in their faces from a skirmish line. Starting at a trot, and finding no obstacle in the earlier part of the distance, they soon broke into a brisk canter. Several miles were passed without a sign of an enemy. Presently they came to a low lineal heaping of dirt and fence rails extending on either side of the road, thrown together evidently for the protection of men lying down for firing. They had been abandoned. A second line of defense was reached soon after, and then a third. As they drew on, these lines were built nearer together and grew more formidable. Their desertion of a skirmish line indicated that the enemy had fallen back from their main defenses.

Emerging from a wood, the fortifications about the town of Tullahoma suddenly appeared before them. Though it was plain now that they were not to be defended, the advancing force half expected to see a cloud of smoke burst from them. But they were silent and impotent, without troops to man them.

Dashing from the edge of the wood Colonel Maynard, followed by Jakey and the rest of the staff, rode over the intervening space and in a few minutes were climbing the slanting sides of the earthworks. A point had been gained which, without the previous maneuvers, would have cost thousands of lives. Even Jakey Slack, who can hardly be called an educated soldier, experienced a certain comfort on riding unopposed over breastworks so formidable. Once within them he got off his horse, and seeing a big siege gun from under which the carriage had been burned, climbed onto it and sat straddle, waving his hat and cheering as vociferously as if the victory had been exclusively due to his own genius.

His hilarity was suddenly quenched by the colonel, who, riding up to him, told him that the brigade was ordered forward in pursuit of the retreating enemy, and that he must go back to his father and sister. Jakey begged hard to go on, but his appeal was un-availing. His brief dignity must be resigned; from aid-de-camp on the staff of the colonel commanding the ——th brigade "to be obeyed and respected as such," he must be reduced to the level of a small boy.

The colonel gave him a hug before parting, and told him that he would send a trooper with him to see him safely on his way. Had Jakey been a soldier, his action on this occasion would have been considered by any court-martial rank mutiny.

"D'y think I hain't nobody nohow? Didn't I go with y' last summer ter Chattanooga when y' war nuthen but a scout? 'N didn't I stay in jail with y'? And now yer talken 'bout senden a sojer with me fo' a nurse."

"All right, Jakey; go it alone, if you prefer it."

The colonel rode away and Jakey, shorn of the plumage he had worn so becomingly for a whole half day, proceeded on his return journey. He first in-quired the most direct route to Hillsboro, and having been directed to it he set off at a brisk trot. He had eaten nothing since early morning and was ravenously hungry. At a farmhouse by the way he secured a meal for himself and a good feed for Tom. Then the old woman who furnished it gave him a kiss and started him again on his journey.

Jakey had not gone far before he came to a road connecting Hillsboro with the MacMinnville branch of the railroad at a place called Concord. The road on which he was traveling forked into the other at an acute angle, the two running nearly parallel for a short distance. Looking ahead toward the fork, he saw a rig which struck him at once as being astonishingly familiar. It was none other than the rawboned horse and paint-bereft buggy he had seen several times before. As it drew near Jakey could see someone in the buggy, and he was not long in recognizing the peculiar dress of Miss Betsy Baggs.

"Hello, Miss Baggs, whar y' goen at?" he called.

Never a word spoke Miss Baggs. She sat bolt upright in her buggy, regarding the boy fixedly as "Bobby Lee" triangulated onward. As she passed she turned her head slowly, keeping her spectacles on Jakey with an unearthly stare. There is something superstitious in all human beings, and epecially in boys. Something like a shiver ran down Jakey's back at sight of this singular person, who knew him perfectly, yet who passed him, her head turning mechanically, without uttering a word. For a moment he was tempted to believe that Miss Baggs had perished, and this was her ghost going to seek rest in some other land than war-scarred Tennessee. But this feeling was momentary. Throwing it off he shouted:

"Shell I give yer love t' Rats when I see him?"

If Miss Baggs was trying to make the boy believe he was mistaken, or that he saw her disembodied spirit, her effort failed signally at this point. A peal of suppressed laughter came back on the breeze to Jakey. Looking after her he saw the back of the buggy, from which streamed the tatters of the top, and under it "Bob Lee's" four legs mingled in inextricable confusion, doing some of their best work.

"She'uns hain't bent on no good," said Jakey to himself as he gave Tom a jog, "reckon she's up ter somep'n."

Jakey rode on musing upon Miss Baggs. He had noticed her kind treatment of his sister, and as Jakey was disposed to regard Souri the most important person on earth after Colonel Maynard, Miss Baggs had thus found her way into that youthful something or other which for want of a better name may be called Jakey's heart. His remark was made with great seriousness. Jakey felt that it was his duty, as a Union sympathizer, to put someone on Miss Baggs's track. "She mought be worken fo' the Confederates," he mused, "'n then agin she moughtn't." The latter view was most agreeable to him, because he liked Miss Baggs and would grieve to see any harm come to her.

While he was jogging along turning the matter over in his mind, he saw several horsemen in blue and yellow come tearing down the road. They reined in when they came up with him and opened a volley of questions.

"Say, boy, did you see a woman with a striped dress and goggles go by?"

"'N a long-legged wind-busted critter?"

"Yes."

"'N an ole rattlin' buggy?"

"Yes."

"What d'y want with her?"

"Never mind that. Have you seen her?"

"Wal, never mind whether I have or not. Git up, Tom!"

This brought the questioner to terms.

"Are you a Confederate boy?"

"Don't I live in Tennessee?"

"I suppose that means you are Confederate. We've no time to lose. The woman in that buggy is —is——" he was conjuring up a story to deceive the stupid-looking boy before him and get the required information, but he was not good at invention. Jakey came to the rescue.

"Wanted by you'uns general or colonel or somep'n?"

"Yes."

"Fo' ter keep her outen danger 'coz she's like 'nuff to run inter a guerrilla camp?"

The man looked wonderingly at the boy, who was making a story for him unasked.

"Y-e-s," he replied, uncertain what to say.

"Wal, she's gone along thar. When y' git ter th' fork 'n th' road take th' left fork."

"All right. Thanks, my little man," and the party galloped away, to take the wrong road on reaching the fork.

Jakey pursued his course meditatively.

"Reckon that warn't me done thet. T must 'a' ben some'un else. I air a Union boy, I air. She'uns's Confederate. Like 'nuff some'un got s'picion of her. Reckon I can't be Union ef I helped her out. Wal, she likes Souri anyway. Reckon she won't do no harm."

Notwithstanding the view taken at the close of Jakey's soliloquy he felt very much dissatisfied with himself. He rode on thoughtfully, wondering what Colonel Maynard would say if he should know what he had done. He soon met a soldier on a lame horse. Jakey inferred that he belonged to the party ahead but had been obliged to drop out of the chase.

"Say, mister," called the boy, "what them'uns chasen thet woman in the buggy fo'?"

"Did you pass her?"

"Yes."

"Put 'em on the track?"

"Reckon."

"She tried to slip through the lines on a forged pass. The guard was suspicious and took the pass to headquarters (after letting her go through, like a fool), when the trick was discovered."

"Wal, reckon they'll ketch her," and Jakey rode on.

Meanwhile the father and sister awaited Jakey's reappearance anxiously. Both had great confidence in his ability to make his way anywhere, but Jakey was pretty young to be riding about in a strange country in such turbulent times, and his sister, on learning his mission from her father, never ceased to be troubled about him during his absence. Neither Mr. Slack nor Souri said anything to the woman with whom they lodged as to the real cause of Jakey's absence. Slack remarked at breakfast that he thought he heard someone knocking during the night, but was very tired and fell asleep again without paying any attention to it. Of course Jakey's absence was noticed, and the farmer felt it necessary to invent some excuse to account for it.

"I don't know what can hev become o' Jake," he said. "Last night I hearn the critters stampen 'n stampen 'n maken a fuss, 'n' I tole Jake ter go 'n see what was th' matter. He didn't come back no mo'."

As the dusk of the evening was coming on Tom was seen far down the street advancing at a jog trot, and on him Jakey, bobbing up and down, his elbows stuck out on each side, and his little legs at an obtuse angle with the rest of his body. As he approached, his father scanned his face to learn whether he had succeeded. Jakey, unmindful of the important service he had rendered the Union cause in carrying the information he had taken, was at the time absorbed with his recent dignity as volunteer aid-de-camp. The consequence was that his countenance shone with a proud look that convinced his father that he had not failed. Riding up to the little porch in front of the house, Jakey slid down from Tom's high back with as much dignity as he could command on descending from such a height. The whole household, including the children, were there to receive him, and Jakey was about to give them an account of how he had served on Colonel Maynard's staff when he caught his father's eye.

"You, Jake," said Mr. Slack, "didn't I send y' out ter th' barn ter look arter the critters last night, 'n now yer been ridin' all over, nobody knows whar. Whar y' ben?"

"Wal," said Jakey, taking his cue readily, "I foun' Tom loose, 'n I follered him all over the *U*nited States."

"I'm glad y' got him," replied the father   'Go in 'n git yer supper.''

VII.

IT was the middle of August before the different columns of the Army of the Cumberland began to cross the mountains between it and Chattanooga in pursuit of the Confederates, who had withdrawn to that place and there intrenched themselves. Meanwhile the Slack family had arrived at their home, near Jasper, in the Sequatchee Valley. Much to Souri's surprise everything about the place looked uncouth. When she left it a year before it was all she had ever known. A ten months' residence in the North, surrounded by every comfort, associating with the daughters of refined people, had made a great change in her. Now the furniture appeared dilapidated, the rag carpets rough; indeed there was a disappointment about "sweet home" that she had not expected. Nevertheless she did not sit down and repine over it. She had no means of procuring anything better, but she found that she could do a great deal of patching. With considerable forethought she had brought some cheap material of different kinds with her from the North, and this she used to the best advantage. She made neat valances for the beds, cushions for her mother's rocking chair, scarfs for the bureaus; in fact with

69

very little she made quite a revolution in the house.

Her great anxiety was her brother. Jakey had attended well to his studies while at school, but his teachers had found it impossible to change his methods of expressing himself. As soon as he reached Tennessee he began to relapse into the state of semi-barbarism in which he had lived befoie the coming of his advantages. Souri knew that there was no hope for improvement in her father and mother. Instead of troubling them when their ways of acting and speaking shocked her, she refrained from comment, but when Jakey dropped into his old ways she tried hard to check him. Besides she felt that it was necessary to keep a strict guard over herself, for she had noticed that when under any excitement, or when her feelings were deeply touched, she was apt to forget herself and be once more the "poor white" girl of former days.

There was another cause of solicitude as to Jakey. It must be admitted, notwithstanding Jakey's good points and a certain original shrewdness there was about him, that he never was the same boy after his few hours of service on Colonel Maynard's staff. It was constantly "When I war Colonel Maynard's aidder-camp," or "When the colonel 'n me rode into Tullyhomy," or "When I carried the news of the *r*evacuation." Then he would strut about with his hands in his pockets, much to his father's amusement, and Souri's dread that he would run away and join the Union army. But one day when he threatened to do so, Souri took him to task for it and made him prom-

ise that he would not. This ended her anxiety, for
Jakey would as soon have forgotten his military hon-
ors as break a pledge to his sister.

The Army of the Cumberland, in three *corps
d'armée* commanded by Generals Thomas, McCook,
and Crittenden, the whole under General Rosecrans,
was now advancing by every possible route toward
Chattanooga. One of the routes taken by the Union
army lay through the Sequatchee Valley and directly
past the Slacks' little farm. One evening Souri was
leaning over the gate thoughtfully, when she saw several mounted men in blue, with yellow facings, come
trotting down the road. They were the first blue
coats to appear of the host that was coming. There
is a certain jaunty air, a devil-may-care appearance,
about a trooper who becomes used to being always
on horseback. Each man and horse seemed the same
animal. Their sabers clanked in unison, and they
were chatting and laughing as if they had come to the
South with only the most peaceful intentions. When
they reached the gate where Souri stood, one of them,
lifting his hat politely, asked:

"Would ye mind me goen to the well for a little
water?"

In the brilliant display that was revealed by the
lifting of the man's hat Souri recognized a head she
could never forget—the head of Corporal Ratigan.

"Why," she said, "ain't you Corporal Ratigan?"

"I am, me young lady, and if Oi'm not mistaken,
ye're one o' the party that was goen through the lines
one day a few weeks ago."

Jakey at this moment came around the house in a fashion at which he had become very expert at school. This was turning handsprings sideways like a cart wheel. Seeing soldiers he suddenly remembered his dignity as former volunteer aid-de-camp, and straightening up, pulled his hat down over the back of his head and tried to look military. True, his hair was in his eyes, but his military training had only been for one morning and Jakey's hair was always in his eyes. Doubtless it would have required months of training from a drill sergeant to get it to growing any other way. Approaching the fence he climbed it, and sat with one leg on each side of it.

"Do ye know me, me boy?" asked Ratigan.

"Does I know one o' them signal lights on th' mounting?"

"O Jakey," sighed his sister.

"Well, me lad," pursued the corporal, laughing. "Who am I?"

"Rats."

"I see ye have a good memory. Rats. It's quare ye should have remembered that." And the corporal chuckled good-naturedly.

"Mebbe *you* remember some'un's name."

"And who is that?"

"Miss Baggs."

"Certainly I do," said the corporal, somewhat startled and confused.

"I sor her t'other day."

"Ye don't mean it?"

"Reckon I do."

"Where?"

"She war a trotten thet ole critter o' hern, goen No'th like shot from a squirrel gun."

"Upon me word!" ejaculated the corporal, evidently much interested.

"Reckon she war up to somep'n."

"What makes ye think so?" And Ratigan changed his position in his saddle uneasily.

"Wal, when we'uns met her——"

"O Jakey, please don't say we'uns," interrupted Souri.

"Wal, when we met her outen the reach o' you'uns" (Souri gave a despairing look but said nothing), "she talked peart 'nuff 'n she knowed me too, but when she passed me on th' road t'other day, no'th o' th' Union army, she only stared at me through her goggle eyes 'n did'n say nothin' nohow."

"And what do ye suppose that was for?"

"Reckon she war in a hurry 'bout somep'n 'n didn' want ter stop 'n talk or nothen."

"Did you speak to her?"

"I asked her ef I c'd give her love to Rats when I sor him."

Corporal Ratigan's Irish good nature triumphed over his desire to reach down and give the boy a cuff. Jakey's countenance was solemn as usual, and did not break into a smile in response to the corporal's embarrassed laugh. He opened the gate and Ratigan rode into the yard, followed by his troopers. They refreshed themselves from a gourd which hung in the wellhouse; then filling their canteens they rode away.

But Souri and Jakey were destined soon to meet one who was of far more consequence·to both than Corporal Ratigan. The next morning, while Souri was setting the house to rights, she heard the beating of innumerable horses' hoofs. Going to the window and looking up the road, which stretched northward for a long distance, in full view she saw a column of cavalry approaching. There is something singular in the sight of a large body of troops marching through a quiet country used only to the plowman, the corn hoer, or the farmer lashing his ox team slowly along the road. Through long years of peace one is used only to seeing soldiers parading through the streets of cities, with crowds to admire, and friends waving handkerchiefs to them from windows. Such indeed were the scenes through which the Union troops during the Civil War passed at leaving for the seat of war. But once among the broad Southern plantations, in the moss-covered woods, or amid the silent hills, there was no one to gaze at them except the simple country people, who had never seen anything more gaudy than an occasional bright necktie, or bonnet feathers adorning city people, and then only at rare intervals. Suddenly Souri saw the road alive with a brilliant cavalcade. First came a mounted officer surrounded by subordinate officers and orderlies. Then the solid column, its officers and non-commissioned officers with shoulder straps and chevrons, the men sabered and pistoled and carbined, each man a miniature citadel in himself. Above the heads of all waved a line of bunting, from the stars and stripes near the center of each regiment to the more frequent guidon; the staff of each resting on the stirrup of the man who bore it.

Before the head of column had reached the house the whole Slack family were standing in the yard gaping. Being Unionists, their faces were wreathed in smiles. These were their own men, whom they had so long hoped for and prayed for to shield them from the terrorism of neighbors who differed with them in loyalty. No handkerchief was ever waved from city mansion at responsive smiling troopers with more zest than that with which Souri waved to the passing squadrons. And as for Jakey, he stood on the fence and flinging his hat in the air shouted himself hoarse.

Two regiments passed, though each seemed like an army, for cavalry occupies three or four times the space of infantry. Between the second and third regiments was a gap of a few hundred yards. In this rode an officer especially noticeable for his youth and manly beauty, attended by his staff and escort. On approaching the Slack cabin he motioned to these to go on; and wheeling his horse from the road, unattended, rode up to the party of lookers-on. Jakey, who was standing on the fence, gave a spring and was caught in his arms.

"Aha, little brother, we meet again."

But there were others to engage the speaker's attention. Dropping the boy to the ground, he dismounted and was soon warmly shaking all by the hand.

"Yer Mark Malone, I reckon," said Farmer Slack, "though y' don't look much like the common sojer ez kem 'long hyar a year ago and changed yer uniform fo' our Henery's store clothes."

"Not Mark Malone—that was a fictitious name—but Mark Maynard. No. I'm not a private any longer; I command this brigade. And it's a splendid body of men; I'm proud of it."

When Colonel Maynard came to salute Souri there was an unspeakable interest, sympathy, even tenderness in her expressive eyes.

"Why, Souri, you're a woman; how you have improved!"

A slight flush on her cheek showed the pleasure the words gave her.

"Hain't I improved?" asked Jakey.

"Improved? Certainly. Have you conquered your old habit of answering people with questions?"

"Did I lick Johnny—— Oh, yes," suddenly recollecting himself. "I purty nigh got over thet."

"So I perceive," said the colonel smiling. "You're a perfect paragon at expressing yourself."

"Won't yer come in 'n set down?" asked Mrs. Slack.

"Not now. If we remain long enough in this vicinity I'll ride over and make you a call. I am going to meet my wife, whom I have not seen for nearly a year. I expect to find her at her mother's plantation near Chattanooga. You remember how she hid me when my neck was in a halter on that very plantation; how I came North in disguise with her; how I came here one night where I had left my horse and uniform and dashed away to the Union lines; how she followed me and we were married by a chaplain. Well, I've never seen her since a week after our marriage. 'Old Pap' is famous for not allowing women in camp, and he made no exception in Mrs. Maynard's case, except for one week's honeymoon in recognition of service rendered the cause.''

"And yer wife's gone back onter the plantation?'' said Mrs. Slack.

"She has. You see in June a recruit entered our family quarters in the shape of a ten-pounder boy. Before that happened Mrs. Maynard went through the lines to join her mother, Mrs. Fain. As the youngster is not old enough to report to his father since his enlistment, I suppose his father will have to report to him."

"Whar th' Confederates gone ter?" asked Slack.

"To the other side of the Tennessee. They've escaped us once more. You see we maneuvered them out of Tullahoma, expecting to force them to fight us on open ground; but it rained every day of our advance. This delayed us so (especially the artillery) that they were enabled to give us the slip."

"I reckon Mrs. Maynard 'll be right glad to see you," remarked Souri feelingly.

"I shall certainly be right glad to see her. And that must account for my leaving you so soon. I owe you all a great deal in this household, and now that our forces occupy the country, if you require anything let me know it. What can I do for you?"

There was silence for a few moments, which was broken by Mrs. Slack.

"Wal, now, colonel, d'ye know I hain't had a cup o' coffee fo' night onter a year."

"You shall have some as soon as I can reach my commissary. Anything else?"

Souri frowned even at the request of her mother, and no one named any other requirement.

"Jakey," said the colonel, "you haven't forgotten how, when I went through here a year ago, I asked you to go with me on my way to Chattanooga to get information of the movements of the Confederate army?"

"Hev I forgot when I war yer aidercamp? Oh, no, no—I hain't forgot."

"Well, I hadn't much inducement to offer you then, unless the sharing of a prison may be called an inducement. Now if you will go along I'll promise you the best that Mrs. Maynard can provide at the plantation. Will you go?"

"Will I? Course I will. Paw, can I hev Tom?"

"Sartin, boy," and the farmer turned and went to the barn.

"Won't you need a—a luncheon?" asked Souri, whose hesitation was an effort to avoid the word "snack"; the only name she had known for a cold bite before she went North to school.

"Oh, no," said the colonel. "We shall ride directly to the plantation; we'll get plenty to eat when we arrive."

Meanwhile Jakey had followed his father to the barn. Mrs. Slack stepped into the house to make up a bundle for the boy. Maynard and Souri sauntered aimlessly in the yard. Presently they found themselves at the wellhouse. Souri leaned over it and looked down into the well. There was something she wanted to say, but found it difficult.

"I thank you very much for what you've done for me," she said.

"Why, Souri, what have I done for you compared with what you did for me?"

"Didn't you find me a 'poor white' girl a year ago, and haven't you sent me to school, with Jakey, and helped me to look into a world that would have been always closed to me except for you?"

"And wouldn't my world have been entirely closed to me except for you?"

Souri was silent.

"Souri, when you speak to me of obligation you remind me how deeply I am obliged to you. When I was imprisoned at Chattanooga, charged with being a spy, tried, convicted, and about to be hanged, you came and effected my escape. Why, child, were it not for you my bones would this minute be moldering in the jail yard at Chattanooga."

"But Mrs. Maynard, she——"

Souri paused. She was bending low over the side of the wellhouse, her face in the palms of her hands, her elbows resting on the board beside the bucket, and looking down as though seeking for something in the dark disk below.

"She completed what you began," the colonel finished for her.

"It was more for her to do. 'Twasn't noth—any-thing for me. You'uns—you was Union and so was I. *She* was Confederate."

There was a depth of feeling in Souri which threw her off her guard and made it difficult for her to adhere to her training in expressing herself.

"Souri, I am indebted to two lovely women for every breath I draw. You opened my prison doors. She who is my wife concealed me when I was hunted for my life. Let us talk no more about it. The very mention of the narrowness of my escape gives me a choking sensation about the neck."

Jakey came trotting out of the barn on Tom, the rim of his felt hat flapping up and down at each step.

The farmer followed, and Mrs. Slack came out with Jakey's bundle. Then with a handshaking all round, and a "God bless you, my little girl," from Maynard to Souri, the two started on their way, not on foot, as on their former journey, but each with a good mount.

VIII.

THE two wayfarers started in the direction the cavalry had taken, but after going a short distance Colonel Maynard reined in his horse.

"Stop a bit, Madge," he said. "I want to consult my staff as to the route." Then to his attendant, " Jakey, I think I know a shorter route than this."

"So do I."

"The one you and I took when we went to Chattanooga before."

"To bring back information," added Jakey proudly.

"We'll take it again. It's off the main road and we'll be less liable to be murdered for our boots."

"Reckon," said Jakey, wrinkling his brow and drawing down the corners of his mouth with an intensely deliberative expression, as though the problem having been submitted to him it behooved him to consider it carefully.

They rode back past the house, and keeping on for about a mile turned into a byway. This they followed till they reached the Chattanooga road.

Colonel Maynard was in the most exuberant spirits. He had turned over the command of his brigade for a day or two to the colonel next in rank to himself, and

8*

was on his way to join his young wife, from whom he had parted a week after his marriage. The two acted on his spirits like champagne. He laughed without having anything to laugh at; he bantered Jakey, he talked lovingly to his favorite horse Madge. In short, Colonel Maynard appeared just what he was in years, little more than a boy.

His services as a scout had attracted the attention of the army, and had led the general for whom he scouted to advance him. He had stepped from the ranks to a high position on the staff, and soon after a cavalry regiment being badly in need of a lieutenant-colonel (the colonel being inefficient and some junior officer being needed to practically command), Maynard was placed in the position. When the colonel of the regiment was gotten rid of, Maynard was made colonel. Soon after, his command was attached to a brigade wherein he found himself the ranking regimental commander. This gave him the command of the brigade.

He entered upon his duties with misgivings. He knew he was well fitted for the duties of a scout, but doubted if he could command the respect of three thousand men. Besides, he knew there lurked within him a spirit of antagonism to conventional methods; he feared impulses that might wreck not only himself, but his brigade—perhaps a whole army. True, there was often a kind of illegitimate nobility about these impulses, but it did not render them any the less dangerous. On hearing the news of his appointment to the command of a brigade, he mounted his horse and dashed over to the headquarters of the general to whom he owed nearly all his advancement, with a view to protesting. On arriving there he stammered out reasons which had no coherence, and was dismissed by the general with the remark that he was suffering from an attack of ill-timed modesty, the general adding: "You are a born soldier, Colonel Maynard, and if the war lasts long enough to give you an opportunity, you will reach a much higher command than that of a brigade."

Once on the road he and Jakey had passed before on their journey together to Chattanooga, Maynard took infinite delight in talking over their "campaign," as he called the mission they had pursued. Jakey became more puffed up with pride at having been with the colonel on that occasion than having ridden with him into Tullahoma. Others had been on his staff on the latter occasion, but he, Jake Slack alone, had been his boon companion, his confidential friend, on his mission to Chattanooga. When Jakey considered this double honor he felt that he must certainly have been born in uniform and deprived of it by some malignant fairy soon after coming into the world.

The Chattanooga road was by no means deserted. Wagons under guard, couriers, staff officers followed by orderlies, citizens, negroes, indeed all manner of people and vehicles passing between the different corps of the Army of the Cumberland, met them or were passed by them on the way.

"Jakey," said the colonel, "I remember every moment of the time when I came along this road on my way back from Chattanooga. I was traveling, as the dignitaries say, *incog.*"

"Yer mean by thet ef they'd a knowed what a 'portant person y' war they'd a showed ther respec' by hangin' y'."

"Exactly. They would have put several feet between mine and the waving summer grass below. You have a forcible way of expressing yourself, but considering that I'm the subject of your remarks, my throat feels clearer at my own more delicate drawing of the picture."

"Reckon," said Jakey, with proper solemnity, remembering that the topic was likely to wound the colonel's feelings.

"On that occasion, Jakey, I did not meet even a mule without my heart jumping up into my throat."

"A rope harness must a skeered y' outen yer skin."

"Especially when I noticed the knots in it. But seriously, Jakey, that experience has filled me with a peculiar dread. Now suppose some day a Confederate spy should fall into my hands."

"Reckon you'd hev lots o' fun hangen him."

"You're far out of the way there, my little Solomon. I fear it would be absolutely impossible for me to do such a duty if required of me."

"Yer needn't take him, in the first place."

"It might be my duty to do so."

"Y' mought do like Tom. Tom he can't never see me when I want ter drive 'im outen pastur. He can see well 'nuff when I get a ear o' corn fo' 'im, though."

"A good idea, Jakey. With that subtle sophistry of yours you could reason a Methodist minister into dancing a hornpipe; but I fear it's hardly sound enough to enable one so used to deceiving others as I was when a scout to deceive himself. I should do my best, should I take a spy, to turn him over."

" 'Sposen 'twar a woman."

"O Lord, Jakey, don't suppose any such thing. I'd have to do my duty in that case just the same as if she were a man. What kind of a looking 'go-cart' is that coming down the road?"

A horse was visible in the distance, its long neck stretched out in front of its body, coming toward them at a rapid gait. The rattling of a buggy, which it dragged, reminded the colonel of the band of a newly recruited regiment. Within sat a woman in a striped dress, sunbonnet, and glasses. In short, Jakey Slack at once recognized his old friend Betsy Baggs.

"Howdy, Miss Baggs," he said as she drove by.

Miss Baggs was the Sphinx she had been to Jakey when he met her near Tullahoma. She leveled her spectacles at him, but had no recognition whatever for him.

"Who's your friend?" asked Maynard, as the buggy rattled away.

"Thet's Miss Baggs," said Jakey.

"And who's Miss Baggs?"

Jakey paused a long while before replying. There was a problem in his mind, suggested by the meeting of Miss Baggs so soon after his conversation with the colonel about capturing a woman spy. For Jakey had a suspicion that Miss Baggs was in some way a Confederate emissary.

"Wal," he said at length, "I reckon she's sweet on Rats."

"Jakey," said the colonel, "there is occasionally a lucidity about your explanations—a shining brightness which makes my eyes blink. But on the present occasion I think there is dust in them. Would you mind giving me a pointer as to your meaning? By rats, do you mean rodents?"

"What's rodents?" asked Jakey.

Meanwhile the rattling of Miss Baggs's buggy was dying away in the distance.

"Real rats are rodents."

"Not them'uns; Rats is a corporal in Major Burke's critter company."

"The corporal's name is quite appropriate to the one you have given his regiment. The woman in the buggy looks as if she'd make a fit vivandière to a 'critter company,' and a fit sweetheart for a corporal by the name of Rats."

Jakey made no reply to this; he was evidently weighed down with some concealed responsibility. The colonel tried to draw him again into conversation, but even "their campaigns" were not sufficient. At last the colonel, realizing that they were near their destination and his young wife, became occupied by his own thoughts. Suddenly he caught sight of a large frame house set back from the road. He gazed upon it with a singular mingling of different feelings. In it he had first met his wife; in it she had con-

cealed him from men and hounds; and there she was
now his wife and the mother of their babe. He gave
his horse the spurs. Jakey suddenly drew rein.

"Colonel!" he called.

"What?"

"Miss Baggs."

"Confound Miss Baggs. What of her?"

"Reckon thur's somep'n wrong 'bout her."

"What do you mean?"

"Mebbe she's a 'Federate spy."

"You little imp, why didn't you tell me that before?" cried the colonel angrily.

"Wal, I hain't sartin' 'bout 't nohow, 'n I
thought yer moughtn't like fo' to hold onter a
woman."

"Jakey," said the colonel impressively, "you have
done very wrong. You should have told me of your
suspicions at once. Remember I'm a colonel commanding a brigade in the Union army."

The colonel sat irresolute. What should he do?
Miss Baggs was now miles away. Jakey only suspected her. His young wife, whom he had not seen
for nearly a year, was within a stone's throw of him.
Suddenly he drove the spurs again into his horse's
flanks and rode on to the gateway of the plantation.
There was no need to open the gate, for there was no
gate to open. The two rode on to the house through
an avenue of trees, and Colonel Maynard dismounted
before his horse reached the foot of the steps leading
up on to the veranda. A young woman flew through
the open front door with all the impulse of a summer

storm. In a moment she and Colonel Maynard were closely locked in each other's arms.

"Mark!"

"Laura!"

Jakey sat on old Tom, viewing this collision very much as he would watch two tempest clouds meet in the sky. "Reckon them 'uns hez got 't bad," he remarked sotto voce, and with a solemnity that was intended to be reverential.

There was rejoicing at the Fain plantation at the sudden appearance of Colonel Maynard. All remembered the circumstances attending the brief stay he had made there the summer before, and were anxious to see the man who had left them a private, hunted for his life, to return a colonel in the Union army. As soon as the news of his arrival reached the negroes they came from the cabins in rear and surrounded the house, peering in at every window, or waiting at the doorways to get a view of their old acquaintance. Being informed of their desire, Colonel Maynard stepped out onto the veranda and spoke a few words to them, thanking them for their devotion to the family of which his wife was a member, and telling them that a sympathy with the Union cause was not necessarily incompatible with such devotion.

But the happiest moment of the welcoming was when the young wife took her husband by the hand, and both impatiently mounted the staircase to a chamber in which there was a cradle. Drawing near it Laura Maynard drew its canopy aside, and there was the round face of a boy two or three months old. He opened his eyes at the moment and stared wonderingly in the face of the man bending over him; his interest being largely enhanced by the two rows of brass buttons glittering on his father's breast. The face of the colonel was pressed upon the soft round cheek of the child, whose little fingers were at once clutched in the tawny beard.

"I've come to report for duty, my son, and I don't expect to be relieved so long as you live; but for the present I fear you will have to be content with the services of your mother. There; one more kiss in lieu of salute."

The kiss was followed by a dozen or so more before the colonel could tear himself from the canopied cradle. Then husband and wife fell to reminiscences of their hurried meeting and courtship in that very house.

Colonel Maynard's brigade went into camp on the river bank, some five or six miles from the plantation. The colonel insisted on having Jakey Slack with him permanently, and sent him home to ask his father's permission; Jakey at the same time bearing an invitation to his sister to visit Mrs. Maynard, reinforced by a special request from the colonel that it be accepted. Jakey succeeded in obtaining the desired permission, and after much hesitation Souri decided to accept. Jakey entered the army as drummer boy, but was not called upon to flourish the sticks. He was at once detailed for duty at brigade headquarters as clerk in the assistant adjutant general's department, as a convenient way of making him confidential factotum to the colonel commanding. Upon getting on the blue and brass of a Union soldier Jakey was very proud of

himself, and when placed in close confidential rela-
tionship with the commander of a brigade, he nearly
burst with the emotions generated by the dignity of
his position.   He was of great use to the colonel, who
at once appointed him dispatch bearer between himself and Mrs. Maynard.   The domestic nearness of
this office only rendered the boy more consequential.
He snubbed not only the orderlies attached to the
headquarters of the brigade, but would occasionally
approach disrespect toward the officers of the staff.
As this was largely their fault (for they were continually trying to amuse themselves at Jakey's expense),
they bore it good-naturedly.

"Why don't you carry that note like any other
messenger," said an aid to him one day, "in your
belt?"

"Coz I haint like any other messenger," retorted
Jakey.   "D'y' reckon a man what carries the colonel's private corrensponden air a common orderly?"

As there was no gainsaying this argument, without a
seeming detriment of the personal dignity of the
brigade commander, Jakey held the field.

IX.

IT was about a week after the arrival of Colonel
Maynard at the Fain plantation. He had returned
to his headquarters. Laura was sitting at work on
some part of the "recruit's" uniform, while the rain
from a September storm beat against the window-
panes. Souri was with her, and as Colonel Maynard
was expecting orders to cross the river with his brigade, the two had secured Souri's promise to remain
at the plantation till the close of the campaign which
was about to open. Souri was upstairs administering
to the wants of the younger Maynard, to whom she
was devoted. He dropped to sleep, and leaving the
chamber on tiptoe she descended to the sitting-room.
As she entered she glanced out of the window.

"Good gracious! If there isn't Miss Baggs!"

They saw through the rain a horse and buggy making a rapid turn through the gateway.

"Who's Miss Baggs?" asked Laura quickly.

"I met her when coming from the North. She got
through the Union lines by playing the part of a
country girl. I met her again, on this side, and she
was a lady. She's coming up to the veranda."

"Bobby Lee" came up the driveway at such a
rapid gait as to astonish the two women looking out
of the window. The horse had scarcely stopped in

front of the house, when Miss Baggs, throwing down the reins, rushed up the steps and knocked loudly at the door.

"Go and see what she wants, Souri. You've met her before."

Souri went quickly to the door. When she opened it and Miss Baggs saw the girl she had met between the lines, for a moment her countenance brightened. Then suddenly her expression changed on remembering that Souri was a Union girl.

"I've no time to explain anything. Call someone, quick, to drive my buggy to the barn ; and hide me."

Now Souri knew well enough that Miss Baggs was working in the cause of the Confederacy. But she saw a woman in trouble, and this in her eyes obscured all else. She ushered Miss Baggs into the room where Laura sat.

"This girl wishes to rest with us a while. I'm going to take her horse to the barn."

Without waiting for a reply she went out and, jumping into the buggy, drove it around to the barn. There she directed Uncle Daniel, who ruled the stables of the plantation, to put both horse and buggy inside and shut the doors. Having seen this attended to she went back to the house.

Meanwhile Miss Baggs stood face to face with Laura Maynard.

"This is a Confederate household, I believe," said the fugitive.

"It is."

"Thank God! you are one of ours."

"No."

"What, Federal?" she turned pale.

"No."

"Then, for Heaven's sake, tell me what you are."

"I am a Confederate married to a Union officer."

There were quick successive flashes of hope and fear on Miss Baggs' countenance.

"And you will not give me up?"

"Give you up? What do you mean?"

"I am in the Confederate secret service. I have just been recognized by a Union soldier—a cavalry-man. He was not mounted, while I was in my buggy. I heard him cry halt. I gave my horse the whip, and before the man could mount I was away, and soon turned behind a wood. There is a fork in the road. I took the left road, leading here. He must have taken the other, which leads nowhere. He will discover his mistake, turn back, and take the right road. This is the first house he will pass, and he will surely come in to ask if you have seen me."

"Well?"

"You will not betray me?"

Laura thought of the coming of her husband one night months ago, flying, as this woman was flying, for his life.

"No, rest easy on that score. I will do all I can for you."

There was but little time for action, for the words were scarcely spoken before a cavalryman dashed past on the road. He was throwing mud and water behind him, his boots heavy with moist Tennessee clay. Noticing the house, as Miss Baggs predicted, he drew rein and entered the gateway. Riding up to the veranda he shouted:

"Hello, there!"

"Get in there, quick," said Laura, pushing the hunted woman into a closet. Then going out onto the veranda, she sternly demanded of the man what he wanted.

"Did you see a woman go by here just now in an old farm buggy?"

"No such person has passed."

"Sure?"

"Sure."

"Are you people here Union or Confederate?"

"Both."

"You must excuse me, ma'am, but I think I'll look about for myself a bit."

"You will do no such thing."

"Why not?"

"Because this house is protected by a safeguard."

"That doesn't include rebel emissaries. I shall make a search."

"If you do you will regret it."

"Why?"

"I shall report you to Colonel Maynard, commanding the ——th Brigade."

"You have some influence with the colonel, I suppose," said the soldier, puzzled.

"I should have; I'm his wife."

"The devil you are," in an undertone. Then aloud: "Well, ma'am, if you are Colonel Maynard's wife that ends it. I don't see how a Union colonel's wife can give aid and comfort to a rebel telegraph worker, for that's what the woman is." And lifting his hat he rode away,

Returning to the parlor Laura found Souri there, just from the barn. The closet door was opened, and Miss Baggs stepped out.

"Is he gone?"

"Yes."

Taking Laura's hand Miss Baggs covered it with kisses, then turning to Souri, she threw her arms about her neck.

"One of you," she said, presently withdrawing from the embrace, "has risked compromising a husband, while the other has acted against the interests of her cause, to protect me. Your individual sympathy has overridden your sense of a more important obligation. I wish I could be like you, but I can't. My whole being has become absorbed in my country. I see only pictures of the South's desolation. They have dried the springs of my heart for any one human being. I am so steeled against anything that would weaken my purpose to serve the whole, that I would sacrifice my own brother, sister, lover, if I had one, to my cause, if necessary. It is war that has reduced me to this; war, terrible war, striking down our brothers by thousands; war, covering our land with smoking ruins; war, frightful, fiendish war, seeking to reduce us to the level of our own servants. War has hardened my heart and made me not a woman, but—sometimes I think, a fiend."

While delivering herself of these words a cold, harsh look gradually came over her handsome features, till she came to the last words. They were spoken with inexpressible melancholy. Then there was a sudden transition to a look of kindliness, which coming after the other, was like the first warm rays of sunlight bursting through storm clouds.

Mrs. Fain came into the room, and seeing a stranger drew back.

"Mamma," said Laura, "this lady comes to us much as Mark once came from the other side. She is chased for her life."

"A Confederate?" asked Mrs. Fain.

"A Confederate, heart and hand, body and soul," exclaimed Miss Baggs.

"One sympathizing with our cause is welcome here. Unfortunately my family is broken by diverse sympathies. My husband is exiled on account of his sympathies with the Federal cause. My son is fighting for the Confederacy. My daughter here is the wife of a Federal officer. My own sympathies are all with the South."

"Madam," replied the guest, "for the sake of the South, were it necessary, I might stay here long enough to endanger your daughter's happiness, but not for my own. Fortunately it is not necessary. Early to-morrow I must be miles from here. I shall go at midnight."

"Let your departure rest with yourself. You are welcome as long as you choose to stay."

"And now," said Laura, "if you will come with me I will get you some dry clothing."

"I will; but first let me know to whom I am indebted for all this kindness. The family name is——?"

"Fain."

Miss Baggs controlled an ejaculation of surprise.

"Fain?"

"Fain."

"And you are Laura Fain?"

"I was. I am now Laura Maynard. You seem to at least have heard of me."

"I have heard of you. I am a Virginian. You once visited in Virginia. I was then in Italy studying art."

"And you are——?"

There was a brief silence before the guest replied. She seemed deliberating whether to make herself known or not.

"Betsy Baggs," she said at last, and it was evident that if she had another name she would not reveal it.

Supper was announced, after which Miss Baggs asked to be shown to a room where she could rest. A servant was summoned, who led her to the guest chamber, and setting the lamp on a table left her to herself.

When the servant disappeared, Miss Baggs turned the key in the lock and then carefully examined the walls, with a view to discovering if there were openings through which any eye could peer into the room. Her narrow escape, the last of a number of such episodes, had partly unnerved her, and she sat down in a chair to rest, languidly closing her eyes. But not for long. Rising, she drew from the pocket of her dress (everyone knows that there is no better place of concealment than a woman's pocket) a small bundle of papers. Spreading them out on the table she drew her chair near it, and after once more casting her eye about the room began to study them.

Miss Baggs had been endeavoring to secure the information required as to the methods of the general commanding the Army of the Cumberland in following the retreating Confederates, ever since the request had been made of her in June previous. Here it was September, and she had effected nothing. True, she had taken a number of dispatches in cipher from the wires, but they were very long, and the longer the message the more difficult she had found them to decipher. Within a few days she had intercepted two very short ones. Taking them from those before her she began to study one consisting of only a few lines. It read as follows:

WASHINGTON, D. C., August 5, '63.
Banks here army the Benjamin cat to for your report shinney daily are advance the cart orders of peremptory applause.

Here is the other; a little longer:

WASHINGTON, D. C., September 3, '63.
Congress long with as advise applause marble your possible your ago to party was connect soon to movements spot his ordered as to Burton pin of and left ordered Benjamin.

Taking up the dispatch she had intercepted when the Army of the Cumberland began to advance, and some papers showing that she had been trying to decipher it, she began to look them over. This is the dispatch:

MURFREESBORO, June 28, '63.
Volunteers Garfield with circling between you possession turn an he cob Bumble at to get that possible by move Benjamin pony chief rapidity around that

put of the hours ready shingle to notice enemy's Tullahoma your point the by of poliwog of plateau Niggard if desire and hope forward to haha move me right I command and mountain order staff.

Miss Baggs had had this dispatch by her since the latter part of the preceding June, and had puzzled over it for many an hour. She had never succeeded in finding a key, but had at last drawn something of its meaning from the jumble of words. After much study she assumed that the words, when laid down in their proper order, would give the proper meaning. But there were certain words, which either did not mean anything, or stood perhaps for some place or general. She began by taking out a number of such words as "poliwog," "haha," "shingle" and "pony." The dispatch was doubtless from Rosecrans, as the word Garfield (his chief of staff) appeared, and the words "chief of staff" were scattered through it. Therefore either Benjamin, or Bumble, or Niggard, meant Rosecrans. Subsequent dispatches which fell into her hands had convinced her that Rosecrans was designated as Benjamin. Then she began to try to fit words together in this wise:

Your command
between Tullahoma and Niggard
get possession
enemy's right
Circling around the mountain plateau
I desire that you get possession if possible
a point between Tullahoma and Niggard
Move with rapidity
By order of Benjamin (Rosecrans) Garfield chief of staff.

Other groupings gave her better results, till she obtained the following:

To Bumble (probably a cavalry general on the left flank): Be ready to move at an hour's notice.   I desire that you turn the enemy's right.   Move your command, if possible, by circling around the mountain plateau.   Get possession of a point between Tulla-homa and Niggard (probably some point in rear of the Southern army) with rapidity.   By order of Rose-crans, Garfield, chief of staff.

The deciphering, so far as it went, was of no avail since it did not come in time, but it helped her with the shorter and easier dispatches, which she now attacked.   She began with this one:

Banks here army the Benjamin cat to for your report shinney daily are advance the cart orders of peremptory applause.

Miss Baggs had learned that a proper name pre-ceded all these cipher dispatches; possibly having something to do with the key.   At any rate, she threw out the first word (Banks) and the words "cat," "shinney," and "cart" as check words.   "Ben-jamin," she assumed, meant Rosecrans.   Applause must be the signature of the sender; and as the dis-patch was from Washington, it was probably either Lincoln, Stanton, or Halleck.   The word "to" taken with "Benjamin" must mean "To Rosecrans" and "peremptory" and "orders" evidently must go together.   The word "advance" doubtless explained the two other words.   This only left "report" and "daily" as words of importance. These combinations did not come at once, but after getting them she inferred that Rosecrans had peremptory orders to advance and report daily to Washington.

"I have got something at last," she exclaimed, getting up from her chair and walking back and forth excitedly. "This is indeed important."

Then she took up the second dispatch:

Congress long with as advise applause marble you possible your ago to party was connect soon to movements spot his ordered as to Burton pin of and left ordered Benjamin.

Again the words "To" and "Benjamin" were put together, and the words "Congress," "marble," "party," and "spot" stricken out as checks. The dispatch being longer than the other, was more difficult of interpretation. It was some time before the student was satisfied with her efforts. She inferred from it that someone was ordered to connect with someone else. She knew that the Confederate generals feared that Burnside might connect with Rosecrans. So it was probable that Burton meant Burnside, who was at Knoxville, and that he had been ordered to connect with Rosecrans' left "as soon as possible." The remaining words evidently meant "Burnside also directed to report his movements to you."*

---

* By the key, the first word in this dispatch, Congress, signifies that the words are to be laid in five lines, there being five columns of words. Every sixth word is to be omitted as a check word. The key directs to begin at the top of the fifth column and lay the

"This is no less important than the other," mused Miss Baggs. "It is clear from both that Rosecrans has peremptory orders to advance, and Burnside is ordered to join him. I must get this through the lines at once. From here I must find a way across the Tennessee—just above Chattanooga if possible—and perhaps I may strike their line connecting with Rosecrans' headquarters at the front, and gather in the latest news. 'It never rains but it pours,' and I'll get in all I can get while I'm in luck."

Collecting her papers she carefully tied them together and put them in her pocket. Then turning down the light, she unlocked the door and went downstairs.

---

words down under each other. Then go up the first, down the fourth, up the third, up the second. Benjamin means Rosecrans, Burton means Burnside, Applause means Halleck.

Thus :

To	Rosecrans	Burnside	was	long
ago	ordered	to	connect	with
your	left	as	soon	as
possible	and	ordered	to	advise
you	of	his	movements	Halleck

The key to the preceding dispatch is as follows : The first word (Banks) denotes that there are four lines and four columns. Begin at the bottom of the second, skipping every fifth (check) word and lay the words up this column. Then go down the first, up the third, and down the fourth.

The key to the longer or first dispatch is : The first word (Volunteers) denotes that there are nine lines and six columns. Go up the third column, down the second, up the fourth, down the fifth, up the first, down the sixth.

This code, varied as in the above dispatches, was in use during the greater part of the war.

X.

COLONEL MAYNARD was in the habit of making frequent visits to his wife, and without warning. Laura understood perfectly the embarrassing
position in which he would be placed at surprising a
Confederate spy under the same roof with herself and
protected by her. She had no mind to place him in
any such position. When Miss Baggs went upstairs
Laura posted a sentry, in the person of Uncle Daniel,
to keep a sharp lookout and give notice of the colonel's approach, in order that Miss Baggs might be got
out of the way before his arrival. Daniel sat down
on a bench on the veranda and lit his pipe. He was
an old man and prone to dose. It was not long
before Lookout Mountain, across the river, began to
sway among the clouds, the nearer trees began to
rock, the old negro's head fell upon his breast, and
he slept.

It was nearly ten o'clock when Laura, having given
up the coming of her husband that night, and for once
in her life rejoicing thereat, was about to dismiss
Daniel from his responsible position, when she heard
a step on the veranda. Thinking it was Daniel walking back and forth to keep himself awake, she paid no
attention to it. There was a turning of the knob to
the front door, and in another moment Colonel May-

nard stood on the threshold of the sitting-room, looking in upon Mrs. Fain, Laura, Souri, and Miss Baggs.
He was about to enter when, observing a strange person, he hesitated. Laura advanced, and taking him
by the hand led him to another room. He had only
once before seen Miss Baggs and then in disguise,
and did not recognize her.

"Why, sweetheart," he said to his wife, "you're
trembling."

"You came in so hurriedly."

"I *am* hurried. We cross the river to-morrow
morning."

"To-morrow morning! O Mark, why couldn't
they wait a few days?"

"If wives and sweethearts had the giving of orders,
Uncle Sam would have his armies always in winter
quarters."

"Why couldn't this happiness have lasted just a
little longer?"

"And then still a little longer. Come, I have but
a short time to stay. Let me say good-by to the
baby."

Laura led the way upstairs, and drew the curtains
from the cradle, exposing the sleeping infant.

There was something in the innocence, the absence
of force in the little slumberer, so different from the
scenes in which he was wont to mingle, to set in
motion a train of feelings in Mark Maynard to which
he had thus far been a stranger. On the one side
was the wife he loved and the sleeping child; on the
other, what now appeared toilsome marches, nights
spent on wet ground, sickness, mangling by shell, and

bullets, and sabre cuts. A year before he had loved these hardships, these dangers. Now a new element had entered into his life, and, at least while he gazed on the little stranger (the only life that had come to him among the many gone since the war began), he felt a strange repugnance to entering upon the coming campaign.

"My boy, my boy," he said huskily, the thought suddenly coming to him that he might never see wife or child again, "how can I now risk leaving you to struggle on to manhood unprotected?" Then recognizing his weakness, he said with a quick-born smile: "But you have your mother, and I must win the star of a brigadier for you to play with."

But war's quick and imperative demands gave him little time for the indulgence of such feelings. He tried to turn away. Again and again he drew the curtains of the cradle, only to draw them back for one more look.

"Laura," he said suddenly, "all is changed. Before you and he came, I did my duty as a soldier, because it was not hard to do, and because it pleased me. Now it will be hard, and I shall do it that you and he may not be disgraced in me. How can I ever leave a blot on my name and have that child grow up to know it?"

Laura, seeing how hard it was for him to draw himself from the cradle, took his hand and led him away.

Going downstairs they found the house silent. All the family were in bed. Maynard knew that it was time he had departed. It was very late and he must ride eight miles to camp, and be on the march with his brigade before daylight.   But he could hardly tear himself away from the house.   The sleeping child upstairs seemed to have brought, from the Unknown whence he came, a maze of gentler emotions which were drifting like smoke-wreaths about his father, obscuring the way from their peaceful influence.

"Laura," he said impressively, "let us always keep ourselves pure for him.   Do you know that I look back with horror at all the deception I was obliged to practice when a spy—when in this house before. And you—how many fibs you were obliged to tell for my sake!"

"Wasn't it dreadful?"

They were locked in a parting embrace.   Mark kissed her again and again.

"Those were strange circumstances," he said.

"Frightfully strange."

"Which couldn't happen again in a century."

"I hope they'll never happen again to us."

"Somehow I dislike to think of your deception, even for my sake.   You won't do so any more, will you, darling?"

"Never," she whispered.

Suddenly he remembered the strange woman he had stumbled on when he came in.

"By the bye," he asked, "who was the lady with you this evening?"

Laura's promise to deceive no more had been breathed only a moment.   What was she to say?   She could not betray the woman who had thrown herself upon her protection; she could not place her beloved husband in an equivocal position.

"She?   Oh, she was only one of the neighbors who

came in to help me with some things I'm making for the baby."

There was one more embrace; then another last one; then another final one; then a stirrup kiss; and Colonel Mark Maynard rode back through the night to camp.

Not long after his arrival bugles sounded the reveille. It was two o'clock in the morning, and the men were aroused to begin their advance to the front. Sending for Jakey Slack the colonel gave him a note to take back to Laura at the plantation He had repeated his adieus so often in person that one would hardly think it necessary to send any more on cold paper, but Maynard's heart strings were pulling him as strongly away from war as his duty was forcing him toward it. Besides he knew that Laura would treasure every word from him.

Jakey mounted Tom, and rode in the gray of the morning to deliver the note. When he reached the plantation he was obliged to do a good deal of pounding and ringing before he could get into the house. Finally Mrs. Maynard's maid, Alice, let him in, and considering the fact that Mrs. Maynard was in bed and Alice stood in very close confidential relations with her, Jakey consented to deliver the note to the maid, and waited to see if there was any reply. Alice returned and said that her mistress would be down in a moment. Presently she entered, dressed in a morning wrapper.

"Jakey," she said, taking the boy by the hand and smoothing his hair out of his eyes, "can I rely on you to do something for me?"

"Could the colonel?"

"You are all going to the front, and no one can tell what may happen. You'll probably have to meet your enemies sometime, and the colonel says that a battle may come at any day. I want you to promise me that if anything should happen to the colonel you will come here as fast as you can and let me know of it. Do you understand?"

"Y' mean ef th' colonel gits hit on th' for'ead with a cannon ball?"

"O Jakey, don't talk so. I mean if he gets sick or wounded or in any other trouble, will you come and tell me at once?"

"Reckon."

Laura knew that this was Jakey's way of making a promise, and she was satisfied. She told him to wait a few minutes, and went out of the room. When she returned she brought two parcels with her.

"This one is for you, Jakey," she said, handing him one of them. "It's a luncheon. Put it in your haversack, and give the other to the colonel. And hand him this note."

She gave him a tiny white envelope, within which in a few words was concentrated what may be best expressed as three days' rations of desiccated affection.

Jakey took the parcels and placing the note in his cap, went out, mounted Tom, and dashed away after his commander.

Maynard's brigade crossed the river south of Lookout Mountain and passed over the mountain's face where it juts onto the river. The enemy had been dispossessed and Maynard had little to do except to cast an occasional glance down upon the Fain plantation, which he could see plainly and where dwelt what was all the world to him. During the day, with a glass, he could see people on the veranda, and fancied that his wife and boy were there. As the sun was setting, he took a last view before descending to the more level ground below. He was destined to pass through strange scenes, to undergo marked changes, before he would see his beloved again.

His command was but one of the many, all moving forward toward a retreating enemy. The three corps, of which the Army of the Cumberland consisted, crossed the Tennessee at different points. General Thomas, once across, moved to Stevens' Gap, an opening in a range called Lookout Mountain, extending south from near Chattanooga. There he entered the valley of Chickamauga Creek. General McCook seized Winston's Gap, further south in the same chain. General Crittenden crossed from the Sequatchee Valley, moving over Lookout Mountain toward Chattanooga. Bragg, finding his communications threatened by McCook and Thomas, evacuated Chattanooga and retreated to Lafayette, twenty miles south. Crittenden, passing through Chattanooga, pushed on to Ringold.

Colonel Maynard moved his command through Chattanooga to Rossville, situated at a gap in Mission Ridge. From there he was ordered forward, entering what is called McLenmore's Cove, an undulating space lying between two ranges, Mission Ridge and the Pigeon Mountains. There the brigade encamped on a field soon to become memorable as the scene of one of the most desperate, the most dramatic of all the battles of the Civil War—the field of Chickamauga,

XI

MAJOR BURKE'S command was ordered to guard the telegraph line extending south from Rossville. The regiment was strung out to a considerable distance, each troop guarding a certain portion of the line. Corporal Ratigan was placed in charge of a section of two miles. Putting himself at the head of eight men he led them to the end of his section nearest camp, and dividing them into two reliefs of four men each, posted them at intervals of half a mile along the line under his care. At sunset, not being relieved, he prepared to spend the night in bivouac. Selecting a clump of trees under which to rest, and cutting some boughs for beds—or rather to keep the men from the damp ground—the corporal established the relief, off duty, there. The rations were cooked and eaten, after which the guard was relieved. The corporal went out always with the relief, posted his men, and slept between times.

Soon after establishing the camp Ratigan noticed that one of his men was none other than private Flanagan, whose reputation in the regiment for glaring stupidity was well established.

"Flanagan," he said, "how came ye here?"

"Faith, I was ardered."

"It must have been the divil that ordered ye. If

ye'r going to act as stupid on this expedition as ye'r used to acting, the wires 'll be cut a dozen times for all you."

Flanagan, who considered himself treated unjustly, bore the stigma attached to him meekly. His good nature was all that saved him from the consequences of the numerous absurdities of which he was guilty. Instead of attempting to argue the matter with the corporal he occupied his mind in devising ways by which he might soften what he considered his obdurate heart, and induce him to act toward himself more leniently.

Soon after the men had eaten their evening rations, consisting of the ordinary bacon and hard-tack, Flanagan took his carbine and strolled to a thicket near by to see if he could find anything more palatable for the next meal. He was soon rewarded by the sight of a bird hopping about in the branches, chirping all the while and occasionally pausing to look at him quizzically, with its head poised on one side. Flanagan determined to bring it down for the corporal's breakfast, thereby propitiating that spirit of antagonism which, in his innocence, he could not account for. He did not stop to consider whether the bird was eatable or not; indeed he did not know. All he wanted was a peace offering. He approached and brought his gun to an aim. The bird hopped to the other side of the tree. He was obliged to take a new position. The bird flew to the next tree. The private followed. Just as he was about to fire, the bird took wing and lit on a branch still further from the camp. Thus was Flanagan led from one tree to another till he found himself around a bend in the road between the hills.

Suddenly he espied something which drew his attention from the object he was following. An old farm buggy, behind a rawboned horse, stood in the road, while near by a woman was coiling a wire on her hand, one end of which was dangling over a telegraph wire above her head. She turned, and seeing a Union soldier, became suddenly white as a sheet. But this he could not see, owing to the shade of her sunbonnet and glasses,

"Good ayvenen, miss."

"La sakes, Mr. soger!"

"It's a foine ayvenen."

"Reckon 't air."

"What do ye be doen wid the little woire?"

By this time Miss Baggs, for it was she, had recovered some of her equanimity.

"I'm a-rollen 't up."

"And what's it for?"

"Wal, I'll tell y'. Yer see th' stone on th' end? Wal, thet's fo' to kill birds with. I jist throwed th' stone at a bird. By haven it tied to a wire I kin hold onter th' stone, 'n don't hev ter keep picken up stones all th' while, pertickerlerly when I'm a-sitten in th' buggy."

"It's an injaneyous and original device."

"What air you'uns a doen hyar?"

"There's a small party of us around the bend; we're guyarden the telegraph."

"How many of y' air there?"

"A carporal and eight men, includen meself."

"What air you'uns doen out hyar away from all th' rest on 'em?"

"Follyen a burred."

"Oh! It's birds yer looken fo'. Wal, you'uns jist go inter thet thicket 'n y'll git a hull flock."

"Ye don't mane it!"

Miss Baggs pointed up the road to a wood which if private Flanagan should go there he would be still further away from his camp.

"Are ye shure there's a flock?"

"Ther so thick y' can't see the sky."

"Oi'll try for 'em."

Miss Baggs went on coiling her wire unconcernedly, till the private was out of sight. Then she sprang into her buggy and giving "Bobby" the lash drove rapidly away.

"One more attempt to-night," she said, "and to-morrow I'll be off for our camps. I'll make it right here. If the rest of the party guarding the line are as stupid as this one, I couldn't wish for a better chance."

It was two o'clock in the morning when Ratigan started out to post the last relief for the night. The men followed, grum and stupid, having just been wakened out of a sound sleep and not yet thoroughly aroused. The party rode to the extreme end of the section, left a man, and turned back, leaving a man at every half mile. Corporal Ratigan had posted the last man half a mile from the bivouac and was returning, when suddenly, turning a bend in the road running through a wood, he descried a dark object before him beside the road. He drew rein and watched and listened. The dark object, as he fixed his gaze upon it, grew into the dim outlines of a vehicle, but it was too dark for him to see if it contained anyone. The corporal, whose mind had been fixed on the special duty of protecting the line, at once assumed that someone was trying to cut the wire. He put spurs to his horse and called out:

"Halt there! Throw up your hands and surrender, or I'll shoot."

The only response was a swish from a whip which came down evidently on a horse's back, and the dark mass before him vanished around the bend in the road. The corporal dashed on, but before he could get round the bend the object had turned again. He could hear the rattling of wheels, and sounds of a horse's hoofs digging into the road at a gallop. Whoever was behind that horse must be driving at a frightful pace, for urging his own beast to his best he seemed to lose rather than gain ground. Coming to a straight piece of road he could again see the object before him, but in the darkness it was simply a darker spot than its surroundings.

The corporal found himself started in a chase which from the first promised to be an unequal one. True, the animal with which his own was vying was dragging some sort of a vehicle, while the corporal's steed had his load all on his back. There was a hundred and eighty pounds of human flesh, some thirty to forty pounds of weapons and ammunition, besides clothing, and several pounds of cavalry boots. Whether or no the odds were in favor of the one or the other, the two animals had passed over a mile, and

Ratigan could not tell whether he had lost or gained. There were strange sounds mingling with the more distinct rattling of wheels in front, but the corporal's sabre, as it gyrated in the air, knocked against his left leg, thrashed under his horse's belly, made such a clatter that all other noises were but whispers in a storm. Then there was his carbine to pound against him and his horse's side, threatening at each beat to break a rib. Indeed the corporal, after vainly trying to carry both sabre and carbine in one hand, while he held the reins with the other, and dug his heels into his horse's flanks, began to think that he could do better in a wagon than so hampered on a horse's back.

Then he decided to try what effect a bullet would have on the fugitive. Dropping both sabre and carbine he drew his revolver and fired a couple of shots. He did not aim directly at the flying object, for he did not know what he was firing at. The only effect produced seemed to be a renewed effort on the part of the steed in front.

Suddenly the ears of the corporal caught a sound that filled him with astonishment. It was a voice urging forward the horse he was chasing. Ratigan had supposed that whoever was trying to escape was a man, yet this voice was different from a man's tones; it sounded like that of a child or a woman. The corporal was puzzled. Then it suddenly occurred to him that perhaps he was chasing Betsy Baggs.

Now, the corporal was as conscientious a man as there was in the Army of the Cumberland, and one of the most gallant, but when the suspicion fell upon him like a chill, that he was after a woman whose presence, for the brief period he had been with her, had thrown a strange spell over him, he ceased to urge his horse with the same pressure as before. In the midst of the chase there had come a contest within his own breast between two conflicting emotions. If Betsy Baggs were in front of him, what would be the result if he should catch her? He must turn her over to the military authorities, and the chances were she would be executed for a spy. On the other hand, supposing he permitted her to escape, he would be liberating an enemy far more dangerous to the army in which he served than a dozen batteries. In short, he would be a traitor to his comrades and his cause.

The corporal turned these two alternatives over rapidly in his mind, dwelling first on one and then on the other, till he thought he would go mad. At one moment his sense of duty, acting all-powerful, would drive his spurs into his horse's flanks till the blood flowed. Then he would see a picture of Miss Baggs, as he had once seen her standing up in her buggy under the protection of Confederate troopers, her eye lighting with delight at his confusion, her hair half undone, the bewitching smile that revealed her white teeth. He would suddenly turn from this picture to the woman standing before a file of soldiers to whom he, Corporal Ratigan, had turned her over for execution. One feature held him on to the chase. It was that he did not surely know whom he followed. He suspected Miss Baggs, but for all he knew it might be someone else. So he pressed on and did his best.

Miss Baggs, for it was she, had passed many pickets, had experienced many lucky escapes. She had browbeaten officers, and had cozened soldiers. She had gone through a dozen places where a man would surely have been arrested. For months she had been in quest of information that would give her cause the victory in the West. When surprised by the corporal, she had just taken off telegrams revealing the whole situation of the Army of the Cumberland. She had withdrawn her wire, had closed her box, and when the corporal came up was preparing to start. And now, after passing so many dangers, on the very eve of success, she suddenly found herself in the most critical of all the situations she had ever been placed in.

Meanwhile the long legs of "Bobby Lee" were getting over the ground at an astonishing pace. It was not the triangulation of a former race for sport with Corporal Ratigan, but the quick, short jumps of a race for life. And Bobby seemed to know the stake. Never in his former flights had his ear been turned back so eagerly to catch the low tones of his mistress. Never had there been so much feeling in that mistress' voice. It was: "Go on, Bobby! Good old horse. Get up! On! on! on! That's a dear boy. It's life and death with me, Bobby"; a continued stream of broken words and sentences, all of which Bobby seemed to understand and act upon as if he had been a human being.

The fugitive knew that the chase could not be a long one. Her crazy vehicle was like a rotten hulk in a storm without sea room. To the north was the Tennessee River, and no means of crossing. Ahead was Chickamauga Creek, but between her and it lay the scattered forces of the left wing of the Union army. She knew the ground well, and had as good a knowledge of the positions of the troops as one could have of an army constantly changing. The point from which she had started was half a mile west of Rossville on the Lafayette road. A mile of chasing had brought her near a fork, the left road leading across Chickamauga Creek by Dyer's bridge; the right leading directly south. By the former route three miles would bring her to the creek and in proximity to the Confederate outposts; by the latter, she would have to traverse double the distance and pass the camps of a whole corps of the Union army. But even the scattered forces on the shorter road seemed an impassable barrier to her, and it was not probable that any bridge across the creek would be left unguarded. There were as many fords as there were bridges, and if she could strike one of these she might possibly find a free passage. She determined to take the left-hand road, intending, if she should succeed in reaching Dyer's Mill, about a mile from the creek, to strike a ford some distance below that she remembered having once crossed.

These possibilities flashed through her mind like messages over a telegraph wire, while the thud of hoofs and the clattering of her pursuer's swinging sabre were sounding in her ears.

"On, on, Bobby, for Heaven's sake, go on."

Would it not be best for her to leave her horse and buggy in the road and take to the woods? No. They would mark the point where she had left them. But her pursuer would not know which side of the road she had taken, and there would be an even chance that he would follow on the wrong side. Something must be done; the race could not last forever; the man behind seemed to be gaining; and then the dread of coming upon a Union camp!

She was about to bring her horse to a stand and jump from her buggy, when the clatter behind her—Ratigan had turned a slight bend in the road—sounded so loud, so near, that instead of doing so she gave him a cut with the whip.

"There's no time now, Bobby. We must put a greater distance between us and the Yankee. Get up, Bobby! Oh, go on! Why haven't you wings?"

Heavens! what is that ahead? Tents white and ghostly in the gloom! And how many of them! The whole field is covered!

Nearer comes the clatter from behind. In front is a sleeping regiment, brigade, perhaps a whole division. It was not there yesterday. It must be in transit. Oh, why should it have halted just in time to block the way?

"God help me, I must take my chances and go on."

Sentinels were pacing on their beats about the camps. In some cases the beats led along the road, but not across it. Right through these chains of sentinels, right into the heart of this sleeping multitude of armed men, dashed the woman whose only weapons of defense were Bobby Lee and her antiquated vehicle.

"Halt!"

"Go on, Bob."

A shot, a bullet singing like a tuning fork, in ears which already sang loud enough in themselves with excitement.

"*Turn out the guard!*"

Following Miss Baggs came Corporal Ratigan, to find the road in front of him blocked by half a dozen men with as many muskets pointed right up in his face.

He uttered an involuntary "thank God!" He must be delayed; the responsibility for the escape of the fugitive would be with them. If indeed she were Miss Baggs he would regard himself fortunate at the delay.

"What's the matter?" asked one of the men.

"I'm chasing some one in front. I suspect a tele- graph breaker."

"Ah! That's it, is it? Well, go on; we've stopped the wrong person."

The corporal regretted that the interview had been so brief, the interruption so short. He had no option but to dash on.

Before the fugitive there stood a man in the middle of the road with a musket leveled straight at her, or rather at the coming mass which he could not distin- guish. Miss Baggs did not see him till she got within a dozen feet of him and heard:

"Halt, or I'll fire!"

Rising in her seat and concentrating all her strength in one effort, she brought her whip down on the horse's back, at the same time holding him in the center of the road by the reins. The man was knocked in one direction, stunned, and his musket went flying in the other.

And now each one of the chain of sentries through which the fair dispatch stealer's horse dragged her and her swaying buggy with a series of lunges, hearing shots, the cries of guards, the clatter of horse's hoofs, the rattling of wheels, and seeing something coming through the darkness as Miss Baggs approached, shouted "Halt!" "Turn out the guard." "Who comes there?" and a score of other similar cries, to none of which Miss Baggs paid any other attention than to fly through and from them as from the hand of Death. A score of shots were fired at her along half a mile of road while she was running the gauntlet.

And now the last sentry is passed and the woman shoots out from between the rows of white tents into a free road ahead. The noises are left behind. But amid the confusion of distant sounds is one which, coming with a low, continued rattle, strikes terror into her heart. A familiarity with war has taught her its calls. She hears the beating of the "long roll." The whole camp is aroused. A legion of Yankees may soon be in pursuit.

Corporal Ratigan was stopped by every sentinel who had tried to check Miss Baggs. After an explanation to each he was suffered to go on. The men who stopped him transmitted the information at once to the guard tent that some one—doubtless an enemy —was being chased. The force was a division of infantry, with no cavalry except a mounted escort to the general commanding. Some of these were ordered in pursuit. There was a hurried saddling of horses, sprinkled with oaths at the delays encountered, and three cavalrymen mounted, and dashed after Miss Baggs and her pursuer. But before they started, a couple of miles had been placed between her and the camps.

The gray of the morning was by this time beginning to reveal objects with greater distinctness. Ratigan, coming to a rise in the ground just beyond the camps, saw the buggy about two miles ahead swaying like the dark hull of a ship rolling through the billows of an ocean. For a moment he hesitated between his duty as a soldier, and that quick, sharp something, be it love, bewitchment, or a natural sympathy of man for weaker woman, while beads of cold perspiration stood on his forehead. It seemed to him that if he should do his duty he would be acting the part of an executioner; not only that, but the executioner of a woman—a woman whose image had got into his heart and his head, and never left him a moment's peace since she first threw the spell of her entrancing personality about him. It was a hard struggle, and from the nature of the case could not be a long one. Duty won. He shouted to his horse, gave him a dig with both spurs, and dashed forward.

There was a depression in the ground down which the corporal plunged. Then the road ran along a level for a while, with another slight rise beyond. As he rode down the declivity the fugitive was on the crest of the second rise. She stood up and turned to catch a glance behind her. She saw a horseman—she was too far to recognize the corporal—dashing after her. Below her was a wooded space, and she noticed that which gave her a glimmer of hope. The road forked. Urging her horse onward she aimed to get on one of the two roads beyond the fork while her pursuer was in the hollow back of her, trusting that she might escape as she had escaped before, by forcing him to choose between two roads, and trusting that he might take the wrong one.

Down the declivity her racer plunged while Ratigan was galloping down the one behind her. So steep was the road and so swift her horse's pace that the danger of death by mangling seemed greater than death by hanging. She reached the bottom, where the road ran level to the fork and the wood. Hope urged her. It was not a hundred yards to the point she was so anxious to reach.

There is a story of a wonderful one-horse shay, which had been made so perfectly that, no one part being weaker than the rest, it never gave out till at last the whole collapsed together. Miss Baggs' buggy was one she had found in a countryman's barn, and had been donated to the cause. It had been an excellent vehicle in its day, though when she acquired it, was in extreme old age. Its forlorn appearance suited her purpose admirably, and after numerous tests she had come to place greater reliance on its endurance than on that of a newer conveyance. But there came a time when if no part would give way all must give way. That time was now at hand. Passing over a rut at the very fork of the road that seemed her only chance for escape, the old buggy gave a dismal groan, as much in sympathy with the mistress it had served so well, as a death rattle, and flew into a hundred pieces.

XII.

CORPORAL RATIGAN had been worked up to such a fever of excitement by the chase and his complicated feelings toward the object of it, that when he shot over the rise in the ground that hid the fugitive from his view, his visage was distorted from the expression of good nature usually stamped upon it to one which can only be called demoniac. His eyes were wild; that portion of his hair which extended below his forage cap seemed to glow with unusual redness; his body leaned forward like a jockey in a race—the whole forming a picture of eager ferocity. In short, Corporal Ratigan resembled an escaped lunatic chasing a flying fiend who had been torturing him.

On the crest of the second rise he strained his eyes after Miss Baggs. Nothing appeared to denote her presence on the landscape except a horse in harness, which he dragged in the dust, trotting back toward a heap of rubbish on the road. A sudden dread took possession of the corporal. It was plainly evident there had been an accident. He had been chasing a Confederate telegraph stealer, that he might turn her over to the military. authorities of his own army to be hanged, and now he was suddenly plunged into terror for fear she had been killed. He went on, but with

124

a new object distinct in his mind. It was not to injure Miss Baggs, but to succor her.

He soon came to the heap of splinters and iron which marked the point of collapse of Miss Baggs' buggy. Miss Baggs was not visible. Had she taken to the wood beyond the fork of the road? For a moment there was a delightful sense of relief, but it was soon followed by the animal instinct of the savage chasing an object of prey. Stimulated by this or a return of a sense of duty, or both, he was about to ride into the wood, when looking down on the long grass by the roadside he descried the unconscious body, the face apparently white in death, of the woman he sought.

In a moment the corporal was off his horse and on his knees beside her. The chase in which he had been so eager, and the cause, were both forgotten on seeing Miss Baggs lying apparently cold in death at his feet.

"Darlin', are ye hurt?"

There was agony in the corporal's voice. He put an arm under her head to raise it; with the other he grasped her hands.

"To the divil's own keeping with the war anyway. What's 't good for, except to injure innocent women and children?"

In that non-resistance of unconsciousness he forgot that this woman had been engaged in what the world condemns openly, if not secretly, as illegitimate warfare. To him she was innocent. Not that he reasoned upon her acts, but because a mysterious something—a breath from spirit land—had made her more to him than all the world beside. He laid his head down upon her breast to listen if the heart beat; he chafed her hands and arms; he took off his cap and fanned her. Still she lay limp in his arms without a sign of life.

"Darlin', darlin', come back to life. Come back, if it's only long enough to tell me ye forgive me for me cowardly chasen ye. Oi've killed ye. Oi know 't. Oi wish some one would run a bayonet through me own rotten heart."

A slight murmur, something like a groan, escaped her.

"Praise God there's life! If it 'd only grow stronger. Ah, thank Heaven! there's water!"

Laying her head down in the grass, he went to the side of the road where there was a runnel of clear water. Scooping some of it in his two hands he threw it in her face.

She opened her eyes.

Corporal Ratigan never forgot the look with which his prisoner regarded him when she recognized who he was. There were two expressions following each other rapidly—the first, reproach; but when she noticed the pain with which it was received, it melted into one of tenderness.

"Ah, Rats," she exclaimed faintly, "how could you do it?"

He put his great hands—brown from exposure— before his eyes to shut out the face which at every glance kindled some new emotion to rack him. Now that she had come to life, another terror came to him to administer an added torture. He knew that mounted men were following, that they would soon appear over the crest just behind them, that his prisoner would be taken, tried, and condemned.

"They're comen! They'll be here in a jiffy!" he cried wildly. "Tell me that ye forgive me; tell me that ye don't hate me as I hate meself."

"For doing your duty, Rats?"

"Duty! Is it a man's duty to run down a woman like a hare? Don't talk to me of duty. If ye suffer for this, Oi'll desert and go. back to Oirland; and God be praised if He'll send a storm to sink the ship and me in it."

Corporal Ratigan was talking incoherently. He was so tortured by the position in which he had placed a woman who, he had now suddenly discovered, had captured his heart from the first moment he saw her, that a torrent of words, unmeaning of anything save his agony, poured out from his lips like bullets from a repeating rifle.

"There's a drop in me canteen—a drop of whisky. Will ye take it, darlin'—I mean—I don't know what I'm talken about. Let me put it to ye'r lips. Take a swallow. It'll revive ye. No?" She appeared to be passing back to unconsciousness. "Take it for moi sake, sweetheart. Only take a good swallow an' ye'll be righted."

She opened her eyes. Evidently she had heard. There was an expression on her face indicating that his words had produced that effect upon her which might be expected in a woman who hears a strong man, unconsciously and unintentionally, declaring his love.

"Why do you wish me to live, Rats? Don't let me live. If you do I'll die on the gibbet."

"Oh, darlin'," he moaned, "don't be talking that way. Oi'll die meself first. Oi'll raise a mutiny. Oi'll——"

He could not go on. His words mocked him. He well knew their futility. "Take a drop, sweetheart; only a drop for moi sake."

What a change from the day he had jokingly asked her to take an oath for "moi sake."

"For your sake, Rats; give it to me."

He put the neck of a battered tin canteen to her lips and she drank a little of the liquid. It produced a beneficial change at once. A tinge of color came to her cheek and she breathed more easily.

"Now if ye'r buggy were only sound," he said. "I'd put ye in it an' ye could go on. Oi'd ride back and throw them from the scent—the hounds!"

"No, you wouldn't, Rats. You're an honorable soldier. You have done your duty, and when put face to face with it another time you will do it again."

"For God's sake, don't tell me Oi'll iver do me duty when it brings death or destruction to you."

"You will, Rats."

"Niver. Oi'll brain the man that dares lay a fin-ger on ye, if it's Old Roscy himself."

A clattering of horses' hoofs, a clanking of sabres, mounted figures standing out against the morning sky on the crest behind them, and three cavalrymen are dashing on to where lies Miss Baggs and kneels the corporal.

"Promise me, Rats, that you will do nothing foolish," she asked pleadingly.

"O God! O'im going to draw me revolver on 'em."

"Promise."

"I can't."

"For *moi sake*, Rats."

The faintest trace of a smile, despite her desperate situation, passed over her face as she imitated the corporal's pronunciation. The quaint humor, mingled with so many singular traits prominent in her that could show itself at so critical a moment, touched a responsive Irish chord in his Irish heart and brought him to terms.

"For your sake, darlin', Oi'll do 't," he said, in a despairing voice.

There was scarcely time for him to speak the words —indeed they were whispered with his lips touching her ear—when the three cavalrymen rode up to where the two were.

"What's it all about, corporal?" asked one of them.

"I found this—this lady—lying here. Her buggy is broken—she is badly hurt." The corporal spoke the words haltingly and drops of sweat stood out on his forehead.

"Who is she?"

"Well—that's to be found out some other time. One of ye'd better ride back for an ambulance and a surgeon."

"Never mind the surgeon," said Miss Baggs, faintly.

"Well, bring the ambulance anyway," said Ratigan. "Ye can all go back if ye like. Oi'll stay with her. She's me own prisoner."

"There's no need of all going," said the man who had spoken. "I'll go myself."

He turned and rode away, while the others dismounted and threw the reins of their bridles over a fence rail. One of them caught Bobby Lee, who was cropping the grass near by, occasionally looking up as though suspicious that something had happened. The men loitered about, now and then approaching to take a look at the prisoner, but soon turning away again, quite willing to be free from the responsibility which Corporal Ratigan seemed disposed to take upon himself.

"Rats," said Miss Baggs, who was now rapidly recovering strength and coolness, "it will not be long before I shall be separated from you. Before then I wish to thank you for the kindness, the interest, even the tenderness with which you have treated a fallen enemy. And I wish to ask your forgiveness for the deception I practiced on you once when you were deputed to see me through the lines."

"What was that compared with what *Oi've* done?" he moaned.

"Do you forgive me?"

"Oi do. But Oi've nothing to forgive."

"And, Rats, you have unconsciously let me know that you—you feel more kindly toward me than——"

"You've robbed me of me heart intirely."

"Well, I'm both glad and sorry. It is delightful to be loved, but sad to think that your very love must make you grieve. Our meetings have been few and strange—very strange," she added musingly. "Who are you, Rats? I know you are well-born. I can see it in every word and motion."

"Oi'm second son of Sir Thomas Ratigan, Esquire, of County Cavan, Oirland. At his death me older brother succeeded to the estate. So I came to America to shift for meself. A year ago Oi enlisted in the Union ranks and here Oi am. Oi wish to God me brother was in his coffin and Oi in possession of the estates, that Oi could give them all to save your life."

"No, no, Rats. You are a soldier and an honorable man. Remember what I have told you. You will do your duty hereafter as you have done it heretofore. Your words in that respect are meaningless. Your sense of honor will always triumph over your sympathy when that sympathy is alloyed with dishonor. For this I have conceived for you an unbounded respect. Perhaps—were I not so soon to be——"

"Don't speak 't; for God's sake don't speak 't."

"Well, Rats, we will try, for the brief time we shall be together, to fix our minds on a pleasant picture. Let us think of that day when the South will be independent, or at least when North and South will be at peace. This region, now trodden by soldiers wearing the blue and the gray, will be given up to those simple people who till the soil. Instead of the sound of shotted guns there will be the lowing of cattle. Instead of the singing of minie balls there will be the songs of birds. There will be peace, blessed peace. Oh, if I could only live to see it. Then perhaps I may take you by the hand and say to you—— But, Rats, this can never be for us. It is only a fancy picture I've drawn to relieve that terrible suffering I see in your face. You've aged ten years in as many minutes. Don't look at me in that dreadful way; I can't bear it.''

The two cavalrymen's backs were turned. They were strolling toward the woods. Ratigan put his arms about her and both yielded to a long embrace. There were no more words spoken. Words would have added nothing to what both felt. There was more pain and more pleasure concentrated in the bosom of each than had been there in all the years they had lived.

XIII.

"TURNED OVER."

THERE was a rattling of wheels on the soft road, and looking up, Ratigan saw the messenger returning, followed by an ambulance. Driving to Miss Baggs, who was still lying in the grass, the driver backed it up to her, while the messenger dismounted and opened the door. The cavalrymen stood ready to lift the prisoner into the vehicle. But Miss Baggs waved them all away except the corporal, and taking his hand rose to her feet and stood for a moment supported by him. The effort was too much for her; her head fell on his shoulder, and for a moment she lost consciousness. Ratigan took her off her feet and, lifting her into the ambulance, laid her on the cushions.

"Oi'll ride at the foot," he said to the others. "One of ye lead me horse."

The men were relieved at this proposition; for the care of a woman in such a condition was by no means pleasing, and they feared she might die before they could get her into camp, and turn her over to some one else. Ratigan sat at the foot of the vehicle, with his feet on the step, while the men, seeing that their prisoner was in no condition to escape, besides being guarded by the corporal, gave her no especial care, riding together some twenty paces ahead.

"Darlin'," whispered Ratigan, as soon as they were out of hearing.

She opened her eyes. He leaned forward and caught one of her hands. It was cold as ice.

"Ah, Rats, where am I? Where are you taking me?"

"Don't ask me," he answered with a groan. "Are ye better?"

"Oh, yes. I'm not badly hurt. I'm bruised, and I've had a shock. But what matters it how I am?"

"If it were only night, ye might slip out and away."

"But it isn't night, Rats, and you are guarding me."

"A fine guard I'd make if there were a chance for ye to get out of this."

She gave a groan as the driver carelessly passed over a rut.

"You wouldn't see me go, when your duty is—to keep me? would you, Rats?" she asked languidly and mechanically.

"Not I. I'd shut me eyes as tight as iver I could."

They came to the place where each had successively emerged from the camp through which Ratigan had followed her before daylight, and found the road lined with soldiers, whose curiosity brought them there to see the woman who had succeeded in breaking through a whole chain of guards. They had all heard of the exploit, and crowded around the ambulance as it passed, but were kept away by the guards in attendance, who dropped back to the sides and rear. This prevented any further conversation between Ratigan and Miss Baggs, except an occasional whisper; but the corporal managed to keep her hand in his under a blanket, unobserved. At last the ambulance pulled up before the headquarters of the division whose camp they had entered, and Ratigan suddenly became conscious of the fact that he must turn his prisoner over to others, doubtless to be dealt with summarily, for he well knew the case would naturally receive prompt attention.

"Oh, darlin'," he exclaimed, "Oi must part with ye. What'll Oi do?"

"Keep steady, Rats. You couldn't help it. It was fated. Or rather He intended.it." She cast her eyes mournfully, but with the light of faith in them, upward. "I only regret that my people will receive no benefit in my death."

An officer, with a captain's shoulder straps, came out from headquarters and surveyed the ambulance. He was a dapper little fellow, fat and red-faced.

"Who've you got there?" he asked of Ratigan.

"A lady, sir."

"The woman who ran the guards last night?"

"Oi captured her on the road below."

"H'm. The guard duty of this division is in a fine condition when a woman can run a whole chain of sentinels. Get her out o' that."

"She's badly hurt, captain," said Ratigan, who had stepped down onto the ground and saluted.

"I can alight," said Miss Baggs feebly. And getting as best she could to the door of the ambulance, Ratigan helped her out. She looked faint, but stood by the aid of the corporal's arm.

"Take her in to the general," said the little captain; "he wants to see her."

As the tent was an ordinary wall tent, there was no great room in it. Miss Baggs went inside, while the corporal stood directly outside with his hand on the tent pole.

"What's she been up to, corporal?" asked the general, a man who seemed to realize perfectly the importance attaching to his position.

"How do Oi know, general? Oi simply chased her and caught her."

"Have you anything to say for yourself?" asked the general of the prisoner.

"Nothing."

"What were you doing, corporal, when you gave chase?"

"Guarding the telegraph line."

"And what was she doing; taking off dispatches?"

"Oi didn't see her doen 't, general."

"I must have you searched," said the general to the prisoner. Then he added, somewhat hesitatingly, "it's rather awkward not having a woman in camp."

"I will relieve you of the necessity," said the prisoner with dignity; and putting her hand into her pocket she drew forth a bundle of papers which she handed to him.

"What are these?" asked the surprised commander.

"Copies of intercepted telegrams."

The general uttered an exclamation, and taking the papers ran them over with his eye.

He looked up at the woman, who, save for the pallor occasioned by her fall from the collapsed buggy, stood apparently unmoved. There was admiration in the eye of the man who gazed at her. He could not but wonder at the daring that had enabled her to remain within the Union lines sufficiently long to capture dispatches bearing dates from June to the middle of September; he was astonished at the coolness with which she handed him documents that would warrant his hanging her to a tree without a moment's delay; and above all there was about her a divine consciousness of having done a duty, a look of triumph under defeat that compelled his reverence, as well as his admiration.

"Are you aware," he said, "that with these dispatches in your possession, and beyond our lines, you would hold this army at your mercy?"

"I am."

"And that captured with them on your person your life is forfeited?"

"Certainly."

There are people who cannot brook a steady stand in one who may be naturally expected to break down in their presence. The general was one of these. In proportion as he admired her firmness, was his desire to force her to show some giving way. He did not analyze his feelings and attribute his desire to any such cause; he yielded to it without realizing that the cause existed.

"The natural method of procedure in this case," he said, looking at her sternly, "is for me to report your capture and the circumstances attending it to headquarters. Do you remember the case of the two Confederate spies captured when this army was in front of Murfreesboro, during the past summer?"

"I have heard something of it."

"Two Confederate officers came into our lines in United States uniform, one of them bearing forged papers as inspector-general in the United States army. They left the colonel, whose lines they first entered, at evening, to go on their tour of inspection. Suspecting something wrong, they were recalled and detained while the case was reported. Word came back that there were no such officers in the United States army; that they were doubtless spies, and the colonel was directed to try them by "drum-head" court-martial and hang them at daylight the next morning, or instructed to that effect."*

While the general spoke he watched his prisoner closely.

"But how does this concern me, general?" she asked calmly.

A slight color came to his cheek at this failure to impress her.

"I will tell you, since you do not seem in a state of mind to readily draw conclusions. I report your case to headquarters. Word comes back to try you by 'drum-head' court-martial and hang you to-morrow morning."

"Well?"

"Well, that is the end of the story."

There was silence for a few moments, while they regarded each other.

"It is *not* the end of the story, general. The story of a life has no end. Death is but a transition. I shall pass through it, as a chrysalis is transformed. It pleases the Great Commander to assign me a fruit-

* A historical fact.

less task.   It is not for me to ask why.   I am but one
of His soldiers, fighting with my brothers—for my
people.''

She had conquered.   There was something so forcible in her words, something so truly grand in her
manner, that the man who would break her spirit
desisted.   He regarded her admiringly and was
silent.

"All I ask, general," she said presently, seeing
that he did not speak, "is that there be no greater
delay than necessary.   Now I have a strength which
may be worn away by long waiting, with death staring
me in the face.''

Still the officer did not speak.   He was thinking—
thinking how he could get rid of so unpleasant a duty
as the trial and execution of this splendid woman.
He feared that should he report her capture to headquarters, he would get the same reply as in the case
he had cited.

"*I* will not harm you," he said presently.   "Some
one else must take the responsibility of this complica-
tion of death and a woman.''

"It does not matter who does the work, so long as
it must be done.''

"Perhaps not to you.   It matters a great deal to
me.   My hands are clean; I don't care to stain
them.''

While this conversation was going on Corporal
Ratigan was listening and observing the speakers
with a palpitating heart.   There was something so cold
cut in the general's tones that the corporal felt a
repugnance at his prisoner being in his especial keep-

ing.   He preferred that she should be sent to some
one else, and was relieved when he announced his
intention to shift the responsibility.   Besides, the
corporal hoped that he would himself be intrusted
with her keeping until she should arrive at some camp
where the commander would be willing to receive her.

"Shall Oi take her to headquarters, general?" he
asked.

"Ah, my man," said the general, as though awakened from a reverie, "are you here?   I had forgotten
you."

"Oi can conduct her to headquarters if you desire
it, general."

"I am not in the habit of receiving suggestions
from my brigade or regimental commanders, much
less a corporal."

Ratigan saw that he had made a mistake and said
nothing.   The general regarded him with his shrewd
eyes.   It was plain to him that the man was interested in his prisoner.

"Corporal, you may go to your camp."

"Yes, sir."

The corporal brought his hand up in salute.   His
soldierly deference was all that he could give to the
general; his heart, his eyes, were all for the prisoner.
He stood for a moment with his hand at his cap,
while his glance, full of meaning, full of despair,
rested on Miss Baggs.   She returned it with one of
encouragement.   The weaker physical woman was
supporting the stronger physical man.

"Well, corporal, are you going?"

"I am, sir."

Yet for a moment the corporal could not withdraw his eyes. The order was imperative; the general was waiting. At last he turned abruptly, and strode away rapidly without once looking back.

"Orderly," called the general to a man standing near, "take this woman to the ambulance."

As Miss Baggs passed out the eyes of the two were fixed again on each other. While the general did not use words, he could not resist a last attempt with his presence, his masterful countenance, his piercing eyes, to overawe his prisoner. She met that gaze firmly, unflinchingly, till she was without the tent, then with a final glance of contempt she turned and walked toward the ambulance.

The general called her back.

"You do not seem well satisfied with my treatment of you," he said, in a tone in which there was something of sarcasm. "We soldiers must do our duty."

"It is not your doing your duty, general, that fails to win my respect; it is that you have not the manliness to do it yourself, but must needs put it upon some one else."

Again the two pairs of eyes met and clashed. The victory was with the woman. The general lowered his to the ground.

"You may go," he said.

As soon as she was gone he went to a tent where there were writing materials, and wrote a note, which he sealed and addressed. Giving it to the little captain he directed him to send it, with the prisoner and the dispatches captured on her, to the officer whose name was on the envelope.

XIV.

IT was eight o'clock in the morning. Colonel Maynard pushed back the tent flap, intending to step
outside and go to the mess tent for breakfast. The
brightness of the morning seemed reflected in his countenance. His step was firm, his bearing full of
youthful, manly vigor. He had been rapidly gaining
the confidence of his officers, and was coming to be
admired and beloved by his men. All misgivings as
to his fitness for his responsible position had melted
away. Colonel Mark Maynard was the man most to
be envied of those no older than himself in the Army
of the Cumberland.

He had scarcely passed from his tent when, glancing
down the road beside which his camp was located, his
attention was arrested by an ambulance coming slowly
along driven by a man in a soldier's blouse and smoking a short clay pipe. On either side rode a cavalryman. The colonel paused to watch the coming
vehicle and its attendants. Had it not been guarded
he would have supposed it to contain a sick soldier
going to hospital. As it was, it must either hold an
officer of high rank or a sick or wounded prisoner.
Whatever it contained, there came to the man watching it an uncomfortable feeling that it was in some
way a link between himself and misfortune. The

bright, happy look of a moment before disappeared, to be replaced by a troubled expression, though he could not have given a reason for foreboding. When the ambulance stopped opposite his tent he muttered with a knitted brow:

"What does this mean?"

One of the attendants dismounted, went to the door of the ambulance, opened it, and handed out a woman, who descended to the ground with some difficulty, as though in a weakened condition. The two then came directly to where Colonel Maynard was standing.

The woman was attired in a striped calico dress; her head and face were bare. The colonel knew at a glance that he had seen her before, but could not tell where. She walked slowly, for she seemed scarcely able to drag herself along, and he had time to study her features as she came on. The two stopped before him; the soldier saluted, and drawning an envelope from his belt handed it to Colonel Maynard. The colonel took it without looking at it. He was still studying the features of the woman.

"A communication from General ——, colonel," said the man who handed him the paper. As the soldier spoke Colonel Maynard recognized the woman he had met at Mrs. Fain's. His hand trembled as he grasped the envelope and tore it open.

HEADQUARTERS —— DIVISION,
ARMY OF THE CUMBERLAND,
IN THE FIELD, September —, 1862.
COLONEL MARK MAYNARD,
Commanding ——th Cavalry Brigade.
Colonel: I send you a woman who this morning was caught tampering with the telegraph line, and who

has evidently been taking off our dispatches. Being in transit and about to move on this morning, I take the liberty of sending her to you under guard, with the suggestion that you do with her as seems best to you. I have use for the limited number of men present for duty on my escort, and this is my apology for troubling you. Yours is the nearest command to which I can send her.

I am very respectfully
Your ob't serv't,

BRIG. GEN.

Colonel Maynard read the missive over twice, slowly, without looking up. He had not read a dozen words before he knew that he held in his possession one whose life was forfeited as his own life had been forfeited to the Confederates a year before. His keeping his eyes on the paper was to gain time—to avoid speaking when his utterance was choked with a strange emotion. His thoughts were far away. He stood on the bank of the Tennessee River, below Chattanooga. It was in the gray of the morning. He saw a skiff tied to the shore. He jumped down to seize it and found himself among a group of Confederate soldiers. Personating a member of General Bragg's staff, he commanded them to row him across the river. They started to obey. As they left the shore, suddenly a boat swung around Moccasin Point. It was full of armed men. He was taken back to Chattanooga, tried, and condemned to be hanged for a spy.

All this passed before his mind's eye as he stood pretending to study the communication before him.

Not this bare statement of it, but each detail, each feeling of hope, fear, despair, as they rapidly succeeded each other from the moment of his capture till his escape and safe return to the Union lines.

Looking up at last with an expression of commiseration which surprised the prisoner, he said:

"Madam, will you please accept my heartfelt sympathies."

Miss Baggs, who had already recognized Colonel Maynard, simply bowed her head in acknowledgment without speaking, but fixing her large dark eyes upon his. When placed in a similar position Maynard had met his enemy's glance with affected coolness, in a vain hope of deception. Not so the woman before him. The time for deception had passed with her. She was a Charlotte Corday, knowing that the guillotine awaited her—a martyr in whose eyes gleamed the divine light of a willing sacrifice to a cause she believed to be sacred.

The colonel spoke again:

"Madam," he said, "it is my duty to report your case to my commanding officer for transmission to the headquarters of this army. There is a little house across the road; if you are able to go there, you will be more comfortable while we are awaiting the reply."

"As you like, colonel."

"Perhaps it would be better to use the ambulance."

"I can walk. I would prefer it."

"Will you accept of my assistance?"

She took his offered arm and the two walked slowly

toward a farmhouse a few hundred yards distant. As the colonel passed a sentry he directed him to have the officer of the guard summoned and sent to him. On reaching the house and mounting the few steps that led up to the door, they were received by a farmer's wife and ushered into a small sitting-room. Bowing to the prisoner, Colonel Maynard stepped outside to instruct the guard. It was not essential that he should hasten, but he did not feel equal to an interview.

After seeing a sentinel posted on each side of the house Maynard turned to go to his tent. He was drawn by some unaccountable instinct to look once more at the abode of his prisoner. She was gazing out at him, with a pair of eyes melancholy, unresisting, full of resignation.

What fiend had suddenly thrown this beautiful woman, this queen of martyrs, into his keeping; with death staring her in the face, and he, perhaps, to inflict the penalty? Why, if he must suffer this turning of the tables by Fate, could not the victim have been a man? some coarse creature who would die like a brute? And why had it not come upon him before love had introduced him to that instinctive delicacy, that gentleness, those finer heart impulses of woman?

"O God!" he murmured, "suppose—suppose she were—Laura?"

He could not bear to look, and could not turn away. For a few moments the two gazed upon each other, while the woman's natural feminine discernment told her that she was pitied; told her something of what Maynard suffered; that her enemy was really her friend. She gave him a faint smile in recognition.

There was something in the smile that was even harder for him to endure than had she shed a tear. Hers was a winning smile, and her position was so desperate. She was so brave, so ready to sacrifice for her struggling people. She bore her trial with such gentleness, yet with such firmness.

She was a woman, and she must die.

He turned almost fiercely and strode back to his tent. Reaching it, he found the man who had brought the prisoner, waiting for him. The soldier saluted and handed him another envelope.

"Why did you not give me this with the other?" asked Maynard, surprised.

"I handed it to you, colonel, but you did not see it."

Maynard stared at the man without making any reply. He had been preoccupied, deprived of his ordinary faculties. Opening the envelope, he took out a small bundle of papers, on the back of which was endorsed:

"*Intercepted dispatches found on the person of Elizabeth Baggs, captured September —th, 1863.*"

Without looking at their contents he dismissed the man who had brought them, and turning, went into his tent.

The hours were long while he waited the return of the messenger he sent to report the presence of the prisoner at his camp. He hoped that he would be directed to send her forward. Why had he not thought to do so, without first reporting her capture? Such a course would have been no shirking of a duty, and they would likely have kept her and attended to her case at headquarters. Now they might leave her with him. They might order him to try, and execute her. He ground the heel of his boot into the soil and cursed his want of forethought.

"Orderly!" he cried. "Mount quick! Ride after the courier who went to headquarters—No. Never mind; it is too late; you couldn't overtake him."

It was not too late for a courier to overtake the one who had gone, and Maynard knew it. He had suddenly changed his mind. He had a vague dread at sending the prisoner away. While she was with him perhaps some way might be found to save her. In the hands of those who were not especially interested in her, her doom was sealed. No, he was not prepared to part with her.

He paced back and forth in front of his tent like a sentry on post. The members of his staff saw that there was something unusual weighing on his naturally buoyant spirits, and left him to himself, not addressing him on any matter, except of moment. It was necessary that his report should go first to division, then to corps, and then to general headquarters, and likely the answer would come back by the same rounds of the military step-ladder. And all this time he was obliged to wait, chafing like a caged lion.

Miss Baggs' capture came at a very inopportune moment for any chance there might otherwise be for mercy. Following a retreating enemy, the Army of the Cumberland had acquired a dangerous confidence. The nature of its own offensive operations had rendered essential a separation of the three different corps of which it was composed. Bragg suddenly had taken a stand with his whole army at Lafayette, whence he could easily strike either one of the Union corps in detail. A dread of disaster was coming to those Union generals, who, with a proper military foresight, took in the situation. Besides, it was known that the Confederates were being heavily reinforced. Instead of the previous blind confidence a cold wave of solicitude crept over the Army of the Cumberland.

It was noon before the courier sent to announce the capture of Miss Baggs rode up to Colonel Maynard's headquarters and handed him a dispatch. It was as Maynard feared. He was informed that in the present exigency the matter could not be given attention at general headquarters, but it was deemed important to deal summarily with spies, be they male or female. He was therefore ordered to convene a "drum-head" court-martial, try the prisoner, and if found guilty execute the sentence, whatever it might be, without delay.

When Colonel Maynard read this order every vestige of color left his face. He could not believe the evidence of his senses. Was it possible that he, Mark Maynard, once condemned to be executed for a spy, was called upon to superintend the trial and the execution which would doubtless follow, of another, for the same offense, and that other a woman? Yet there were the instructions duly signed "By order," and only one meaning could be attached. He held it listlessly in his hand for a while, and then handed it to his chief of staff.

"At what hour shall the court come together, colonel?"

"I presume at once. The order so directs; doesn't it?"

"How about the witnesses?"

"You will have to send to the source from which the prisoner came to us."

"In that event I will fix the hour for three o'clock this afternoon. The judge advocate will require a little time to prepare the charges and specifications."

"As you think best."

Colonel Maynard turned and went into his tent. Hours passed and he did not come out. "The colonel is in trouble," said one. "They say he was once in the secret service himself," said another. "Then he knows how it is to be in such a fix as the woman up in that house." "He's been there." "It was at Chattanooga a year ago. They say he brought the news of Bragg's advance into Kentucky." "Well, if he has to execute a sentence of death on a spy, and that spy a woman, I wouldn't be in his boots for the shoulder straps of a major general."

And so the comments went on while the colonel kept his tent and Miss Baggs peered dreamily out of the window, watched by guards.

XV.

TRIED.

WHEN Corporal Ratigan left Miss Baggs with the
general, to whom he had unwillingly conducted
her, he was in such a condition of mind that he forgot
all about his horse and started to walk toward his
camp. When a cavalryman shows such evidence of
absence of mind, it is a sure sign that he is in a condition bordering on insanity. Ratigan walked some
distance before it occurred to him that he was pursuing an unusual means of locomotion; then he turned
back to get his horse. When he arrived at the place
from which he had departed, Miss Baggs had gone.
Mounting, he rode to his own camp, and upon reaching there he first went directly to his tent; then, shun-
ning his comrades, stole away to a wood and threw
himself on his face in the shade of a large tree, and
gave himself up to grief.

It is difficult to recognize in this lugubrious person
the man who half a dozen hours before was dashing
on in a mad chase after the very woman whose capture
now so distressed him. But the transitions of war are
rapid and unexpected. Its lights are brighter, its
shadows far deeper than in ordinary life. Then to
the corporal had come that greatest of all complications, a moving of the human heart. For months he
had dreamed of Betsy Baggs; he had found himself

thinking of her in his waking hours, on the march, on picket, amid the roaring of guns. He had sought to banish that picture of her standing in her buggy after having duped him, which had so long haunted him, and had failed. But Corporal Ratigan had never been in love, and was entirely unacquainted with the symptoms. Suddenly circumstances had brought about an interview with her under a strange situation. Then he had discovered what it was that had been tormenting him so long.

The corporal, lying on his face, unmindful of the sweet rustling of the leaves above him, his mind tossed hither and thither by Miss Baggs of the past, Miss Baggs of the present, Miss Baggs whom he had been instrumental in capturing, and Miss Baggs treated as a spy, was not the soldier he had been. From a man of brass, he had become a man of clay.

"O Lord, O Lord," he moaned, "if they'd organized corps of lovely women to be attached to each division of the army and the enemy, there'd be no more fighting for either cause. Each would fight the other about the women and the cause would have to take care of itself."

"Corporal Ratigan!"

The corporal put his hands to his ears and groaned.

"Corporal Ratigan, I say."

Still the corporal would not hear. He knew that some one was approaching, for whether he would or not he could not help hearing his name called, each time more distinctly. Presently a soldier stood look-ing down at him.

"Corporal Ratigan," he said, "ye'r wanted at the

headquarters of Colonel Maynard, commanding the
——th brigade."

"What's that for?" asked the corporal, without
changing his position.

"Witness for court-martial."

Why will people ask questions explanatory of dis-
agreeable events or misfortunes, the answers to which
they know well enough already? And why, when the
information comes, will they deny its truth?

"If ye say that again, Conover, Oi'll brake every
bone in ye'r body."

"What's the mather wid ye, corporal?"

Ratigan by this time had got up from the ground,
where he was lying, and approached his tormentor.

"Don't ask me, Conover, me boy."

"Why, Rats, ye're looken as if ye were goen to be
tried ye'rself."

"Tried? Oi'm to suffer on the rack as one o' me
ancesters did once in the old Tower in Lunnon."

"How's that?"

"Oh, don't ask me, don't ask me. Oi can niver
endure this trial. Oi'll doi, Oi'll doi."

"Come, brace ye'rself, me boy. Ye're in no
condition to be goen before a court. What is it all,
anyway?"

"What is it all? A woman to be tried for her
life. And I caught her. Oi'm to bear witness
against her. O God, if they'd let me off by tying me
up by the thumbs, bucking and gagging, carrying a
log on me shoulders, drummed out o' camp with
shaved head and feathers behind me ears. O Lord,
O Lord, Oi'll doi, Oi'll doi."

The corporal mounted his horse and was soon jogging along at a snail's pace toward Colonel Maynard's headquarters. There was a problem in his brain which he was revolving. It was the question of leaving the case of the United States *versus* Elizabeth Biggs without a witness. This, of course, meant desertion. Desertion meant, if caught, being riddled by a file of his own comrades. This did not impress Ratigan so unfavorably, considering the terrible condition of mind he was in, but he doubted if this course would save Miss Baggs. If his desertion, even should it result in his own ignominous death, would save the life of the woman who was to be tried that afternoon, he would desert at once. But there were the dispatches found on her person. Why did neither of them think to destroy them? Miss Baggs certainly would have thought of it, except for two reasons: First, she had been dazed by her fall; second, there were love passages going on at the time the work should have been done, between her and Ratigan, which occupied the attention of both to the exclusion of all else. Ratigan put his good sense in command and it told him that his desertion would probably not save Miss Baggs. Then he remembered her singular confidence that he would in any event do his duty, and her wish that he should do it. This settled the matter and the corporal was saved from the ignominy of desertion. He rode on and dismounted at the house where the court was already assembled.

"Corporal Ratigan, you're late," said the president sternly.

The corporal saluted, but said nothing. He was

directed to wait till some preliminaries had been disposed.of, and he took position in a corner. It needed all the strength of which he was possessed to maintain himself on his legs, and he tried to keep his eyes from looking about the court room. He feared that if they rested on the prisoner, even for a moment, he would sink down on the floor, a heap of blue uniform and boots. Nevertheless the eyes will not always be controlled. Despite his efforts, Ratigan's gave involuntary glances here and there, until suddenly they rested on the object they were expected to avoid, sitting opposite, surrounded by guards, pale, but self-possessed, and a pair of glorious eyes looking at him with such sympathy and encouragement that the poor man felt as if the windows of Heaven had been opened and an angel was looking out to give him strength. Once his eyes were riveted on hers there was no getting them away, until he was suddenly aroused by a voice.

"Corporal Ratigan!"

Mechanically he staggered to a place designated as a witness-stand, and holding on to the back of a chair steadied himself to give his testimony.

"State how you first saw the prisoner tampering with the telegraph line on yesterday morning, September —th," said the judge advocate, an officer very tall, very slender, and very serious looking.

"Oi didn't see her at all."

"What?"

"It was too dark to see anything."

"Well, state what you did see."

"I only thought I saw something."

"Come, come," said the president sternly, "we have no time to waste; tell the story of the capture."

Thus commanded, the corporal braced himself to give the desired account.

"Oi was riding to camp—after having posted the relief, and coming along the road—it was the road Oi was coming along, Oi—Oi—— Colonel, it was so dark none of ye could have seen ye'r hand before ye'r face." The corporal stopped and gáve evidence of sinking on the floor.

"Well, go on."

"There was something black in the road, or by the side of 't. Oi stopped to listen. Then Oi thought some one might be tampering with the line—mind ye, Oi only thought it—and Oi called on whoiver it was to surrender. Then Oi heard a 'get up,' and whativer it was dashed off. Oi followed it as fast as iver Oi could, calling on 'em to stop, and firing me Colt. Divil a bit did anyone stop."

The corporal paused again. It looked as if he were not going to get any further.

"Go on, my man."

"Well, then we came to the camp of General ——'s division, and I was halted by the guards, while what Oi had seen got ahead. So Oi lost sight of it en-tirely."

"Proceed."

"Well wasn't it the fault of the guards stopping me and letting the other go on—and no fault of mine?"

"Go on."

"What's the use of going on? Oi lost sight of what was tampering with the wires."

"But you overtook it."

"How can I swear it was the same?"

There was a smile on the faces of those present. The questioner seemed puzzled at the corporal's device to avoid testifying against the prisoner.

"Did you not ride on and overtake what you had seen?"

"Divil a bit."

"I know better. You went on and found something in the road. What did you find?"

"Oi didn't find what I'd seen."

"What had you seen?"

"Didn't Oi tell ye it was so dark that I couldn't see anything?"

"That won't do, corporal; you certainly followed something. Now, on coming up with it, what did you find it to be?"

"It wasn't what Oi followed. That, whatever it was, had gone out with the morning light. Oi reckon it was something ghostly."

"Nonsense. Did you not find the prisoner lying in the grass?"

"Oi did," replied the witness, as if his heart would break, and he again showed signs of collapse.

"And you had reason to believe it was the person driving the buggy you followed?"

"I didn't see any buggy. It was so dark——"

"Well"—impatiently—"the person driving whatever it was you saw."

"How could I know that?"

"It was natural to infer that, there being a horse and buggy near, the prisoner had been driving it."

"There was no buggy."

"Well, the pieces."

"Now, I would ask the court," said Ratigan, steadying himself to impress the members with the probability of his position, "if the person or whatever it was I saw tampering with the wire moighten't have turned off on another road an' Oi suddenly lighted on this one."

"That'll do, corporal; you may step out and give the next witness your place."

The next witness was an officer from the camp to which the prisoner had first been taken after her capture. He testified that upon a proposition to search her, she had voluntarily produced the dispatches, which were shown to him in court, and he identified them as the same as those she had given up.

A reading of these dispatches was called for and they were read.

In addition to those Miss Baggs deciphered when at the Fain plantation, were two others, which were as follows:

CRAWFISH SPRINGS, GA.,
September 14, 1863.

Mobile Burton you when on has from other bob from reinforced Quadroon count us that to wet applause will can your undoubtedly century points orange Benjamin and beer coming we join * telegraphs.

---

* Key. The first word, " Mobile," denotes that there are seven lines and four columns. Begin at the top of the second ; down the second, up the first, down the third, up the fourth ; omitting every eighth word.

Pinned to this telegram was a paper bearing an attempt at explanation in the prisoner's handwriting.

To Burton (probably Burnside)
on your coming
can we count
when can we count on your coming?
Applause (some person, probably the signer) tele-graphs
been reinforced from
some one telegraphs that Quadroon (probably Bragg) has been reinforced from other points.

WASHINGTON, September —th, 1863.
Potts ready we result condition us if separated goes Jack all badly rapidly attack scattered the twentieth and doodle D shall but I in the but well plaster Arabia are up should present dread the concentrated jet be by should our enemy closing we to.*

There was no attempted explanation with this tele-gram. Either the prisoner had made no headway with it, or she had not sufficient time; probably both, though it was more difficult to decipher than any of the others.

These telegrams had been sent to general head-quarters and an interpretation of them furnished, which was read to the court:

CRAWFISH SPRINGS, GA.,
September 14, 1863.
To Burnside: Halleck telegraphs that you will join us. When can we count on your coming? Bragg has

---

* Key. First word, "Potts," denotes that there eight lines and five columns. Go up the fourth, down the third, up the fifth, down the second, up the first.

undoubtedly been reinforced from Virginia and other
points.   ROSECRANS.

CRAWFISH SPRINGS, GA.,
September 16, 1863.

To the Secretary of War: All goes well. We are
badly separated, but closing up rapidly. If the enemy
should attack us in our present scattered condition,
I should dread the result. But by the twentieth we
shall be concentrated and ready.   D.

The reading of these dispatches produced an impression on the court very unfavorable to the prisoner. She had held the very life of the army in her
hands. Had she got through the lines with these two
ciphers and their interpretations she would have
supplied the enemy with such information as would
put an end to all uncertainty, and insure an attack on
the Army of the Cumberland before it could be concentrated or supported by other troops. This would
have resulted in its annihilation.

There was really no defense to make, and the defending counsel simply placed his client on the mercy
of the court, hoping that being a woman death might
not be the penalty. The room was cleared and the
verdict considered. The court were not long in con-
victing the accused of being a spy and amenable to
the treatment of spies; but as to the punishment there
was a great diversity of opinion. Some thought that
imprisonment in a Northern penitentiary would be a
sufficient atonement. There were those who argued
that this would not have any effect to deter others
from similar acts at a time when the army was in so
critical a situation. Then the importance of the dis-

patches Miss Baggs was attempting to deliver to the
enemy; the fact that their delivery would have given
any general prompt to take advantage of an army's
weakness an opportunity to destroy the Army of the
Cumberland, acted seriously upon those who were
disposed toward clemency. Some members of the
court argued that the prisoner had acted as a man
and must take the consequences, the same as if she
were a man. There was none but knew that in this
view of the case she would be immediately hanged.
The disputants soon ranged themselves on opposite
sides, the one in favor of an extreme course, the other
of a life imprisonment. But the critical position of
the army and the enormity of the offense finally won
over the latter, and the case was compromised by the
convicted woman being sentenced to be shot at sunrise the next morning. The verdict and sentence
were approved within two hours of the finding, and
Colonel Mark Maynard was ordered to see that the
sentence was duly carried out.

XVI

SCARCELY had the court-martial brought in a verdict when an order came to Colonel Maynard to move his brigade across the Chickamauga Creek by way of Dyer's Bridge, to be ready early the following day to make a reconnoisance beyond the Pigeon Mountains. He ordered an ambulance for his prisoner to ride in, since he had no option but to take her with him. The distance to be traversed was but a few miles, and although it was nearly sunset before the command broke camp, it was barely dark when the tents were pitched in the new situation. Luckily a house was found for the reception of the prisoner, and the headquarters of the colonel commanding were established near it.

As soon as Maynard's tent was pitched he went inside and shut himself up from everyone. The matter of the life in his keeping, his desire to save his prisoner, the impossibility of his doing so except by betraying his trust and conniving at her escape, was weighing terribly upon him. A desperate struggle between his duty as an officer, and his repulsion at carrying out a sentence upon a woman which had once been passed upon himself, was driving him well-nigh distracted. One thing was certain: he could not save Miss Baggs without sacrificing himself. He was ready to sacrifice himself if he could do so honorably. He might even consider the matter of doing that which he had no right to do, but since the devil-may-care days of his scouting, a new world had opened to him which made the struggle more complicated than it would then have been. He had a wife whom he loved devotedly, and any obloquy he might take upon himself must be shared by her and his son. He knew that if he could conceive it to be his duty, or if he could make up his mind without the approval of his conscience, to connive at the prisoner's escape, he would have a fair chance of success. He was charged with the execution, and this would give him power over her person. On the other hand, such a violation of trust was too horrible even for consideration, and if he did not so regard it, the penalty he must suffer—disgrace, if not death—would well-nigh kill his wife. For a long while he revolved these considerations in his mind and at last came to a decision. He would suffer the torture of carrying out the sentence. He would do his duty to his country, his wife, and his son.

He had scarcely arrived at this decision when a message came from the prisoner asking to see him.

The racking of his whole nature, which had been partially allayed by his decision, came back to him with the summons. He dreaded an interview. He felt that the resolution he had formed was of too little inherent strength to warrant placing himself under so great a temptation. But his memory took him back to the jail in which he had been confined on the eve of his own intended execution at Chattanooga, and he thought how he would have regarded anyone who would refuse him such a request at such a time. He got up, and walked over to the house where the prisoner was confined.

He paused a few moments before entering, in order to collect himself, then walked slowly up the steps. The guard stood at attention and brought his piece to a "present," but Maynard did not see him, did not return his salute. He opened the door, entered the house, and in a few minutes was in a room in which the prisoner was confined. She was standing by a window. As he entered she turned and stood with her hands hanging clasped before her, her sorrowful eyes fixed steadily upon him.

"Colonel Maynard," she said, "I have sent for you to ask you to deliver my last messages. I once met you in the house of one who is dear to you. There I received shelter from the storm which raged without, but which was nothing to me beside another evil that threatened me. I was sore pressed and in great danger of capture. The women in that house—an elderly lady, a young girl who visited there, and your wife—took me in at a great risk to themselves. Your wife certainly had much at stake, for your honor might be involved. I have sent for you now to ask you to say to them that I have treasured their remembrance and their kindness to me."

She waited a moment for him to accept the trust. She might have waited till the crack of doom, without a reply; he had no power to utter a word. He simply bowed.

"I desire also to intrust this keepsake to you, to be sent to my brother."

She took a locket from about her neck, and held it up before him. On it was painted a miniature of a young man in the uniform of a Confederate officer. Maynard looked at it, and started back with a cry as if pierced with a red-hot iron.

"He? he is——?"

"My brother."

"O God!" He staggered to the wall and leaned against it, shivering.

"You know him, colonel. There is no necessity for deceit now. I have long known the singular circumstances that surround you and him: that you both loved the same woman; that you won."

"And that twice—twice he gave me—my life?"

"That he never told me."

"Ah! He never told you that?" replied Maynard, a kind of wonder in his tones.

"When at Mrs. Fain's plantation I discovered under whose roof I was sheltered. Your wife had never seen me, and I determined that it would be best for all that I should not make myself known."

Maynard stood in amazement at these developments, in horror at the situation, as he now knew it to be.

"And you are the sister of Cameron Fitz Hugh?"

"I am. I am Caroline Fitz Hugh."

" *You shall not die.*"

When Colonel Maynard spoke these words there was a grandeur in his tone, his figure, the lines of his countenance, the light in his eye, strangely inconsistent with a resolution he had made the moment before they were uttered. He had on the instant reversed his decision made not ten minutes before to do his duty, in the ordinary acceptance of what that duty was; he had determined to save the woman before him, even if it were necessary to take upon himself far greater ignominy than the death to which she was sentenced. There was silence between them, during which Miss Fitz Hugh stood looking at him in admiration, mingled with inquiry. She knew that some secret charm was at work within, but she did not know what it was.

"How can my death be prevented?"

"I am charged with your execution. I will take you to your lines myself this night."

What was that subtle influence, far stronger than battalions of infantry or batteries of artillery, which gave it to one not present, unconscious of his power, to hold Mark Maynard over a precipice, and to cast him into a black gulf below? Was it circumstances that had, a year before, led Fitz Hugh to accept the very part Maynard was now called upon to play? Was it love that had given Maynard the bride Fitz Hugh was to have possessed? Was it some invisible fiend that had made Maynard a robber of that bride from the man to whom he twice owed his life, and was now bringing on his punishment? These were indirect causes; but they cannot explain that inexpressible, intangible sense of honor which will lead a man—to speak paradoxically—to commit a crime, and sacrifice himself at the same time for another.

The expression on Miss Fitz Hugh's face, as she heard Maynard speak words which would save her from death and give her liberty, underwent a change. For a moment after they were spoken there was a delighted look, but as she realized what they meant to the man who would save her it was transformed into

an expression which can only be described as bordering on the confines of angel land. There was a holy
look in her eyes, a radiance of purity from the soul
expressed in every feature. There was the superhuman attribute of choosing death before life and
liberty at the price of wrong.

"No, colonel, we Fitz Hughs cannot accept sacrifice, and especially wrong, from others; we give; we
are not accustomed to receive."

Maynard stood gazing at her with a look as if, in
refusing the sacrifice, she had stabbed him.

"What then," he said at last, "can I do?"

"Send the news of my condition, of my expected—"she shuddered at pronouncing the word—
"execution to our lines. Knowing that I am condemned they can bring what influence they may be
able, to save me."

"It will avail nothing."

"Try it. Fate, luck, Providence works strangely
at times. Let us push on and leave the rest to a
higher power."

The colonel looked at his watch. "It is now half-
past nine. We are but a few miles from the Confederate lines. Your brother is——?"

"In ——'s cavalry division and on the Confederate
right. I heard from him only a few days ago. He
was then at Ringold."

"That is not far from here."

"There may be time," she said hopefully.

"Someone must steal through the lines. If not
shot, he may accomplish something. In half an hour
I shall be——"

"You?"

"Yes, I! I will not trust this only thread on which your life hangs to anyone else. Though I confess," he added gloomily, "I have no confidence in it."

"No, colonel, I cannot accept this from you. You are the commander here, and are all that stands between me and death. You must remain here, and send a messenger."

"Who would I dare intrust with such a message?"

"Send for the man who captured me, Corporal Ratigan; let him bear the message."

"He?"

The colonel looked at her a moment, as if to question why this man should be so trusted, but her eyes were lowered. He knew there was a secret which it did not become him to pry into.

"I will send him, if he can be found at once. If not, I will go myself. And if the mission fails——"

The words were not finished, for he well knew how precious time was, and turning from the room and the house, strode rapidly toward his tent.

He had gone but a dozen paces before he heard someone call.

"Colonel!"

He did not hear. The call was repeated.

"Colonel!"

A man approached him, whom in the darkness he did not recognize.

"Is there no hope, colonel?" the man asked in a choked voice.

"Who are you?"

"The man who captured her," pointing to the house. "Oi'll never draw sabre again."

"Corporal Ratigan?"

"The same."

"This is fortunate. Come with me."

The two started together to a thicket, wherein they would neither be observed nor heard.

"Oi'm hangen round, ye see, colonel. Oi'm away from camp without leave. Oi hope they'll shoot me for a deserter."

Colonel Maynard did not speak till they reached the thicket. Then turning and facing Ratigan, he said earnestly:

"You would like to save her, would you not?"

"God knows I would."

"Then go to the picket line and get through unobserved, if possible. Go to Ringold and find a Confederate officer—Cameron Fitz Hugh, if he is there. Tell him that his sister is condemned to be shot at sunrise to-morrow morning. Say that Colonel Mark Maynard sends him this information, that he may use whatever influence he possesses—take any measures he may consider honorable—to save her. Tell him," the colonel lowered his voice, "that I offered to attempt to do so, taking ruin upon myself, but she would not accept the sacrifice. Go, there is no time to lose. When the sun rises it will be too late."

"Oh, colonel," cried the man in agony, "there is so little time."

"Go! It is not yet ten o'clock. We have six hours."

The corporal was moving away, when the colonel stopped him.

"You will need the countersign."

Ratigan returned, and the colonel whispered it in his ear. "Carnifax Ferry."

XVII

RATIGAN'S MISSION.

THE extreme left of the Army of the Cumberland, from which Corporal Ratigan started to go through the lines, was held only by cavalry and mounted infantry, and these widely separated. There was no regular picket iine, such as usually exists between armies confronting each other where the different branches of the service are represented in one continuous line. Consequently the corporal had a far better chance to get through than under ordinary circumstances. Passing over the Pea Vine Ridge, he descended the other side sloping to a small stream called Pea Vine Creek. It was essential that he slip through between the Union vedettes unseen, for if observed he would be taken for a deserter and either shot or sent into the headquarters of his regiment. The videttes were principally on the roads, and the corporal, believing that they would be looking for an enemy on routes over which cavalry could best advance, selected one least advantageous for a horse to follow. Wherever he could find a thick clump of trees or low growth, a knoll, a ravine, indeed anything difficult for a horse to pass, he would go over or through it. Now he would stop to listen for some sound such as a horse is liable to make, and now would steal on his hands and knees or crawl on his belly over some eminence where, if he should stand upright, his body would make a silhouette against the sky. On crossing a bit of level ground he suddenly heard a horse's "splutter." He was near a clump of bushes, in which he lost no time in concealing himself. A cavalryman rode by within fifty feet of him, walking his horse slowly, the butt of his carbine resting on his right leg, and in a position to be used readily. He was patrolling a beat. Ratigan waited till he had gone past, then darted onward to trees which, from their irregular line, he judged grew beside the creek. He was not disappointed and was soon standing in shallow water, resting for a few minutes under a low bank.

Ratigan's eagerness to get on, and the consequent temptation to carelessness, were restrained by his remembrance that on his getting safely through depended that slender chance on which Caroline Fitz Hugh's life hung. His faculties were strained to their utmost acuteness. Had he been flying for his own life he could not have been so wary. His ears took in the slightest sound; his eyes, soon becoming used to the night, gave him views of distant objects with surprising distinctness; and now, crossing the creek under the shadowing trees, even his touch came to his assistance, and enabled him to grasp roots by which to drag himself upon the other side.

Once past the creek he felt that one-half his danger was ended. He had doubtless got beyond the range of his own comrades, and now came the greater danger of meeting the Confederate pickets. Men on picket, with an enemy before them, are not apt to trifle with those coming from their front, and Ratigan knew that if he should suddenly come upon a vedette he would be more liable to receive a shot than a challenge.   Leaving the creek he ascended a slight eminence, and made a survey of the surrounding country.   All was silent, except that he could hear an occasional sound like a distant burst of laughter, or a shout from the direction of Ringold, in his front. Presently he heard the unmistakable rumble of a train coming from the South.

"It will pass right down there behind that clump of trees, and go through the cut," said the corporal.   "I wonder wouldn't it be a good plan to take advantage of its noise when it passes to slip through the outposts.   They'll be thinking of the train, and I can follow in its wake."

He advanced cautiously to the trees beside the track, and waited for the train.   It came on slowly. Southern railroads at that time were not in a condition to warrant fast traveling, and the road in question was no exception.   Ratigan waited perhaps ten minutes beside the cut through which the train was to pass, but so eager was he to get on, so little time lay between life and death, that it seemed half an hour.

Presently the headlight of a locomotive shot out from around a curve.   The corporal had forgotten that its light would reveal him to the engineer.   He crouched down out of sight with a high-beating heart, and none too soon, for had he stayed where he was the light would have shone directly on him.   He waited while the engine puffed slowly by.   It was drawing a long train of mixed passenger, cattle, and platform cars; every car crowded with troops.

"They're preparing to give us a brush in earnest. Like enough these are reinforcements," muttered the corporal.

Ratigan determined to follow the railroad north to Ringold, which he judged to be only a mile distant. The train loaded with Confederate troops having just passed, the guards he might meet would probably not be very suspicious of an enemy. He walked on the track for a short distance, expecting a challenge with every step.

He received one suddenly, just before entering a wood. A man on horseback aimed a carbine at him and gave the customary:

"Who comes thar?"

Ratigan at once threw up his hands, which his challenger could distinctly see, and cried out: " I want you to take me to Colonel Fitz Hugh."

"What do you want with him?"

"Do you know him?"

"He commands a regiment in our brigade."

Seeing that the corporal held his hands above his head the man permitted him to draw near. Once there Ratigan informed him of the nature of his mission, and begged him for Colonel Fitz Hugh's sake to send him to Ringold at once. The vedette was convinced from Ratigan's earnestness that he bore a message of importance, and calling his comrades ordered one of them to dismount. Then taking the precaution to blindfold the stranger, he mounted him, and placing a horseman on either side of him, sent the three clattering toward Ringold.

It was not a long distance to the town, but all distances, all periods of waiting, seemed long to the corporal. Was not the terrible event to take place at sunrise? And now it must be near midnight.

"What is the time?" he asked of his conductors.

"Twenty minutes to eleven."

"Let's go faster. Colonel Fitz Hugh would be as anxious for me to get on as I am myself, if he knew my errand."

"All right. Let's light out, Pete." And Ratigan felt the motion of a gallop in the horse he rode.

And now comes a "halt" from a guard, and an answer, followed by "advance and give the countersign." One of the men goes forward for the purpose. Then the party goes on again, but what they pass, or where they are going Ratigan knows nothing. He only knows that they are moving, and that they are not moving fast enough to suit him. Presently they stop, and the corporal can hear one of the men dismount. There is a stroke of a clock evidently from a church spire. He counted "one," "two," "three," and on to "eleven."

"Dismount."

He lost no time in throwing himself from his horse and was led forward. The air became warmer. He must be in an inclosure. The bandage was taken from his eyes.

He was standing in a tent lighted by a candle fixed to the end of a stake driven into the ground. There was but one other person present, a Confederate

officer. He was a tall, slender young man with long
black hair, a mustache and goatee, and an eye honest,
respect-inspiring, and with all the gentleness of a
woman's.

"Are you Colonel Fitz Hugh?" asked the corporal,
making a salute as if in presence of an officer of his
own side.

"I am."

"I have a message from your sister."

Colonel Fitz Hugh turned ashy pale. No one
could come to him from her without striking terror
into him, for he knew the work in which she
was engaged. For months he had lived in dread of
her capture. If the messenger had been a citizen or
a Confederate soldier, it might not speak so clearly of
danger, but coming from a Yankee trooper, quick
reasoning told him that she had doubtless met with
disaster.

"Indeed," was all his reply to the corporal's
announcement.

"Oi'm sorry to inform ye, sir," said the corporal,
in a voice which he vainly endeavored to keep steady,
"that Miss Fitz Hugh, passing under the name of
Elizabeth Baggs——"

Fitz Hugh put his hand on Ratigan's arm and
stopped him, while he gathered his faculties to bear
what he knew was coming.

"Was pursued by a contemptible cur of a Yankee,
who deserves to be hanged for chasing a woman——"

"Yes, yes. Go on."

"Was captured and——"

"O God!"

"Condemned to be shot for a spy to-morrow morning at sunrise."

Fitz Hugh sank back on a camp cot and covered his face with his hands. For a few moments the corporal respected his grief by silence, but time was precious, and he soon continued.

"Thinking ye might exercise some influence to save her, Oi've come to inform ye of the—distressing fact."

The last two words were spoken in a broken voice.

"By whose authority?"

Fitz Hugh rose and stood before the corporal. He had nerved himself for whatever was to follow.

"Colonel Mark Maynard, commanding the ——th cavalry brigade."

"Do you mean to tell me," said Fitz Hugh, with a singular, impressive slowness, "that *my sister* is at the mercy of *Mark Maynard?*"

"He is charged with her execution."

Colonel Fitz Hugh shuddered. "That man is my Nemesis," he cried in a voice filled with a kind of despair.

" 'Tis he that sent me to ye."

"He?"

"The same."

"Does he wish to save my sister?"

"He does."

"Why then does he not do so?"

"He can only save her by his own disgrace. Your sister will not accept the sacrifice."

"A true Fitz Hugh," said the brother proudly.

" 'Then Miss Fitz Hugh suggested that he might send me to inform ye of the situation, that ye might

have opportunity to use any influence ye would consider wise and honorable to secure a reprieve."

Fitz Hugh thought earnestly with his head bowed,
his eyes fixed on a spot on the ground.

"There is nothing that I can do," he said at last.
"Threatened retaliation is the only recourse, and that
could not be effected under the circumstances without
implicating Colonel Maynard."

"Then ye see no way open?" asked the corporal
despondently.

"It is impossible for me to act intelligently alone.
If I could see Colonel Maynard, perhaps together we
might hit upon a plan."

"Would ye meet him between the lines?"

"There is not sufficient time."

"There's five or six hours."

Fitz Hugh stood pondering for a few moments
without reply. Then suddenly starting up, he said:

"Go tell Colonel Maynard that I will meet him as
you suggest. Let the point of rendezvous be—let me
see—where do you consider a feasible point? You
have just come through."

"Oi would name the bank of the creek at a point
due west of this."

"How long a time will be required before the meeting can take place? It is now a little after eleven."

"It may be an hour, it may be longer. If ye will
be there, colonel, at twelve o'clock, we'll meet ye as
soon after as possible."

"You will find me there at twelve."

"It would be well, colonel, to concert a signal by
which each should know the other."

"Suggest one."

"Oi'll doubtless be with Colonel Maynard. Oi'll cry '*Oireland*,' and you can respond——"

" *To the rescue.*"

Colonel Fitz Hugh called to those waiting outside, who had brought in Corporal Ratigan, and directed them to blindfold him and take him to the Federal lines; and, if possible, insure his getting through without injury. They were to report the result to him in any event.

Ratigan knew nothing but the gallop of the horse on which he sat, with a handkerchief about his eyes, until the party conducting him drew rein and he was directed to dismount. Then he was asked if he would be escorted to a Union vedette known to be on a road leading around the north end of the ridge, or whether he would go alone.

"Oi'll go alone," he said. "If ye go with me they'll think it a midnight attack."

Starting forward, the corporal trudged over a short distance between him and the vedette. As he drew near he began to sing a few lines from a play popular at the time.

> " Thim's the boys
> What makes the noise,
> Is the Ry'al Artiller*ie*."

"Who comes there?" cried the vedette, cocking his piece as Ratigan came in sight.

"Friend with the countersign, to be sure! Who d'ye suppose?"

"Advance, friend, and give the countersign," called

the man. He was a good deal puzzled at hearing the Irish brogue coming from that direction; but it reassured him; he did not have much fear of an enemy, unless it were a trap to get him at a disadvantage. Ratigan drew near and whispered: "Carnifax Ferry."

"What are you doing out there?" queried the man.

"Looken out for trains bringen in troops. One came in half an hour ago loaded."

"You don't mean it? Guess they're getten in reinforcements."

"I believe ye, me boy."

Ratigan walked on toward the camp till he got out of sight of the vedette; then he ran till he dropped breathless in Colonel Maynard's tent.

XVIII.

RATIGAN was so exhausted as to be only able to give Maynard a few detached sentences, conveying some idea as to what he had accomplished. There was little that it was essential should be told except that Colonel Fitz Hugh would meet him between the lines as soon as he could get there. Casting a glance at his watch, Maynard noticed that it was twenty minutes to twelve. The distance to the point of rendezvous, as near as they could estimate it, was two miles. Every minute was precious. It would be midnight before they could meet, and then they would only have about six hours in which to take measures to secure a reprieve. They could only do so by communicating with general headquarters some fifteen miles away. In any event, the case was desperate. However, Maynard had been used in his scouting days to sudden transitions, and had himself escaped from prison on the very night before his intended execution. Calling his striker he bade him saddle Madge, who, he knew, could carry him over the ground at no laggard pace, and ordering a mount for the corporal at the same time, the two waited impatiently till both animals were led up before the tent.

Mounting, they began to climb the Pea Vine Ridge. Ratigan, who had been over the ground, led the way.

They reached the top of the ridge, and the corporal pointed out the position on the creek, due west of Ringold, where they were to meet Colonel Fitz Hugh. Descending the slope they came upon a Union vedette, and were challenged with the usual words, "Who comes there?"

"The colonel commanding, with an orderly, inspecting vedettes."

They were advanced, gave the countersign, and passed on. Taking a route between two roads, and meeting no more guards, they cautiously approached the place of rendezvous.

On reaching the bank of the creek they descended it, the corporal riding ahead and peering through the darkness to discover what they were looking for. Presently the dark figure of a horseman emerged from a clump of trees on the opposite bank, and rode forward, toward the creek. Ratigan saw him, and believing him to be someone in attendance upon Colonel Fitz Hugh, called:

"*Oireland.*"

"*To the rescue,*" called the man in a low voice, and rode up to the margin of the creek.

The two men arranged that Colonel Fitz Hugh and Colonel Maynard should advance to the respective places they themselves occupied, as soon as they had withdrawn. Then wheeling, each rode back to his principal, and in a few moments more the Union and Confederate officers faced each other from opposite banks of the creek. The distance between them at this point was but a few yards, and the night was not so dark but that they could plainly see each other.

The equestrian figures stood silent, each waiting for the other to speak. The only sound came from the gurgling of the stream which flowed between them. Somehow a couplet from "The Brook," a poem which had always been a favorite with Maynard, got into his head, and the waters were continually saying:

> " Men may come, and men may go,
> But I go on forever."

It seemed that the silence, so painful and embarrassing, would last forever. Maynard tried to think of some remark by which to break it and open the interview, as Fitz Hugh evidently expected of him; but no words came. Those of the couplet kept chasing each other through his mind, and so long as they occupied it there was no room for any others. Fitz Hugh waited for Maynard to begin. The gravity of the situation could not disturb his sense of propriety. He had made an analysis of the etiquette attending such a meeting, and concluded that Colonel Maynard, having opened the question between them by sending a messenger, and that messenger having suggested the interview, it was Maynard's part to speak first. And so it seemed minutes—it was only seconds—that the dark figure in blue and the figure in lighter gray sat upon their horses and gazed at each other from the opposite banks of the stream, while the hours were flying toward the rising sun and death; and he who was expected to break the silence could think of nothing but

> " Men may come, and men may go,
> But I go on forever."

At last Maynard broke out, "You are Colonel Fitz Hugh, I believe."

"I am. I recognize Colonel Maynard's voice."

"I heard yours last on a certain evening a year ago; an evening memorable to both of us. Then you gave me my life, and by doing so placed yourself in a position to be shot for a traitor to your cause."

"Not for your sake, colonel; for the sake of another."

"It matters not for whose sake; the act remains. Once before, you spared me when you found me under a roof which covered——"

"Then I respected the laws of hospitality sacred in the South. Let us not dwell on these matters, colonel. Let us proceed with that upon which we have met for consultation."

"You are right; time presses. Your sister stands convicted of the same offense as mine at the time of which we have been speaking, and sentenced to die at sunrise. We meet to concert a method to save her."

"At my request. But any proposition must come from you, Colonel Maynard. I am unfamiliar with the feeling on the part of those in power in the Federal army as to executing a sentence of death upon a woman."

"Circumstances which I cannot explain—for they pertain to the situation in which these two armies are placed—render the feeling against your sister very severe."

"You have suggested my exerting influence from our side."

"It was your sister who suggested it.   I have little faith in it."

"What did you propose?"

"That which your sister would not accept."

"And that was?"

Maynard whispered in a strange, savage tone:

"To use my authority, as commanding the brigade charged with her keeping, to place her within your lines."

"And now?"

"I listen for some suggestion from you."

"I can think of none except, with your permission, to enter a protest over the signature of our command- ing officers of highest rank."

"It would avail nothing."

"Then there is nothing to save her from this sacri- fice which, though she has always been prepared for it, and doubtless will now meet it, like the remarkable woman she is, with becoming fortitude, is still hard for those of us who love and respect her, to bear. We will revere her memory as a martyr's."

During this dialogue each man sat on his horse, without any movement, and spoke in measured, formal, automatic tones.   Maynard's words were quicker than Fitz Hugh's, who held to the slower fashion of speaking common in the South.   After the last sen- tence spoken by Fitz Hugh, there was a long silence. They had met for a purpose; their meeting was a failure.

It seemed to both that they could hear their watches ticking away the seconds that lay between Caroline Fitz Hugh and death.   Neither knew the agony suffered by the other, unless he judged that other by himself. Neither had the heart to terminate the interview, though both knew that it was fruitless. A night bird set up a dismal cry. It seemed a death knell.

Then Maynard broke the silence.

"Colonel," he said in a set voice, "remain here, or meet me here at any time after an hour. It may be the small hours of the morning. It will be, if at all, before sunrise."

"What do you propose to do?"

"What I propose to do neither you nor your sister shall know till it has been accomplished."

"I will remain here, or near by, and at one o'clock you will find me where I now am."

"Adieu," cried Maynard, as he turned his horse's head and galloped away.

"Adieu," replied Fitz Hugh, in the stately tone to which he was accustomed, and raised his hat as politely as if he were saluting in a ballroom.

Fitz Hugh rejoined his companion and rode away in the direction of Ringold, and Maynard, followed by Ratigan, started back toward their camp. Maynard's brain was in a fever. Time had been expended to no gain. The small hours were coming on, and only six of them would pass before the event he so much dreaded would take place. He had formed his resolve. Whether wise or foolish, right or wrong, practicable or impossible, his resolution was taken. Once determined upon his course, he spurred his horse on without thought of obstacle. Turning from the rough ground on which he rode, he was about to take the road, on which he might get on faster, when he was suddenly startled by the firing of a bullet and the sound that came with it. The shot rang close to his ear, almost brushing his temple.

Knowing that he had by his carelesness suddenly come upon a Union vedette, he called out:

"Cease firing. Friends!"

In answer to a call to advance, Ratigan rode forward and found a vedette, who had mistaken them for an enemy. On making themselves known they were suffered to pass on, and Maynard, feeling that he was too incautious to lead, gave way to Ratigan. They proceeded on their way with more caution, and passed through a gap in the ridge leading to Reed's Bridge.

The good footing of the road enabled them, after getting well into their lines, to proceed rapidly. After they had passed the ridge, they left the road and turned northward. Soon after they reached camp.

XIX.

IN THE SHADOW OF DEATH.

ONCE inside his tent Colonel Maynard said:
"Corporal, I want you to get me the uniform of
a private soldier. You must do so without exciting
suspicion."

"Oi don't know how Oi'll do 't, colonel, withovt
going back to me own camp."

"I fear that will take too long. Can't you steal
one from one of the tents near by?"

"Oi moight be able to do 't, an' Oi might spend the
whole night trying. Oi can get one at me camp
certain."

"I would take your jacket, but I want your assistance. There's no other way but for you to go to
your camp."

"Colonel, Oi'll ride hard."

"Ride, and remember that every moment is worth
years at any other time."

Ratigan lost no time in mounting, and was soon
galloping on his way. Once out of the camp from
which he started he found no guards to pass, and was
able to drive his horse to the utmost. The night
before he had chased the woman whom he had then
known as Betsy Baggs in a mad race to capture her;
now he was tearing along in a mad race to save her

from the consequences of his capture. Past woods and waters flew the corporal, over bridges and hills, through hollows and rivulets, till he came to his own camp. There he at once sought the quarters of private Flanagan.

"Flanagan," he cried, shaking the private, "ye'r wanted."

Flanagan, seeing the corporal bending over him, and supposing he was aroused to go on some duty, got up at once.

"Never mind putting on ye'r clothes," said Ratigan, "do 'em in a bundle and come along. Ye'r wanted for a special duty, and that right quick."

"Duty in me drawers, is it? How would Oi look foighten that way? But all right, carporal," and Flanagan, gathering up his belongings, followed Ratigan outside the tent and away from his slumbering tent mates.

"Flanagan," said Ratigan.

"What is it, carporal?"

"Let me take ye'r clothes, and ask no questions."

"Take 'em. And divil a question will I ask except what ye do be wanten 'em for."

Ratigan seized the bundle and, with an injunction to Flanagan to keep his mouth shut if he wanted to save himself from future trials, mounted his horse and was again flying over the ground back to Colonel Maynard's headquarters.

It was now the small hours of the night. The corporal cast his eye to the east and saw a faint streak of white light there. Digging his spurs into his beast's flanks and urging him with his voice at the same time, rider and horse sped on in a race between life and death.

"Go on, ye beast," cried the corporal. "Go on, me darlin'. Stretch ye'r cussed legs; for I don't care if ye kill yersilf if we lose no time. What's ye'r loife compared with hers? On with ye, me beauty. Win the race with the sun that is showing his light there, and Oi'll worship ye forever."

With such contradictory and incoherent phrases Ratigan urged his horse till he could go no faster. Again did hills, vales, woods, waters, fences fly by, till at last the corporal dismounted at the camp he rode for, and in a moment was in Colonel Maynard's tent.

The corporal started back. A man stood there whom he did not recognize for a few moments as Colonel Maynard. He had no beard, while the colonel had had a heavy one. His hair and eyebrows were black, while the colonel's were light, and the hair which had hung below his hat in short curls was now cropped.

"Give me the clothes, quick."

The corporal handed him the bundle and Maynard lost no time in getting into them.

"Corporal," said the colonel, "let me explain what I am about to do. I know something of the blood that flows in the veins of Caroline Fitz Hugh. She will never accept her life at the price I intend to pay for it. She must not know that I intend to save her by violating a trust, by incurring my own downfall, or she will not leave her jail. Do you understand?"

"I do, colonel. She would chide me if she knew I was doing the same."

"While you have been away I have placed three horses in the wood yonder."

"I see, colonel."

"Corporal Ratigan, every man has his own part in life to perform. The distinctive feature in mine seems to be to decide quickly between conflicting duties. I am going to violate a trust, to perform a sacred obligation. If you will aid me, follow me."

Taking up a slip of paper lying on his camp cot, on which he had written an order, the two left the tent. They were challenged by the sentry on post, but giving the countersign proceeded till they were again challenged by the guard at the temporary prison. There the colonel advanced and gave the countersign, and passed into the house.

The sergeant in charge met them, and asked what they wanted. The colonel handed him the paper he had brought with him. It was an order for the person of the prisoner. The place was only lighted by a candle, and the colonel took care to stand with his back to it. But this was not necessary, for his disguise was complete. Corporal Ratigan remained without the door, on the porch.

The sergeant looked from the paper to the man who stood before him, inquiringly.

"This is very strange," he said.

Maynard made no reply.

"Here is Colonel Maynard's order," the sergeant added, reading it over again, "do you know what he wants with her?"

"Do you suppose I don't know any better than to ask questions when I get an order?" replied the spurious private gruffly.

"And I suppose you think I've no business to do so either. There's all sorts of games practiced in these cases, but an order's an order, and, as you say, I've no business to ask questions when I get one."

"Well, then, don't keep me waiting. I don't care what Colonel Maynard wants with the prisoner; he's sent me for her with a written order, and that's all there is about it."

The sergeant went into the room where Miss Fitz Hugh was confined and led her out, pale and wondering.

"It isn't sunrise," she said, in a voice which it was difficult for her to keep from breaking.

"Come," said the colonel. She followed him to the porch and Corporal Ratigan joined them, but it was too dark for the prisoner to see who he was, and he did not dare to make himself known. As soon as they had got to a safe distance he whispered:

"Darlin'."

"Rats!"

"Not a word till we get further away."

They walked on at an ordinary pace, though all desired to hasten. After passing some distance from the house, Maynard turned and glanced back. He saw the sergeant watching.

"We must go to the tent," he muttered, and the three walked on. Before entering he looked again. The sergeant was still watching. He evidently wished to make sure that all was right. All entered the tent, while the colonel, standing at the front and peering between the tent flaps, watched for the sergeant to go back into the house. Presently he did so and left the way clear.

"Now come on."

Leaving the tent they walked a short distance down the road. Not a word was spoken. Presently they turned aside and entered the wood. There they found the horses.

"Mount," said the colonel to the prisoner.

Putting a foot in his hand she sprang up onto a horse's back. There was no sidesaddle for her, but the high front of a "McClellan" served very well, and she was so good a horsewoman that she could have ridden sideways on the animal's bare back. The stirrup was fitted, the colonel and Ratigan mounted, and the three rode rapidly away.

"We must dodge the picket," said the colonel. "Even the countersign might not avail us with a woman in the party."

"What does it all mean, Rats?" asked Miss Fitz Hugh. "I thought you were going to do your duty at all hazards."

"Well, there's different kinds of duties, and sometimes they won't work together. If saving a woman's life isn't a duty, then me mother didn't bring me up right."

"Who's the other?" she asked, while Maynard was riding a little in advance.

"One who this night makes me his slave."

"And I from this night will be indebted for my life to both of you, if you succeed in saving it. But I can't bear to have you sacrifice yourselves for me. You may be committing an unpardonable sin toward your comrades, but I cannot believe you are committing a sin toward Our Father. And one day it will be all ended, Rats; and then who will care?"

"Oi know those who will rejoice."

Ratigan now took the lead, having passed over the route before several times, and being familiar with the best way to get between the vedettes. Colonel Maynard dropped back beside the prisoner.

"Who are you?" she asked.

"One who serves you."

The voice sounded familiar, but was disguised, and she did not recognize it as Colonel Maynard's.

"Were you sent by Colonel Maynard?"

"No."

"Why should you try to save me?"

"Ask me rather why I should not."

It was plain the man, whoever he might be, desired to remain unknown, and she desisted from further questioning.

"After all my death would not profit the Federal cause," she said. "My lips will be sealed to any information I may possess."

"Your information would be too late in any event. Had it been otherwise this plan would not have been attempted."

"Why so?"

"Your commander-in-chief of the Army of Tennessee has delayed too long already. He will attack us almost immediately. Your information would not now hasten that attack."

"How do you know?"

"We have captured prisoners showing that your men have been reinforced from Knoxville and Virginia. General Bragg has ceased to retreat and is about to fall upon us with a concentrated army."

"You are right in assuming that neither you nor I can have any influence for or against either side now. These troops have been coming from Virginia for a month. They are nearly all arrived; you may expect to hear the opening shot of a great battle at any moment."

The corporal, who was in front, reined in his horse and held up his hand in warning. They were on the edge of a wood and within a few hundred yards of the creek, and could see to the right and to the left.

"My God!" exclaimed the corporal, "there are vedettes there, and vedettes there," pointing north and south. "And they are both coming this way. We must go back."

Colonel Maynard rode forward to see. He glanced at both parties of vedettes, then in front of him. From that front at that moment there came a horse's neigh. It was answered by a neigh from behind the three on the edge of the wood.

"Your people are where that horse neighed. Can you keep your seat in the saddle for a dash?"

"Yes."

"We are surrounded; it is the only chance. Are you prepared? Ready! Go!"

The two men dug their spurs into their horses' flanks and all three shot out toward the creek. They had not gone a hundred yards before they heard:

"Halt there," immediately followed by a shot. They paid no attention to either, but dashed on over the uneven ground, the two men riding close on either side the prisoner for fear she would lose her balance. Her horse stumbled, but recovered. A volley came from the vedettes riding from the south, but no one was hit. In crossing a gully Miss Fitz Hugh tottered sideways, but Maynard caught her and righted her.

"On, on," he said, "a few hundred yards and you are saved."

Then came another volley; this time from the party advancing from the north. Corporal Ratigan swayed in his saddle, but recovered himself.

"They are advancing to meet us! Quick! Down the bank! Through here! it is not knee deep!"

A third volley came, but it did no harm. It was too late to stop the fugitives now. They rode right into a party of Confederate officers.

Friends gathered about Miss Fitz Hugh. Her brother, being in presence of others, restrained his desire to throw his arms about her neck. He lifted his hat to her as politely as if she were as nearly related to the rest as to himself, then took her hand and kissed it. Suddenly, in the midst of a shower of congratulations—a wild, irrepressible cheer that burst spontaneously from the party, Caroline Fitz Hugh gave a shriek. Corporal Ratigan had fallen from his horse, and lay white and bleeding on the ground. Springing from her own horse she bent over him and raised his head.

"O God! he's dead."

XX.

THE DARKEST HOUR.

THE cheer, the shriek, Miss Fitz Hugh's words, sounded in Colonel Maynard's ears as he put spurs to his horse and dashed away up the stream in a direction parallel with the Union lines. The cheer was the announcement of the completion of an act by which he had parted with what he held most dear, the confidence of his superiors, his peers, and the rank and file of the army. He had given to Caroline Fitz Hugh to see the rising of the sun whose light was now broadening in the east. He had called down upon himself what to him was the bitterest of all degradation; perhaps to meet the fate that had been intended for her. Riding up the creek on the bank nearest the Confederate lines he approached a wood. This he entered, crossed the creek unobserved, and emerged to see the men by whom the escaping party had been chased returning toward the ridge. Not caring to be questioned by them he rode back into the wood until they were in a position not to see him; then he trotted slowly to the ridge and over it, making his way back to his tent.

It was now broad daylight. As he dismounted he noticed a detachment of cavalry marching on foot, under the direction of an officer, toward the house where Miss Fitz Hugh had been confined. On arriving there they halted and the officer went inside. In a few minutes he came out and strode over to Colonel Maynard's tent. The colonel had gone in. He had thrown off his cavalry jacket and was waiting for what was to follow. The officer entered the tent and, not recognizing Maynard, shorn of his beard, asked for the colonel commanding. ·

"I am Colonel Maynard."

"Ah! I did not recognize you, colonel. I have just called for the spy in the house where I expected to find her, and was told by the sergeant that he had delivered her soon after midnight to two men bearing an order from you."

"Well?"

"I suspect something must be wrong. Was the order a forgery?"

"No."

"Then the prisoner is in your keeping?"

"No."

"Escaped?"

"Yes."

The officer was too astonished to ask any more questions at once.

"Who is responsible?" he asked presently.

"I am."

"You?"

"Yes, I. You will march your men back to camp. You need not make any official report of the matter unless you choose. I will report the escape myself."

The officer bowed and, with the same astonishment on his face that had been there throughout, turned from the tent, and going to the men standing in the road marched them back to camp.

Colonel Maynard came out of his tent and mounting his horse rode to the headquarters of his division commander. He rode slowly, his head bowed almost to his saddlebow. Reining up before the general's tent he sent in his name by an orderly, and was soon admitted.

"General," he said, "I have come to prefer charges."

"Indeed," said the general. "Why not forward them in writing in the regular way?"

"It is because of the person against whom I am going to prefer them."

"And that is?"

"Myself."

The general looked at him with a puzzled expression.

"Colonel, are you ill?"

"No, general."

"I suppose it would be ridiculous to ask a man if he is all right here?" and he tapped his forehead with his finger.

"I am sound of mind and body."

"Well, well, colonel, what does it all mean; it's too early in the morning for joking," and the general yawned.

"I have to report that the spy left in my charge has escaped, and through my connivance."

"Good Lord!" exclaimed the general, "that *is* a serious matter."

Maynard remained silent.

"And the explanation?"

"There is none."

The general looked into the melancholy eye of Colonel Maynard, and felt a cold chill creep over him. He knew there was some reason for the act which would explain, if not excuse it.

"Colonel, you are a dashing fellow, with a tinge of romance in your nature. I trust you have not yielded to an absurd notion as to taking the life of a woman."

"No. I have not."

"Then give me some explanation. I fear it will go hard with you, but I will do all I can for you if you can give a satisfactory reason."

"I have no reason to give."

"Of course I must report the matter. Better speak now; it may be too late hereafter."

"I have reported the fact. That is all the report I have to make."

"Then, colonel, it is my duty to order you to your tent under arrest. You may leave your sword here with me, if you please. An order will be issued placing Colonel —— next in rank, in charge of your brigade."

Colonel Maynard unhooked his sword from his belt, and handed it to the general. Then he rode back to his tent, and as he entered it he felt that he had left his former self outside; that, as in the case of a fallen comrade, he would never see this being of the past again. As for his present self, that, if suffered to live, could only live a life in death.

The news of the singular act by one of its most

promising, its most popular colonels, rapidly spread among the army. It was received with different feelings by different persons. Some were so averse to the shooting of a woman that, if they had had a reasonable explanation, they would gladly have excused the act in their hearts, though they could not but condemn it openly. To the great majority it was a traitorous breach of trust, a violation of all the instincts of a soldier, that could merit no less punishment than that which had been intended for the prisoner. Knots of men discussed it at the mess tables of officers and by the camp fires of the soldiers. All regretted that the blow had fallen on Colonel Maynard, so young, so recklessly brave, so promising; and there was scarcely a man who did not secretly rejoice that the Army of the Cumberland had been spared the obloquy of executing a woman. It was supposed that the spy carried important information; that she possessed dispatches which would seriously endanger the army, and this fact tended to bring down most of the condemnation which fell upon the man who had assisted her to escape.

The result of this feeling was the ordering of a court-martial to try Colonel Maynard with as much dispatch as had attended the trial of the escaped woman. The charge was "giving aid and comfort to the enemy," the specification "himself aiding in the escape of a spy in the service of said enemy."

The court met on the afternoon of the day on which Maynard had reported his act. Men of his own grade, or near it, sat about a pine table in a wall tent and proceeded with the formalities attending the case. As Maynard pleaded guilty to both charge and specification, there was little to do except to come to a verdict. Before doing so the president asked the accused if he had anything to say in his behalf, any explanation to make.

"No," was his reply.

"Colonel Maynard," said the president, "you have served this army with distinction. You have been respected, trusted, beloved as few other men in it. You have confessed to having committed one of the most atrocious crimes that can come under the jurisdiction of a military court. Nothing can excuse it. There may be something to palliate it. I conjure you to speak before the court brings in a verdict and names your punishment."

"Mr. President," replied Maynard, "for my act toward this army I am accountable to you as a court-martial convened to try me; for my act as one of right or wrong, of honor or dishonor, I am accountable only to a tribunal with which you have nothing to do. Do not waste valuable time. Before the sun sets twice, if I mistake not, you will have a more important work to do in the reception of the enemy. Do your duty as a court, and do it with dispatch."

There was not an officer present but looked at Maynard with a curious admiration. It was plain that he had sacrificed himself, though it was not entirely plain why. Even those who condemned him most bitterly seemed to hesitate to bring in a verdict which would naturally carry with it the punishment of death.

"You are mistaken, colonel," said one of them,

referring to Maynard's predictions, "the enemy have been in full retreat ever since we left Murfreesboro. I only fear he's going to give us the slip again."

"I regret your confidence, sir," replied Maynard. "I am aware that others feel as you do; and it is a mistake which will cost this army dear."

"Nonsense. Haven't we——"

"This is not the place to discuss problems for which only our commanding general is responsible," interrupted the president. "Let the prisoner leave the court."

Maynard was led away, and the court proceeded to consider a verdict. There was little time spent on it, for there was but one thing to do, and that was to make it "guilty of the charge, and guilty of the specification." Then began a discussion of the punishment. One of the members stated that it was personally known to him for a fact that the accused had one year before visited Chattanooga as a spy, when the place was held by the Confederates, had been captured, tried, condemned, and sentenced to be hanged. That Jacob Slack, a boy who was now serving as his orderly, had been with him; that he had contrived to get news of Maynard's condition to Missouri Slack, his sister, at Jasper, Tennessee; that she had gone to Chattanooga, had entered his jail, had exchanged clothes with the prisoner, and thus effected his escape; that he had been concealed, and afterward helped through the lines, by a Miss Fain, whom he had married on reaching the Union lines. "I put it to you, gentlemen," he concluded, "could one whose life had been saved by women, carry out a sentence of death upon a woman for the same offense for which it was intended he should suffer?"

The speaker knew nothing of the relations existing between Maynard and Fitz Hugh. It is impossible to know what might have been the effect had he possessed this knowledge. The court acted only on the information communicated by the officer who told the story of Maynard's experience as a spy, and the main facts in this were known throughout the army. The circumstances of the accused's sentence by Confederates to be hanged for a spy and his escape, the valuable service he had rendered the Union cause, the reasons he had for not wishing to shoot a woman, saved his life. The sentence of the court was that he be dismissed the service with forfeiture of all pay and emoluments.

When this sentence was communicated to Colonel Maynard, he was in his tent, waiting to know his fate. He had expected to be shot. He hardly knew whether he was more moved by the leniency shown him, or more disappointed at being obliged to live a disgraced man. But one reason gave him comfort that he was not to die: his wife. He knew that, although all others looked upon him with horror, she would love him all the more that he suffered.

XXI

A MILITARY PROBLEM.

THE events attending the capture and escape of
Caroline Fitz Hugh, and the dismissal of Colonel
Maynard from the service, all happened in such quick
succession that Jakey Slack was not aware of what
was taking place until after it was all over. It must
be confessed that Maynard had not treated his most
devoted adherent with the consideration he merited.
But it is the way of people who are rising to eminence
to gradually leave off familiarity with those formerly
most intimate with them. Maynard had treated Jakey
with mock deference, but had not thought of leaning
upon him for advice or strength, much less comfort,
and during the raging of the fire through which he
had passed Jakey Slack had been as far from his mind
as if he had not existed.

One evening as "retreat" was sounding—it was the
evening of the colonel's deposition from his rank and
command—Jakey walked into his tent. Maynard's
head was bowed down on his camp cot. Hearing
someone enter he looked up and saw his old friend.
Had Jakey been another boy, when he saw the hag-
gard look, the strongly marked lines of suffering in
the face before him, he would have shown some mark
of the effect such a sight had upon him. Not so
Jakey. There was no expression either of surprise or

grief upon his unexpressive countenance. But the sight of Jakey standing there to remind him that, though a whole army condemned him, there was one in it who never could be brought to think him guilty of any crime, had a different effect on the late commander. He reached out his hand, took that of Jakey and, drawing the boy toward him, folded him in his arms. Thus do those who have been deprived of their greatness go back for sympathy to those from whom they have farthest departed.

Maynard held the boy against his breast, while he gave way to convulsive sobs such as are unusual in a man, and only come when some mental struggle under an intense grief is relaxed, and suffering permitted to get control. Neither spoke. Jakey's presence reminded Maynard the more keenly of those he loved. His mind had been upon his wife and child. Jakey's coming brought also Souri's image, and the trials and triumphs which he and Jakey and Souri had once passed together; and trials and triumphs borne in company weld hearts. Of all who loved him only Jakey was there, and on him alone could he rely for comfort.

At last Jakey withdrew himself from his friend's embrace. He had permitted him to indulge his grief for a few minutes, and this he considered quite long enough.

"General," he began. He had always called his chief "general," contending that he was a general since he commanded a brigade.

"No more of that, Jakey; I am only Maynard now, Mark Maynard. Mark is a good enough name for me,"

"Wal, that don' make no differ. You'uns got th' same body, 'n arms, 'n legs, 'n all thet. Hev y' done th' fust thing fo' ter do?"

"What's that, Jakey?"

"Tell Mrs. Maynard."

"Jakey, I can't."

"Recken she'll hev ter know 't some time."

"There's going to be a battle. No court can keep me from shouldering a musket or wielding a sabre. I'll go into the fight that's coming, and never come out of it. Then she'll not need to know it."

"What makes y' think ther's goen ter be a fight?"

"I would not have the intuitions of a soldier if I did not."

"Y' haint General Rosey."

"Nor do I need to be General Rosey to divine what's coming. Do you suppose I knew any more about war with eagles on my shoulders than in a private's uniform? If there were some superior being to look into the heads of the men composing this army, and readjust the rank in accordance with fitness, many a star would leave the shoulder where it now rests to light on that of some obscure private."

"Wal, ef we fight 'em won't we wnip 'em?"

Jakey noticed that, with the change of his friend's mind from his grief to war, there was an immediate improvement from the terrible depression upon him. He asked the question for the purpose of keeping Maynard's attention fixed for a time on war, rather than for information.

"Whip 'em? Why, Jakey, we're scattered all over creation." He dipped his finger in a tin cup full of water and began to draw a rude map on the top of an extemporized table, consisting of a square board nailed on a stake driven in the ground.

"Here's the Chickamauga flowing between these two ridges, Missionary and the Pigeon Mountains, from south to north into the Tennessee. Crittenden's corps is here at Lee and Gordon's Mill. Thomas' corps has just passed through Stevens' Gap down here, ten or a dozen miles from Crittenden, while McCook is at Alpine, twenty miles away from Thomas. *We* are off here, near Reed's Bridge, the tip of the left wing, forty miles from McCook, the tip of the right wing.

"Bragg is here at Lafayette, on the east side of the Pigeon Mountains, and opposite our center at Crawfish Springs, where he can strike any one of our corps separately. He can ride up onto the Pigeon Mountains and, looking down on the valley of the Chickamauga, see just where we are located. I was up there myself the other day with a reconnoitering party and came upon one of his scouts, looking at us very much as one would survey a barnyard of fat turkeys before Christmas."

He paused, and seemed lost in some attendant problem. Presently he added absently:

"All I'd be afraid of would be delay."

"What d'y mean by thet?" asked Jakey.

Maynard started. "I was thinking that I was on the other side," he said. "You see, Jakey, in a military point of view the beauty of the situation is all with the Confederates."

"How?"

"They can cut us up in detail."

"Wha 'd you do if you wor him 'uns?"

"I! I'd drive a wedge right in here between Thomas' and Crittenden's corps. I'd destroy first one and then the other. After that I'd eat my rations and have plenty of time to take care of McCook's, which is too far away even to hear the guns."

"That 'ud be hunky," said Jakey, pretending to catch his friend's enthusiasm. "Pity' twasn't t'other way and we had 'em as they got we 'uns. Mebbe ef you 'uns wor in command of our army y' mought do somep'n fo' ter change th' siteration."

"I?"

"Yes, what.'d y' do?"

"That's a poser, Jakey."

Maynard studied his improvised map for a while without speaking, as if it were a chess-board. At last he said:

"General Rosecrans, I learn, has ordered his scattered columns concentrated at Crawfish Springs, the center of his line. Perhaps this is as good a plan as any, at least if Bragg gives him time enough to close up. To me two plans seem to be open. One is to demonstrate along the Chickamauga, principally with cavalry; while——"

"What's demonstrate?" interrupted the listener.

"Make a feint, a fuss, pretend to have a big force and only have a little one. I would leave the camp-fires burning at night, to make them think I was still there, and draw my army away to Mission Ridge. Moving backward on converging lines——"

"What's them?"

"Lines coming to a focus——"

"What's a focus?"

"Confound it, Jakey, we'll be attacked and whipped before I can make you understand. These roads you see come together at Chattanooga. From Chatta-nooga, if necessary, the army could be crossed——".

"I thought we 'uns was a-folleren them 'uns!" observed Jakey, surprised at the turn the campaign had taken.

"Jakey, did you ever hear of the man who held his adversary down by placing his nose between that adversary's teeth?"

"No."

"Well, that's the way we're holding our enemy; but your remark leads to the other side of the problem. Desperate diseases require desperate remedies. If I were a general I'd never be on the defensive if I could help it, cost what it might. It sets a man to wondering what his enemy is going to do, instead of doing something himself. Now our southernmost column might be pushed out here,"—putting his finger on the line denoting the Georgia Central Railroad,—"to cut the Confederates' avenue for supplies. Bragg might turn and crush it, but he can do that now. The trouble is, Jakey, we need troops for quick marches; flying col-umns to move without camp equipage. Such a column down there could strike, retreat, strike at another point, and so confuse an enemy that he wouldn't know what was to happen next."

Jakey was too young to understand the phases of the war problem in which Maynard's mind had become engrossed to the obliteration of his trial, disgrace, wife, child, friends, comrades, everything but the game that charmed him. But Jakey's mind was as much on his friend as his friend's was on the problem, and he determined to go on fostering the awakened interest. Unmindful of the demonstration made thus far he suddenly broke out:

"Supposen I wor th' general commanden this hyar army 'n you 'uns wor th' general commanden t'other army. Now, how would 't do fo' me ter march out in the middle o' the night 'n just knock the stuffen right out'n you' uns?"

Maynard smiled. It suddenly occurred to him how little Jakey knew of the game of war; how useless had been his explanations.

"What would be your plan of attack, general?" he asked, wishing to humor the boy.

"Wal," said Jakey, who had no more idea of what he was talking about than the fourteen-year-old boy he was, "I reckon I'd put the big guns in a long line on top 'n th' Pea Vine Ridge hyar, 'n jest scatter shot 'n shell like chicken feed."

Maynard burst into a laugh. Jakey surveyed the altered expression of his friend's face with his bright little eyes and chuckled, but his own face was as imperturbable as usual.

"General," said the boy-commander's supposititious enemy, "what would you do if I were to draw my troops out of range?"

Jakey was puzzled. He made a desperate effort to conjure up a reply.

"Wal," he said presently, "I reckon I'd jest wait fo' you 'uns ter do somep'n."

"Your ground would be strong enough in itself, but weak on the flanks, especially your left, and in case of retreat you would have the creek to cross in face of an enemy—a hazardous undertaking. I would turn your left and get possession of the roads to Chattanooga. Perhaps I could defeat you and force you to recross the creek. While you were doing so I would knock you to pieces. If you succeeded in crossing you would find my troops in your rear between you and Chattanooga."

Jakey neither understood nor even heard a word his opponent said, but he looked as seriously studious over the problem as if he were the general commanding.

"Are you whipped, general?" asked Maynard.

"Wal, mebbe ef I air whipped I don' know nothen 'bout 't, 'n I'll jest go on fighten till I make you 'uns think thet you 'uns air whipped."

"Like Grant at Pittsburgh Landing."

The reference was lost on Jakey, but it led him to think that he had made a point; he looked very wise and said nothing. He was thinking on a line which he feared might be of some practical importance to his individual self. He was not certain but that it would be necessary for him to make the connecting link in person between his friend and his friend's wife. So he turned the conversation on lines of retreat.

"Now suppose," he said, "just supposen I war busted, right hyar, how'd I git away?"

"That would depend on the condition of things. If I were the general opposing you, you'd never get away safely. I'd never stop till I had driven you into the Tennessee River."

"How could I get thar from hyar?"

"This part of your army where we are now, could only fall back on Rossville. There the flanks would be better protected for a stand. You could go from Rossville to Chattanooga by this road" (pointing to it on the map). "If you should be successful in keeping your enemy far enough from you and long enough, you might cross the river there, and save your army. You might perhaps stay there if not too reduced in numbers, and if you could keep your line of supply open."

"This air th' bridge I'd cross the creek on, I reckon," pointing to Reed's Bridge on the map.

"That's the nearest from where we are."

"Wal, general," said Jakey, in a tone to indicate that the discussion of the campaign was ended; "ef you 'uns bust me I'll retreat that-a-way."

Nothing more was said about the imaginary campaign by either. Maynard's eye was fixed on his water map, and he was lost in study. Jakey let him alone till he saw that he was drifting back to his trouble. Then he endeavored to lead him into war again. At last, seizing a favorable opportunity, the boy suggested the propriety of sending some message to his wife.

"Time enough for that after the fight," was all Maynard would say. Jakey was discouraged. He knew that if his friend lived after the fight it would not be his own fault.

XXII.

JAKEY considered himself bound in honor to report to Mrs. Maynard her husband's condition, not only on account of his promise made her on the evening of his departure for the front, but because he had a vague unformulated notion that there are certain exigencies where only women can "do somep'n," and he knew that "the general" required his wife's attention. There seemed to be no way of acquainting her with the condition of affairs except to go and tell her himself. Jakey, being in the army, could not leave it without permission. The question was how to get such permission. Not being a quick thinker Jakey spent several hours on the problem without any result. At last he determined to make a beginning, at least, and going to the headquarters of the new commander of the brigade, he sent in word that "General" Maynard's clerk wished for an audience. Jakey was ushered into the presence of a gray bearded colonel, twenty years older than the late colonel commanding, who in Colonel Maynard's clerk expected to see a soldier not less than eighteen years old, and standing over the regulation limit of five feet four. When little Jakey Slack appeared before him he opened his eyes in surprise.

"What do you want, sonny?"

"General Maynard, he don't command no mo', 'n I want ter go hum."

"What position do you hold in the service. I see you wear Uncle Sam's buttons."

"Drummer, detailed fo' duty at General Maynard's headquarters."

"In that event, you'll have to go back to the band you started from. I can't let you go home. I have no such power."

Jakey turned from the tent without another word. He had cast his fortunes with "General" Maynard, and, while he was in his element with the army, that army was nothing to Jakey without the "General." He made up his mind that if he could not keep his promise to Mrs. Maynard with permission, he would keep it without permission. Now Jakey had learned enough of army regulations to know that absence without leave at such a critical juncture would be considered as flagrant a breach of army regulations as desertion, and the penalty for desertion he well knew was to be shot.

"Wal," he said after mature deliberation. "I goen ter do what I promised anyway."

A violation of principle, even if it is to right a wrong, will always extend its malign influence. Mark Maynard had made such a violation, and here was Jakey Slack, who looked to him for guidance, about to imitate his example. If his beloved "general" could break an army regulation, certainly it would be no harm for him to do so. At least so reasoned Jakey.

He had always kept the clothes he had on when he joined the army. He felt that he was of quite enough importance to have *impedimenta*, and the only *impedimenta* he possessed was his old clothes. They had been carried in the wagon with Colonel Maynard's baggage and now came in handy. Jakey did them up in a bundle, and as the bugles were blowing the tattoo, he sallied forth to saddle Tom. The horse looked around and, seeing Jakey, submitted himself to be saddled and bridled, after which Jakey, with his bundle under his arm, mounted by the aid of a convenient stump and rode away. He was stopped by a sentinel, who recognizing him as the former brigade commander's factotum, permitted him to pass. Having crossed the creek and reached a clump of trees away from the camps he rode into it, and dismounting took off his blue and brass and put on his old clothes.

"Ef the general air reduced," he said, "I reckon I got' ter be. These air good 'nuff fo' me now."

Having divested himself of the plumage, which, notwithstanding his remark, was very dear to him, he rolled it in a bundle, and fastening it in the crotch of a tree where it would be covered by successive layers of green boughs, he carefully noted the place, which was the only wooded spot near the fork of two roads, so that in case he should want his uniform again he could find it. Then remounting Tom he set off toward Rossville, remembering by the water map that the right-hand road led there.

It was about eleven o'clock at night when he reached Rossville. He determined to rest there a few hours, and making for a cavalry camp, got on the "soft side" of a sergeant, and turned in with his natural associates, the soldiers. Jakey asked the guard to waken him at two o'clock, at which time, after a bite furnished by his friend, the sergeant, and a feed for Tom, he set off toward Chattanooga. At daylight he crossed the Tennessee River and was soon on his way across the neck of Moccasin Point toward his destination.

As Jakey approached the plantation it occurred to him for the first time that the information he bore was not pleasant for him to give to anyone, especially a woman, and that woman "the general's" wife.

"Reckon she 'uns 'll be skeered when she sees me," he muttered to himself. "I don't like this business nohow. Wonder I didn't think o' this befo'. Wish ther' wor some'un ter tell her. Mebbe I'll see Souri first. Ef I do, I'll let her tell."

But Jakey was not so lucky. He reached the plantation just before breakfast-time, and as Laura Maynard cast a glance from her chamber window she saw him ride up to the veranda. She remembered well the promise she had extracted from Jakey, and knew in a moment that he was the bearer of some bad news. Putting her hand on her heart, to stop its thumping, she ran downstairs and out on to the veranda. The boy dismounted and came up the steps.

"O Jakey, what is it?"

Now, Jakey had his own methods of carrying his points, and whether or no they were original or ingenious he carried them. Sometimes his parrying was very clumsy. It was so now. He must gain time at all hazards.

"What air what?"

"There's something happened to the colonel. I know it. Tell me the worst."

"Wal, now, Mrs. Maynard, 'the general' he hain't dead nohow."

"Thank Heaven he lives. Is he ill or wounded? Is the wound mortal? Or is his illness dangerous? Will he recover? Oh, tell me, tell me!"

"Which 'un o' them air questions shell I answer fust?"

Souri came out on to the veranda, and seeing Jakey took him into her arms.

"What are you doing here, Jakey?" she asked.

"Reckon I air a standen on ter th' gallery jest now."

"Mark is ill, wounded, Heaven knows what!" exclaimed Laura, "he won't tell me." She clasped her hands and trembled.

"Jakey, don't give Mrs. Maynard pain by keeping her in suspense; tell her."

But Souri dreaded to have her friend hear bad news, as well as Jakey dreaded to give it.

"Wal," said Jakey, cornered, "the general: he air damned obstinate."

"Obstinate?"

"Yas."

"What do you mean, Jakey?" asked Souri, encouragingly.

"Wal. The general, he reckons ther's goen to be a big fight 'n he's goen fo' ter git hisself killed."

"Heavens!" exclaimed Laura. "What *does* it all mean?"

"Means Miss Baggs."

"Miss Baggs!" cried the wife, bristling. "So it's something about *her*."

" 'T's all 'bout her."

"Tell me what you mean, this instant," said Laura, with flashing eyes.

By this time Jakey had got to a point where he could begin to tell his story. He did so after the following fashion:

"Miss Baggs, she wor kecht taken the telegraphs off 'n th' wires and turned over to the general. The general he wanted to turn her over to headquarters; but they was too smart for him. They tole him 't try her 'n kill her."

"The cruel monsters!' cried Laura.

"Maybe Jakey's got it wrong. They'd not be likely to express it that way," said Souri.

"Reckon that's about it with a spy, anyhow. The general, he tried her, but when it come 't killen her, he wasn't thar."

"The noble man; it is just like him," from Laura.

"Then he found out that she was a sister of a old friend o' his'n."

"Who was that?" from Laura.

"Mister Fitz Hugh."

"Caroline Fitz Hugh?"

"Reckon."

"Who is she?" asked Souri of Laura.

"I—I never saw her. I know who she is, though."

"Then the general he dressed hisself like a private sojer, 'n he 'n Corporal Ratigan——"

"Corporal Ratigan!" exclaimed Souri.

"Yas, he 'n Corporal Ratigan, they run her over the lines."

"Well?" from Laura, breathlessly.

"The general he confessed, 'n they tried him 'n——" Jakey hesitated.

"Sentenced him to be——? O Souri, help me." And Laura tottered against her friend.

"Ter be cashyered."

"Do tell me what it is," gasped Laura, looking imploringly at Souri.

"I don't know; what is it, Jakey?"

"Bein' dropped out'n th' service."

"And is that all?" cried Laura, hysterically. "Only dropped out of the service: and for doing a noble act! Poor Mark! I know that he will consider this a terrible disgrace, but to me it is a blessing. Now I can show him how I love him," and dropping her head on Souri's shoulder she burst into a torrent of tears.

XXIII.

MARK MAYNARD was passing the first night after his sentence. Jakey had left him, after their discussion of the campaign, to relapse into gloom. He blew out his candle and threw himself on his camp cot. Sleep would not come. The events of the past few days caracoled fantastically before him like an army of cavalry goblins in review. They had scarcely got by before they turned and came cantering back again. Thus they marched and countermarched till midnight, and still no sign of sleep. Maynard tossed and turned and pined for day. And what would it bring forth? Surely a battle could not be much longer delayed, and with a battle there was a chance for oblivion.

Scratching a match he reached for his watch. It was twelve o'clock. He felt that he could no longer bear those low-peaked canvas walls above him. He must get out under the broader canopy. Lighting his candle he noticed the uniform of private Flanagan, in which he had aided the escape of Caroline Fitz Hugh. He put it on and, throwing back the tent flaps, stepped out into the night. The sky was covered with thin clouds, behind which the moon shone, giving a light between darkness and moonlight. He set out toward the front. Passing out of his own immediate camp he ascended the slope of Pea Vines Ridge, which stood dark against the eastern sky. Climbing to one of its highest points, where he could overlook the Pea Vine Valley, he seated himself on a rock and gave himself over to meditation. Around him was the dark circle of the horizon, while above was the great dome. Beneath him, on the eastern slope of the ridge, were the Union out-posts, beyond which slept a Confederate army. Back of him, in the valley of the Chickamauga, were the Union troops, the two armies making in all a hundred thousand souls.

And yet these vast numbers seemed dwarfed under the great vault above. The heavens would last forever, but these hundred thousand men must all at last be gathered within the slowly folding wings of time. Many doubtless in a few days; a moiety of the whole, a few gray beards from the now youthful ranks, meeting once a year to talk over their long past campaigns, speak reverently of their fallen comrades and part to convene in smaller numbers the next year. One by one they would join those who had become a part of the fields on which they fought; their better part reforming in their new-born existence, spiritual hosts unalloyed with human passions, to continue an eternal contest between right and wrong.

While Maynard was thus musing there came a distant rumbling from the south. It grew, faded, was lost, and reappeared, the unmistakable rattle of a train. It came on slowly from a distance of several miles, the rolling of the trucks, the panting of the locomotive, growing louder the while, till it reached a point directly east of where he was sitting and a few miles south of Ringold. There it could not only be heard, but seen

by him.   He watched it move on up the road and at
last it was lost in Ringold.   He listened to hear if it
went further, but the sound did not recommence.

Scarcely had the train stopped when another was
heard coming from the same direction.   It, too, came
on, was lost for a time in the tunnel, and passing north,
stopped where the other had stopped.   Then came a
third and a fourth, all moving in the same direction.
In less than an hour Maynard counted five trains, all
of which stopped at Ringold.

He rose from his seat.   "There," he exclaimed,
pointing to Ringold, "is a point from which, if I am
not mistaken, there will soon come an attack on our
lines.   They are bringing troops in those trains to
mass them on our left, where there is so little to oppose
them.   If the trains were going south, it would argue
that the enemy were retreating.   Coming north means
that they are going to take the offensive.   It looks to
me as if this rapid moving of men at this hour meant a
daylight attack right here on the left.   If so, there is no
time to lose.   I must get back and give a warning."

He walked rapidly in the direction of Reed's Bridge,
where he knew all about the forces encamped there
(cavalry and artillery), but as he walked it occurred to
him that his information would likely not be credited
in any event, and as a deposed officer it would be especially liable to be disregarded.   Still he went on, has-
tening his pace, and coming to the headquarters of the
commanding officer of the troops he sought, found an
aide who was on duty all night, the general being ap-
prehensive in his exposed position, and wishing to be
called at the slightest sign of an attack.   To him May-

nard recounted what he had seen, and the general was awakened and informed. He turned a willing ear to Maynard's caution, and at once ordered that the men be aroused, the horses fed and breakfast prepared. Then the horses were saddled, the artillery harnessed, and the baggage loaded into the wagons.

After imparting his information Maynard went to his own camp, called for his horse, and buckling on his saber and pistol rode back to the camp he had left. He arrived just in time to join a reconnoitering party starting to ride over the ridge in the direction of Ringold. Being in a private's uniform he was not recognized by the men—his appearance was much changed by the loss of his beard—and fell in with the last files as though he belonged to the troop.

The squadron trotted up the road leading through a gap in the ridge, and stood on a summit overlooking the Pea Vine Valley. By the light of day Maynard looked down upon the landscape he had seen a few hours before; but ah, how changed. Ten thousand men in gray were coming across the valley.

It is a solemn sight at any time to see an army moving to strike a foe. There was something in the silent movement—too far for him to hear the tramp of the men advancing over the intervening space, still wearing its summer robes of green—to remind him of a thunder cloud rising in a clear sky. There were compact columns of infantry steadily marching, while on either flank cavalry trotted forward, head up, like a troop of lions over jungle. Occasionally there came a confusion of distant sounds—orders—mere murmurings preceding the storm. The advancing host seemed rather a troop of specters, moving with the wind—an army of malicious spirits coming to scatter a plague from their still silent weapons.

This fancy vanished with the first few shots from the skirmishers. They were too real, too spiteful, to attribute to any but human agencies. Back goes the thin line of blue before the scattered Confederates in advance, supported by thick columns of dusty gray. No skirmish line would care to stand against these columns coming silently, not yet in presence of a foe worthy of a volley.

Suddenly there is a rumbling, a shouting, a lashing of horses in Maynard's rear. Turning he sees a Union battery, drawn by horses, galloping up the slope from the bridge. Dashing into position, the horses are swung around, pointing the muzzles of cannon toward the advancing host. The guns are unlimbered; there is a boom, followed by a shrieking shell arching toward the heavens, and dropping with a sound like an exploding rocket over one of the advancing columns.

The shot produces a change in the disposition of the closely packed Confederates, as a turn of a kaleidoscope alters the combination of colors. The closed columns halt, quickly extend wings on either side, joining tips, each while deploying, resembling the continued line, from tip to tip, of some huge distant bird. Now they are in line of battle, and once more move forward, while the Union battery drops shells in their extended and less vulnerable ranks. Marching over open fields, crossing gulleys, now lost in a wood, to appear upon its other edge, bisecting creek and road, a slowly drawing coil, a line of the "ribbed sea sand," a streak of dust before a rising wind, the Southerners move steadily forward. Before them the Union outposts give way, retreating under cover of their guns.

What are those funereal looking wagons driving up and being stationed at different points? those men, with a strip of red flannel about their arms, scattering themselves over the field? To the young enthusiast for war in the distance, who has been impatient to see a battle, these wagons, these men marked with red, composing the ambulance corps, getting ready to take care of dead who have not yet been killed, wounded who have not yet been hit, bring the first realization of what war means. There is none of the harsh music of battle about these grim-looking wagons, these men waiting for victims, to brighten the eye and send the blood coursing through the veins. They go about their work in a methodical fashion that dampens ardor as water quenches fire. They mock a soldier's ambition for glory. There is something in the calculation, the preparation, to remind him that, after all, the gold lace, the feathers, the martial music, are but to cause him, like the pampered sacrifice, to forget what he is for—to be shot.

But Mark Maynard was a veteran, and had seen all this before. He gave the ambulance corps a single glance, and then looking toward a group of Union officers partly concealed from him by the smoke of the battery, saw one of them, with the stars of a brigadier-general on his shoulder, peer northward through a field-glass. Turning his eyes in the same direction he could see a light cloud rising west of Ringold. He watched it and observed that one end of it was trending toward a ford, north of Reed's Ridge. The officer soon shut up his glass, and in another moment aides were galloping away to give orders to retreat. A column of Confederates, extending for miles, were marching to the ford to turn the Union left, and no time was to be lost in getting the little force back to the bridge.

There is a quick limbering of guns, and skirmishers, cavalry, gunners, all hurry back over the ridge. At the bridge they find two regiments ready for any duty to which they may be assigned. They are directed to hold the ford to which the column of dust is moving. Protected in that direction, the force at the bridge awaits more confidently the coming of the advancing Confederates.

They have not long to wait. The skirmishers, a thin line of gray, is soon seen skurrying over the ridge like light scattered clouds before a "white squall." The main line of gray is still tramping over the Pea Vine Valley, keeping the slow pace of their heavy guns. The Union men do not wait for the stronger force; they turn upon these skirmishers and drive them back through the gap to their more slowly moving comrades.

Mark Maynard, following with the rest, soon again found himself on the ridge. There, in the valley below, was the line of battle he had seen, but nearer—a crescent-shaped line extending from the bank of the creek above the ford across the northern end of the ridge into the Pea Vine Valley. Battle-flags appeared above the line at regular intervals; each one of fifteen flags Maynard counted, indicating a regiment. He knew that the little Union force east of the Chickamauga could not stand against what appeared to be at least a division of infantry with a very strong force of cavalry. Nor was he wrong; the scythe swung round as if moved by the arms of a Titan, mowing with its sharp edge the opposing Unionists. They were sent flying back to the bridge and hurriedly put themselves into a position to defend it.

They are ready for the storm when it breaks, meeting it with artillery and charges of cavalry. The Confederates are driven, but by this time their artillery has been got forward and posted at a point north of the bridge, where it can sweep the valley of the creek, the bridge, and those whose purpose it is to defend it.

Now there is imminent danger. Will the little force on the east bank get over or will it be cut off and captured by these overwhelming Confederates? It can only be saved by one portion charging the enemy while the others are moving by twos (the bridge will stand no more) across the structure.

Among those who charged and recharged to keep off the gray coats swarming upon them on that eventful morning, always in the advance, in the spitting line of foam that precedes the billow rolling upon the sand, Mark Maynard was ever present. As each wave rolled from the margin of the Chickamauga broke upon the Southerners, and receded, a number of the Union troops had passed the bridge. Maynard waited till every man was over, then stepping on the bridge he joined a party who were tearing up the flooring, to prevent the enemy from following. At last these left for the shore and he remained alone. As board after board came up, the Confederates pushed nearer, but still he worked on. Bullets sang to each other as they passed from east to west and from west to east, while the air was thick with interminable explosions. At last all was done that could be done. Whether his action had so excited the admiration of his enemies that they had no heart to shoot him, or whether an overruling power would not let him die, he at last turned unhurt and joined his comrades.

He had been exposed as never before, as he might never be again, but he had not met Death.

XXIV.

THE NINETEENTH OF SEPTEMBER.

SELDOM has an army been in a more critical position than the Army of the Cumberland at this
juncture. The Confederates overlapped the Union
front on the north by half a dozen miles, and between
Confederates and the Chattanooga road, leading from
what was both the Union left and rear into Chattanooga, there were only small bodies of cavalry. Bragg
had but to overwhelm these, cross the Chickamauga,
and march a few miles westward to seize this road and
throw himself between his enemy and that enemy's
base—Chattanooga. It was his intention to cross
Reed's Bridge by eight o'clock in the morning, with
one column, and Alexander's Bridge, a few miles
above, at the same hour, the two columns to join and
seize the coveted road, attack Crittenden's left, while
a third Confederate column, crossing at Dalton's Ford,
would attack him in front. Crittenden once crushed
under these combined forces, as it was expected he
would be by noon, the whole Confederate army was to
overwhelm Thomas, still ten miles distant, leaving
McCook, twenty miles away, to be finished later on.

There was nothing on the left to prevent the execution of this attractive plan but the two bodies of cavalry at Reed's and Alexander's bridges. Eight o'clock
came and they were not overwhelmed. The sun stood

high over the valley of the Chickamauga, and still the
Confederates had not crossed at either of these two
points.   The defenders of the bridges were a swarm of
hornets flying in their enemies' faces with many an
effective sting.   At noon they were still stinging.   It
was not till three o'clock in the afternoon that the defenders of Alexander's Bridge were forced to give way,
and those at Reed's Bridge only retired on learning
that the other had been captured by the enemy.   So
the morning and the afternoon passed, and when evening fell but eight thousand Confederates had been
thrown across.   What was to have been executed on
Friday, the eighteenth of September, must be deferred
till the next day.   Will it then be too late?

The moon is lighting up the field, the woods, the
summits of the two ridges inclosing the valley of the
Chickamauga, and a hundred thousand soldiers.   The
air is cold and crisp, and myriads of camp-fires are
scattered over the valley, as a reflection of the starry
heavens upon the bosom of a lake.   All night the
moon gleams upon the steel of the two sleepless armies:
the Confederates pushing across the Chickamauga, the
Unionists marching to cover their unprotected left.
Many a soldier casts his eye up into the serene heavens
and remarks the Queen of Night looking down upon
him, so pale, so cold, so dead, as if in mockery of his
own animate being, and prophetic of what may come
for him on the morrow.

From the southward comes the tramp of dust-cov-
ered men in blue.   At their head rides one who before
the sun twice sets is to take first rank among the heroes
of Chickamauga.   Thomas is leading his men from a

distant point far beyond Crittenden, to the exposed
left and rear; to the Chattanooga road—the road commanding the line of communication of the Army of the
Cumberland. It must be a forced march, for the time
is short and the distance is great.

From the eastward the Confederates are pushing
across the Chickamauga. Every available passage is
occupied, but there is little left of the bridges and it is
slow and hazardous work at the fords. Large bodies
of men are like streams. They flow easily across open
countries, but become choked in narrow ways. Yet
the work goes on. It is a long night; long for these
men wading through water, or standing in the chilly
hours past midnight in wet clothing. It is an eventful
night; for if they get across in sufficient force, and
the way is still unblocked as yesterday, the fate of the
Union army is sealed.

At midnight Maynard lay under a tree, trying to
catch some sleep. The exertion of the day would have
brought it, for he was exhausted; but his position, as
to the army with which he had no place, was burning
him like a hot iron. A few days before and he would
have been leading his brigade through these stirring
scenes. Now he was not even a private soldier. He
was an outcast, a wretch too detestable for the respect
even of menial cooks and strikers, of teamsters, of the
grasping horde of army followers, whose object was to
cheat the soldier and rob the dead.

The moon, finding a convenient opening in the
boughs above him, looked at him in a way that in a
measure quieted him. What an absence of turmoil on
her surface! No guns roar in her valleys, no armies

contend for the possession of her ringed ridges. The thought for a moment chased away his desire for oblivion. He shuddered at her nothingness. The scenes through which he was passing seemed far preferable. He was in the midst of man's coveted action. While that lasted he could not for long be plunged in despair. Thank Heaven, he was permitted to seek solace in such turmoil, such roaring of guns and yelling of men as had come and was coming.

Toward morning his thoughts became less intense, less clear. The sounds coming from a troop of horses, picketed near, became more and more confused; the snores of men, resting after a day of hard fighting, lost their vigor; the branches above him twined indistinctly; he slept.

He was awakened by the sound of a gun. It was broad day. He started up and listened. Then came another dull boom, then another, and in a few minutes there was the rapid firing of a battle on the left. Surely that is not the little body of cavalry in whose ranks he had fought the day before.

Mounting he rode toward it through a partly wooded, partly open country. The fields were gray, but the woods were still green. Then there was the odor of the morning in the country and the chirping of birds, hunting for their breakfast. It would not be long before that perfume must give way to the smell of gunpowder, before the chirping of the birds would be drowned by the sounds of musketry and artillery.

Meeting an aid-de-camp riding at full speed toward the south, he called out, pointing in the direction of the firing, which he could now discern was on or near the Chattanooga road:

"Who's there?"

"Old Pap, with two divisions."

Maynard uttered an exclamation of surprise and pleasure.

"How did he get there?"

"Marched all night."

"Much force in his front?"

"You bet! I'm going for reinforcements;" and in a moment he was out of sight.

A courier came dashing from the opposite direction.

"What news from the right?"

"The head of McCook's column is at Crawfish Springs."

"Good. The army is safe for the present; the game is balked."

Striking the road leading to Alexander's Bridge he found himself in rear of the Union line of battle that had opened on the left. A force hurried by to the support of comrades at the front. The ground he was on had just been fought over, and dead and wounded were scattered everywhere. Entering a wood he pushed forward through it. A young soldier, a boy of eighteen, was sitting on the ground, supported by a tree, gasping for breath. A red stream, running down his bosom, showed that he had been shot through the lungs. "You are thinking of home, my boy," muttered Maynard, and pushed on. An officer lay in his path and begged him for what the wounded crave so eagerly—water. Maynard rode about hunting for a stream or a spring. At last he found what he sought, and filling a canteen rode back to where the man lay. He was dead. In his hand he held a picture of wife and two little children.* Within hearing of the booming in front and shells cutting the trees above him, he had passed from the harshest, through the gentlest of human feelings, to the eternal peace.

Riding on Maynard met an officer he had known intimately. Without thought of his altered condition, the degraded colonel waved his hand in salute and cried out: "How goes the battle, major?" The officer passed by with a look which Maynard never forgot. It sent the hot blood mounting to his cheeks. He could have cloven the man's skull with his sabre. But there was no need of that. Was there not an enemy at the front? Yes, and there was death. He dashed on and arrived at one of the hottest points on the left just as a line of cavalry was moving to a charge.

Joining them he rode down into a storm so wild, so fierce, so full of destruction that surely he thought the coveted Death must come. But the gaps in the ranks were to his right, to his left, anywhere, everywhere, except where he rode. And when the troopers with whom he fought came out of the fight Mark Maynard was still among the living.

So opened the battle of Saturday, September the nineteenth. Throughout that day Maynard rode wherever he saw that the grim specter hovered. At times he was with the cavalry, at times he would dismount, and leaving his horse in the rear go forward with a musket. On one occasion, catching the enthu-

* The incident is related in war memories of an officer: "Steedman and his men at Chickamauga."

siasm of battle, he was forgetting his misfortune, when the officer of the regiment with which he fought recognized him. The two had been at enmity.

"Leave these ranks!"

Maynard turned, saw that he was addressed, and who addressed him. Throwing down his gun, the hot tears bursting from his eyes, he turned away.

Again he was tramping through a cornfield on the flank of a regiment, when he saw a division general inspecting the men as they passed forward to an attack. He recognized the general who had sent the spy to him. Their eyes met. Maynard had by this time come to see through the device by which the other had led him into his present position and regarded the officer steadily. The man turned his horse's head and galloped away. There was one man in the army who did not care to look him in the eye.

Maynard kept Madge, as far as possible, within striking distance, returning to her frequently after his marches on foot. As the dusk of evening was coming on he mounted her and rode forward to get the position of the Confederate line in his front. He was in rear of a Union line lying down and firing. They would fire, rise, move forward a little, fall and fire again. Maynard kept near in their rear, till wishing to see how the line joined on the left, he rode in that direction. He was astonished not to find any troops there. Glancing in his rear he discovered the backs of troops firing in the opposite direction. It at once occurred to him that they were Confederates, who had pushed further forward than their supports. He was about to turn away, when he saw that he was discovered. With that resource for which he had been famous in his scouting days, he determined to play a bold game. It was growing dark, and in his dusty and begrimed condition it would be difficult for anyone to tell what uniform he wore. Putting spurs to his horse he dashed in front of the Confederate line, holding up his hand and shouting:

"Stop this firing. Stop firing."

Those who heard him obeyed. Riding along the line toward the colonel he cried:

"Colonel, you'll kill our own men if you don't cease firing in that direction."

Dashing on, as if he were a staff officer on an important duty, he watched his opportunity, and seeing cover in the distance gave Madge the spurs and amid a shower of bullets (for by this act it was plain to which side he belonged) rode into safety.

"General," he said, riding up to an officer in command of a Union brigade, "there are some Confederates over there in advance of their line. If you will march your men by the flank you'll go in behind them and capture them."

"How do you know?" asked the general.

"I just came from there and saw them myself."

The order was given and parts of two Confederate regiments were captured. The colonel commanding them inquired for the Yankee who had been ordering his men about, but by this time Maynard was off to another part of the field.*

The day passed with a succession of blows upon an

* This feat was actually performed during the war by a young aid-de-camp in the Union Army.

army still too "strung out" for its own good. But they were all successfully resisted. Wherever a place was weak, some brigade or division was sent to strengthen it, usually leaving a place where it had been. But all points were strengthened in time; all damage repaired, at least the damage on which hung defeat; the damage to the dead and thirsting wounded scattered along the line for miles could never be repaired. It could be counted and laid down accurately in the official reports; but who can count or repair the hearts broken with every charge, every defense.

And so the sun went down, over a field on which there was no victory, no defeat; only suffering and death.

XXV

THE night has come again. The smoke has rolled away from the battlefield of Chickamauga. There is neither sound of cannon nor musketry, except here and there an occasional picket firing. There is another sound within the dark forest where Thomas' men are resting, the sound of the wood-chopper's ax. The commander-in-chief of the Confederates hears it and knows with a general's quick perception that another chance of destroying his enemy is passing. He cannot enter that forest at the dead of night to stop that chopping, and he knows as he hears hundreds of axes replacing the more appalling sounds of the day with the clatter of their blades, and now and again some great tree crashing through its neighbors, that by morning his enemy will be entrenched behind breastworks.

Maynard bivouacked on Thomas' line. The two armies lay too near to each other to light tell-tale camp-fires, and as all equipage had been sent to the rear and blankets were scarce the army spent the night shivering. The wood was too thick to see anything above the lower branches. The men needed sleep, but it would be as easy to sleep on the battlefield as in the continuous clatter of those axes. Besides, distrust had come upon the whole army. It was an anxious night to the generals, and the men partook of the solicitude of their commanders. It was known that the enemy had been reinforced from Virginia, Knoxville, and other points. It was rumored that Burnside was coming, but Burnside did not come. To a natural fatigue was added that more appalling weariness of being constantly in the presence of death, and the certainty that when the soldier should rise in the morning the grim specter would rise with him to haunt him for another day.

At midnight the corps and division generals met at headquarters for a council of war. All believed that the Army of the Cumberland had been sacrificed; that they had been pushed forward without adequate preparation or support, and that the enemy from even distant Virginia had been permitted to slip away to overwhelm them. There was dissatisfaction at the past and foreboding for the morrow. As they rode away to rejoin their commands, many an officer ground his teeth and muttered imprecations upon those whose mismanagement they considered had brought an impending disaster.

There is a streak of gray in the east. The commander-in-chief of the men in gray listens for the sound of guns in the hands of those he has ordered to begin the attack at daylight and which are to be a signal for others. The streak broadens; day comes, the sun rises; it is eight o'clock. Still all is silent along the line. It is only a mistake; only an order not received or understood by the general who was to lead off, but in that mistake is involved possible failure. With all the vaunted generalship on the field of battle what is it, after all, that turns the tide except the mistakes?

Mark Maynard, on that Sunday morning, was lying with his body in the dirt and his head on the root of a tree. He dreamed that he had just come in from making a charge at the head of his brigade, and was approaching his commander to report a glorious success; that the general said to him, after thanking him for his achievement: "Colonel, it will give me pleasure to recommend you for promotion to the rank of brigadier——"

"General!"

He awoke and saw Jakey Slack looking down on him. It was he who had spoken the word "General!"

"General," said Jakey, as he saw his friend's eyes open. "'T's ben a damned hard fight."

"For Heaven's sake, my boy, where have you been, and what are you doing here? The battle will open soon again this morning. I wonder it hasn't opened already. You must get back."

"I thort I war a sojer."

"Well, Jakey, you are a soldier; that's a fact; and I'm not."

"Reckon I'll git cashyered. I ben away 'thout any furlough."

"Where?"

"Wal, I thort I'd go 'n see Souri afore the fight, cos I mough'nt hev no chance after it. I mought git killed, 'n then I wouldn't be no good nohow."

"Have you seen her?"

"Yas."

"And Laura?" he started up.

"Yas."

"And you told her——"

"Reckon."

Maynard paused in his questions; he dreaded to know how his wife had received the news. Did she condemn him, with the rest?

Jakey put his hand in the pocket of his coat and took out a card on which was a picture of Laura, holding her child. Maynard seized it and in a moment his eyes were riveted on it, to the exclusion of all other objects; his mind drank in thirstily all it suggested.

"Mark," he exclaimed suddenly. "For these you must win back your spurs."

"Reckon she 'uns 'ud like fo' ter hear y' talk that-a-way," put in Jakey sympathetically.

"Jakey, I'm a changed man. I feel that I am to have a chance to vindicate myself on the field to-day. For two days I have been fighting in the ranks. I have had only a private's opportunity, and that is to furnish material for the sacrifice demanded by the god of war, while the god only smiles on those who lead the victim. To-day—to-day——"

"Somep'n 'll turn up sho', you bet."

"Come, we must get some breakfast. We'll need it soon. This day will decide the fate of the Army of the Cumberland."

Going to a group of soldiers near by, from whose camp-fire emanated the pleasing odor of boiling coffee, the two asked and received a breakfast.

A fog hung over the valley of the Chickamauga which screeend the two armies from each other. Maynard and Jakey were ignorant of their surroundings, a hundred yards distant ; so they munched their "hard tack" and swallowed their coffee, quite willing to be hidden from Confederate fire while they were doing so. Meanwhile Jakey gave his friend an account of his trip, and how he had arrived on the field at noon the day before.

"How did you find me, Jakey?" asked the hearer.

"Wal, I ast a good many sojers and none of 'em knew whar y' war. 'Bout dark I heard one o' th' cavalry of the old brigade, *our brigade*, thet knew y'. He was a tellen how y' went with 'em in a charge. They all liked ter hev yer do that-a-way. I ast him whar I mought find y', 'n he reckoned he sor y' goen up this way. So I kem and found y'. That's all."

As he finished, Maynard exclaimed:

"Look."

The fog had suddenly lifted. They were on a ridge which had been fortified during the night, the works resembling a horse-shoe. Their position was on the left side of the shoe and commanded a view up the Chattanooga road, which ran directly north from where they were. There, a short distance east of the road, and overlapping the Union left, the lifting mist revealed a line of Confederate gray. As Maynard spoke, with a shout they rushed forward and took possession of the prize they had been trying to grasp for two days. They were between the Union army and Chattanooga.

Leaving Jakey where they were, and instructing him to stay there till he should return, Maynard went down to take a hand in the fight. He found a dead soldier, whose musket and cartridge-box he seized, and pushing on to the line of firing, took position with an infantry regiment. The enemy, unsupported, were driven from the Chattanooga road to a ridge near by, where they halted and gave their pursuers a desperate fight. Then the regiment to which Maynard had allied himself was ordered to another part of the field and he went with them. Passing through a thick fire of bullets, which were mingled with the larger missiles of cannon, he encountered a sight that has seldom been seen on the field of battle. Crouching under a log was a little girl * about eight years old, who having got caught in among the disputants, was right in the midst of a battlefield. Maynard never forgot the contrast between the terrified child and the unmerciful scenes surrounding her. Being a volunteer he was under no man's orders, except as he chose to obey them. Falling out of the ranks he went to the child, took her up in his arms and while bullets pinged about them, and shells screeched above them, carried her to the rear, to where he had left Jakey.

"Here, Jakey," he said, setting her down by the boy, "it's time you have a sweetheart, so I've brought you one. She comes to you from the field of battle and probably won't stand any nonsense. So you must treat her with proper deference."

"Golly!" exclaimed the boy, squaring himself before the weeping girl, with his hands in his pockets.

"Take her to that house down there and wait till I come; that is, if I ever do come; and, if I don't, tell my wife to look out for this little one, and if necessary provide for her. I must go; there is hard fighting at the front."

Jakey took the little girl by the hand and led her

* This incident is related in personal memories of an officer: "Steedman and his men at Chickamauga."

away, while Maynard went over to the south slope of
the ridge to see what was going on at the right.
Standing on an eminence he looked down on the contending lines toward the south.

The sun was now standing midway between the
horizon and the meridian.   The day had thus far gone
without any especial advantage on either side.   Finding the left strong, the Confederate commander was
massing troops on the right of the line of blue.   Maynard could see them marching into position for a
gigantic effort.

There was a momentary lull in the firing on the right
and Maynard thought that from a distance he caught
the faintest sound of a church bell.   It might have
been fancy, for congregations would not be likely to
meet near a battlefield, and the continued roar in the
center and left would likely have prevented a bell
being heard.   At any rate, it suddenly occurred to
him that it was Sunday morning.

Sunday morning! What a contrast between that and
other Sunday mornings he had passed.   It was near
eleven o'clock, the hour when people were assembling
for worship, and he pictured the neatly dressed throngs
moving to church, while bells were ringing in the bel-
fries.   All over the broad land congregations were assembling, unmindful of the struggle that was going on
at Chickamauga.   Doubtless in the early morning in
the cities "extras" had announced the battle of the
day before; doubtless in many there was a feverish interest in the news from the front, and in some an anxiety for dear ones exposed there; but the vast throng
of worshipers, North and South, were about to bend the

knee in adoration of a beneficent Creator, while two armies representing them were grappling in a death struggle.

But an event occurred at that moment to put to flight all thought in Maynard of what was passing elsewhere. The enemy were moving to the attack. As Maynard glanced toward the Union line, to see if it was in condition, he saw a division face to the left and begin a march in rear of another division, leaving its place in the line a defenseless, yawning gap.

"Great Heavens! Some one has blundered!"

"Halt! Go back! Great God! what are you doing?"

Who could hear him at such a distance, who would obey him if heard? Oh, the agony of a sight like that! To see men marching not only to their own destruction but the destruction of their comrades; doubtless of the whole army; and without the power to prevent them! Oh, for a battery with which to fire smoke over that death-trap, to conceal it. Oh, for a cyclone to blow dust in the eyes of those Confederates. God grant that the stupidity which prevails in war may seize those Southern generals, now; that they may not reap this offered advantage. May they be blinded. God! this is terrible.

"There! They see it. They are preparing to march through it. There they go. Hear those cheers: that 'rebel yell.' They're near it; they're in it. Our men are breaking on the right of the gap. There goes a regiment, a whole brigade on the left. Heavens! how those gray coats leap forward. It's a splendid sight, if they *are* Confederates. They know it's all up with us. The whole right of the army is giving way; broken, scattering pell-mell over the field, chased by the Southerners pouring volley upon volley after them."

"Stop and rally! No, no one could rally troops on the breast of Niagara. But there's a crumb of comfort: those men nearest this way are bending back like wrought iron. They are not breaking. Good! There's a faint hope for the left. But, O Lord, what's the left, with the right and center gone?"

That historic blunder, followed by that historic disaster, carried away in the maelstrom, the general-in-chief of the army, the leader of a corps, and several division commanders. There was no rallying point till Missionary Ridge was reached, and that was four miles away. Fortunately for the rest of the army some of the troops belonging on the right of the Union line had been sent to strengthen the left. These were saved from the rout, and ready to stand by the still unbroken left.

And now comes a spectacle, a contrast which must always stand out a splendid monument of heroic endurance in the great cemetery of war—the spectacle of an army, one-half routed, gone, driven like dry leaves, before the wind, the remaining half holding in check for more than half a day a force against which the whole had found it difficult to contend. Standing in the center of the "horse-shoe," the fortification of which his wisdom has constructed during the night, General Thomas, intent upon guiding the troops of his own corps, with no word from his commander-in-chief, for a time not knowing, or at least not admitting, that the army is by all the rules that govern the science of war defeated, goes on fighting as if there is but one Army of the Cumberland, and that composed of the troops under his command.

The right put to flight, the Confederates prepare to crush the remainder of the army. All around the "horse-shoe" they gather their forces, and hurl them against the blue-coats. The first onset fails. There must be another. A second wave goes rolling on and dashes against the logs behind which the one-armed Army of the Cumberland is fixed. It recedes without making a breach. It will need more such waves—a constantly beating surf. Surely that curve, with flanks bent almost in a circle, almost touching, cannot be called a line of battle; it may be a curve of battle, but how can such a curve stand against the whole Army of Tennessee?

But this curved array of bayonets is too tough to be broken in front. It must be taken in flank. There is a ridge just beyond the right heel of the "horse-shoe"; it has been abandoned by the Unionists; no one seems to know why. Climb up, Confederates, seize this ridge; it commands the Union right. Once firmly lodged there you can hammer them unmercifully.

And the gray coats do climb the ridge and drag artillery with them.

The Union commander sees them, and at a glance discerns that without a force to drive them from it his army is lost. There is no such force; every man is engaged, and needed where he is. The general's brow is knit and his square mouth sets even more firmly than before.

"There is a cloud of dust rising over there to the

north, General, and men marching under it," said an aide. "I wonder who they are?"

It makes a great difference to the hounded general whether they are friends or enemies. He looks anxiously in the direction pointed out by his aide and orders him to reconnoiter the uncertain column. The officer rides forward to a point where he can get a good view, draws rein, dismounts, and climbing a fence brings a field-glass to bear on the advancing troops. They are far from him; they are covered with dust, and their flags are furled, so that he cannot tell whether they are blue or gray. If they are gray, that means destruction for the troops defending themselves in the horse-shoe. If they are blue, they may serve as a forlorn hope on the ridge commanding the Union right.

The aide not only sees these troops, but the troops see the aide. They too wonder if he is blue or gray. Neither can tell, but from his position they suspect him to wear blue. At any rate, they assume that he does.

Suddenly every flag is unfurled displaying the stars and stripes.

Enough! Mounting his horse the aide rides over the ground between him and the head of the advancing column.

"Who are these troops?"

"The first divison of the Reserve Corps."

Posted at the opening of the struggle to guard a bridge across the Chickamauga, on the extreme north of the battlefield, with orders to hold it at all hazards, this division had for two days listened to the sounds of fighting without firing a shot. The Confederates had made a crossing without using the bridge watched, and the division was a useless guard. On Sunday morning its commander, chafing at inaction, yet dreading the consequences that might occur the blame attending a disobedience of orders, determined to burn the bridge and march to the relief of comrades whom he divined were being hard pressed. Gathering his principal officers in a church near by, he announced to them what he proposed to do. The little church, unused at that hour of that holy day to anything more vigorous than a minister pounding the pulpit or the strains of Old Hundred, rang with the assenting acclamations of soldiers.

Marching through fields of yellow corn, guided only by the distant but continuous roar, the division each moment lessened the distance between it and the army whose fate hung on its quick coming. The direction taken led them toward the north side of the "horse-shoe," and the rear of the Confederates. First a small body of Confederate cavalry, guarding a hospital, were met. These were easily scattered, and the column moved on. Striking the Chattanooga road the division marched on down it. There were heights to the east, and on these were guns. It was plain to the gunners that the advancing column was a rescuing column. They opened fire to delay it. The Union troops did not heed them; there was a more important enemy, a more important work further on.

But they were marching directly in rear of the Confederate line. Filing to the right, through an orchard and open fields beyond, they came to a point where the dim outline of the troops engaged could be seen through the overhanging clouds of smoke. The Reserve halted in a field between the two bent flanks—the two heels of the "horse-shoe,"

XXVI.

STORMING THE RIDGE.

MARK MAYNARD was standing holding Madge by the bridle, surveying the battlefield. He heard a gun fired from the crest of the ridge so important to both armies. He turned and saw the shell it sent, whirl in a spiral, screeching above the heads of two officers, evidently of high rank, standing in a field near the center of the "horse-shoe." One of them, a large, massive man, he recognized as General Thomas. The other was the commander of the newly arrived division. As Maynard looked the latter rode away. He was going with orders to retake the ridge.

Maynard had not seen General Thomas for months. Indeed he had met him but a few times since the days when he was the general's favorite scout. Remembering his disgrace he was about to go away, not caring, in his altered condition, to meet the man for whom of all the army he felt the greatest reverence. But the general turned before he could do so, and looked in his direction.

It was too late to go away unobserved, and Maynard felt a desire to discover if there were not something after all in this great soldier so great that he could afford to give him a kind word. He walked toward the spot where the general stood.

"What are you doing here, my man?" said the commander of all there was left of the Army of the Cumberland, sternly, seeing the begrimed Maynard in private's uniform and not recognizing him. "Why are you not with your regiment?"

"I have no regiment, general."

"Your troop, then."

"I have no troop. I am not a soldier."

"Who are you?"

"Mark Malone."

The sternness on the general's face slightly relaxed.

"Ah, Colonel Maynard. Pardon me. I did not recognize you."

"No, general. I *was* Colonel Maynard; I am now a private citizen. I would be glad to assume my old scouting name, Mark Malone."

"I heard of your — misfortune. I regretted it doubly, remembering your services when you were scouting."

"Yes, general; then my services had some value. I was fitted for a scout, a spy. You thought I was fitted for something better and advanced me. I was vain enough to think you right. I did not know myself. As a spy I needed no conscience; I was not subservient to any principle. When, as a brigade commander, I was obliged to choose on higher ground, I failed, in the choice. I have proven myself unworthy of your confidence. I have sunk to the level from which I started."

The general did not reply; he was watching the newly arrived division getting into position.

"You connived at the escape of a spy, I think?" he said presently.

"Worse. I assisted in that escape."

"A woman: was she not?"

"She was, general."

"H'm. It isn't a pleasant task to shoot a woman. Yet a soldier must do his duty."

Maynard did not reply.

"Colonel, there is going to be a weak spot there. I would like you to go and see that that gap is closed. My staff are all away, as you see, on some duty. Ah! Never mind. They are marching by the flank, I see. Now it's all right."

He was so intent upon the forming of the line that for a moment Maynard thought he had forgotten his presence.

"Who was this woman?" the general asked, presently.

"You remember when I went to Chattanooga to bring you information of Bragg's movements to Kentucky, I met a Confederate officer—a Captain Fitz Hugh, who twice gave me my life?"

"Yes, yes, I remember. They're standing well down there in the center, and with so little ammunition. They'll get their new cartridges presently from those brought by the reserve division. The ammunition comes as opportunely as the men."

"'They're making a good fight everywhere," observed Maynard.

"Let me see; you say you were called upon to shoot a woman. She was some relative to this Captain——"

"Now Colonel Fitz Hugh. A sister."

"That made it pretty hard for you, colonel. But a soldier must do his duty."

"Have the Confederates possession of that ridge, General?"

"They have."

"And are our men going to retake it?"

"They're going to try."

Maynard swept his eye over the position.

"They *must* take it."

The general shot a quick glance at the degraded officer.

"You think it important?"

"The fate of this part of an army—it can't be called a whole one—depends upon it."

"You are right, Colonel. We must take that ridge, or before nightfall be flying over this field like the right and center; or what is worse, be captured. This is not the first time I have observed that your eye is made for war."

Maynard had become so engrossed that he did not hear; he almost forgot his chief's presence.

"I haven't a command to lead up that hill, but I have arms to carry a musket. I'll go in the ranks where I've been since the fight began," and he started in the direction of the Reserve.

"Stay, Colonel," called the general.

Maynard turned and walked back to where the general was standing. He waited for him to speak further; but he did not. Minutes passed, while Maynard watched the absorbed commander, who in turn was watching the line forming below.

"Colonel Maynard," he said at last, "do you see that regiment down there? It seems to be short of officers. So far as I can judge from its movements no one is in command. I shall have to make an infantry-man of you, though you are of the cavalry. Go and lead that regiment in the attack about to be made on the ridge."

"But, general——"

"There is no time for buts, sir."

"I am a civilian, with no right to command."

"You are in the service till the finding of the court that condemned you has been approved." Then to an aide, who rode up at the moment: "Captain, go with Colonel Maynard and place him in command of that regiment," pointing. "And let there be no mistake. If the order is questioned say that the exigencies of a critical moment demand that it be obeyed."

Maynard tried to speak the grateful words that rose to his lips, but either he could not, or he saw that the general's eye had caught a new point of danger, and was absorbed in it. Mounting Madge he rode away with the staff officer.

There was wonder on the faces of the men who saw a new commander in the uniform of a private of cavalry put temporarily in place to lead them. For a moment a murmur ran along the line, but some one recognized him—one who knew his mettle—and word was passed: "It's the cavalryman, Colonel Maynard."

None cared, at that critical moment, for his recent trial, so long as there was one at their head who could lead them in what they all saw must be a desperate effort.

Amid the incessant thunders that burst everywhere around the line of that horse-shoe curve of battle is one place where there is no firing. It is at the ridge, where men are forming at its base for a desperate attempt, and on its top others are preparing to receive them with lead enough to teach them the futility of so presumptuous a move.

All is ready. The line is formed. Seventy-five hundred men are about to push toward the realms of death, and a larger proportion of them are to enter there. At the word ''forward!'' the skirmishers move out into the thicket that covers the side of the disputed ridge, followed by the regular battle line, all climbing the hill together.

Glance the eye along the line. There is the officer, his mind intent on keeping his men up to the trying work before them; the officer intent in keeping himself steady before the eyes of the line he leads. There are the faces in the ranks, most of them, if not all, stamped with a serious cast, a dread under control, with the thought of each that in a few minutes he may be lying, pierced by a bullet or maimed by a shell. A few there are whose remarkable physical nerve, or in whom a natural excitable temperament, gives them an appearance of exhilaration; but such are often the most depressed just before they are well in the fight.

While the line of blue climbs the side of the ridge, all is quiet above; a quiet that brings a suspense harder to bear than a scattering fire. It promises a tempest when it comes. And it comes soon. From a concealed line, near the top, suddenly there is a myriad of explosions. Every missile known to war is sent down to stagger that blue line. The first crop of human flesh lies under the reaper.

There was pandemonium on that hillside for forty

minutes.   It was an eventful fight for many a man, not
considering those who were laid low by missiles of war.
There were a few whose place it was to lead, in whom
a constitutional inability rendered it impossible for
them to face such a storm.   They were ordered back;
their places filled by those made of sterner stuff.
There were soldiers in the ranks who skulked, but their
officers drove them on.   The main force of that reserve
division of Union troops showed a united strength of
purpose, which, if it could be transferred to a different
field, a field of moral heroism, would make an army
of gods.

Mark Maynard climbed with the rest.   For a moment when that storm burst, the instincts of a human
being, acting upon him suddenly, made him recoil.   A
number of quick recollections flashed before him: his
position; the chance given him to redeem the past, the
consciousness that men looked to him for strength in
that trying moment.   They were all as nothing compared with one other; one which prevented any further
giving back.   It was not a desire for death; that was
too near.   It was not a desire to show prowess at a
moment when men were either quailing or making
records as heroes.   At that terrible moment there
came before him, a picture so sweet, so innocent, that
one may well wonder how it could have appeared amid
such frightful scenes.   It was the photograph of his
wife and boy.   With it flashed the thought: ''All for
them; for myself, nothing.''

Whether he needed this to nerve him to do his
duty, certain it is that from this moment he forgot
danger.   One idea absorbed his entire being; that

whether he lived or died word should go back to those he loved better than himself, that he was at least not among the flinchers. Once this idea possessed him, he was a machine—a cog moving three hundred wheels. He knew nothing of the deafening sounds; he was oblivious to bullets or shells. Like the picture of the Sistine Madonna, was ever present the gentle face and figure of a woman holding up a child. Mother and child, in the famous painting, have for centuries stood forth a divine light to lead the world from sin; mother and child, in the eyes of Mark Maynard, were a divine light to lead him out of the depths into which he had fallen by a violation of principle.

The time of probation was short, but not too short for Maynard's bearing to have its effect. Among the few who held the men together, during that brief struggle for the life of the army, he took an important part. The ridge was won, and one of the first regiments on it was that commanded by Colonel Mark Maynard.

The ridge was not only won; it was held. But who can depict the holding? It was by a repetition of struggles like the one that took it, only the gray attacked, while the blue defended. Eight times the Confederates charged and eight times they were driven back. Night came; there was no light whereby to make another. The ridge was in Union keeping; the Army of the Cumberland was saved.

Relinquishing his command Maynard rode through twenty-five hundred dead and wounded of the seventy-five hundred men who climbed the hillside a few hours before, to General Thomas' headquarters.

"Have you any further commands, General?" he asked.

"Ah, Colonel Maynard. Let me thank you, among others, for your work. You men over there have saved us. I want you to go back to the cavalry and command one of several forces intended to cover our retreat. We must get back to-night to a safer position."

"I await your orders, General."

"Colonel," added the general, turning upon him a kindly, approving eye, "there are a number to be rewarded for to-day's work; among them yourself. If we get safely out of this, I shall make a suitable acknowledgment of your services."

XXVII

THE battle of Chickamauga is over. The Army of the Cumberland has withdrawn to Chattanooga, safe for the present, at least, behind breastworks. Their enemies are looking down upon them from the heights that encircle the town, waiting for them to fall an easy prey through starvation. Colonel Maynard is awaiting the result of army red-tape in the matter of his court-martial. The papers in the case were lost in the rout of the right, and were forgotten in his efforts to save the left. At any rate, no one seemed to care anything about them. The ups and downs in military life are rapid, and since the eclat attending his gallant services on the ridge, his comrades were disposed to look upon his sacrifice of himself for another as rather a heroic act, after all, quite in accord with his peculiar personality.

One day—it was perhaps a week after the retreat of the Army of the Cumberland—Maynard was sitting in his tent with Jakey and the girl found on the battlefield. Jakey had turned up in due time and renewed his services with the deposed colonel. True, that colonel's position was somewhat anomalous. He was in no great need of an orderly, but was disposed to avail himself of Jakey's friendship. He had neither seen nor communicated with his wife, feeling a disin-

clination to do so until something definite should
occur to establish his future status with the army.
Jakey therefore continued to be the only friend "present for duty."

"You say," said Maynard to Jakey, on the occasion
mentioned, "that you left her at the house to which I
told you to take her, and took a hand in the fight."

"Reckon."

"Where did you get anything to fight with?"

"Dead sojer. Tuk his gun 'n cartridges."

"Upon my word! I wonder the enemy stood
against such a reinforcement."

"Wal, I shot one of 'em, anyway. We was tuk by
lots more 'n we 'uns, 'n was runnen. Suddent I
hearn a man say, ' Stop, thar, y' little Yankee rascal!'
I turned roun' 'n sor a ossifer on horseback. He
called on me fo' ter surrender, 'n I up en shot him."*

"You don't mean it?"

"Reckon."

"Then what did you do?"

"Wal, tother uns, they went on 'n I skedaddled."

"Well?"

"Then I went back t' the house 'n found Jennie,
'n by that time 't was gitten dark, 'n the army com-
menced t' retreat. We 'uns retreated with the rest on
em."

"On foot?"

"Yas, part o' the way. Jennie, she got tired, so we
sat down by ther road till some cavalry [Jakey had
learned not to call them critter companies] came along

---

* An incident similar to this occurred at Chickamauga. A boy
of twelve years shot a Confederate officer, and was made a sergeant.

after the infantry hed all passed. One on em said,
' Ef that haint Colonel Maynard's orderly.' ' 'N
with a little gal,' said another. Then the fust on em
tuk me on behind him 'n tother un tuk Jennie on
before him, 'n we 'uns all covered the retreat."

" A valuable acquisition to the rear-guard," observed Maynard, and he began to question the little
girl. He discovered that she was the daughter of a
farmer living on the battlefield, who had neglected to
remove his family till the last minute. Caught in the
midst of a fight, all became panicstricken, and the
child was separated from the rest.

While he was gaining this information an orderly
came to his tent and showed him a letter post-marked
County Cavan, Ireland, and addressed to the man who
had assisted in the escape of Caroline Fitz Hugh.
But there were features of the address which led
Maynard to doubt if it was not for some other Ratigan.

" Where did you get this ?" he asked.

" It came in with the mail. It's been lying un-
claimed for several days, as no one knows who it is
for. There was a Ratigan in the —th Cavalry, but
he is among the missing. The letter was taken to
the headquarters of that regiment, and Colonel
Burke suggested that you might know something
about the man."

" Ah, yes," said Maynard, sadly. " You can tell
Colonel Burke that I saw Ratigan killed. But this
reminds me," he added. " I must see if I can regain
his body." Then to the orderly : " I wish you would
say to Major Burke that if he will give me an escort
I'll go out under flag of truce and see if I can find out

anything about Corporal Ratigan, whom I saw fall from his horse in the enemy's lines. Ask him to make out a request for permission to send out the flag, forward it, and let me know the result."

The result was a permission to send out "the flag," and the next morning, after an early breakfast, Colonel Maynard, accompanied by Jakey and the little girl, whom Maynard hoped to restore to her parents, each mounted, and all attended by a lieutenant and twenty men, set out from Chattanooga toward Mission Ridge. They met the enemy's pickets at the base of the ridge, and were conducted to Rossville. Colonel Maynard at once requested that he might be accorded an interview with Colonel Fitz Hugh, if that officer survived the battle. A messenger was sent to summon him, and as he had some miles to go, "the flag" party dismounted, were taken into a house, where they awaited the officer's arrival. Every attention was shown them, and they were made as comfortable as possible. Two hours after the departure of the courier, Colonel Fitz Hugh rode up to the door.

There was always a certain embarrassment between these two men, which under the circumstances was quite natural, but which was heightened by the habitual dignity with which Fitz Hugh bore himself. There was much to force them apart, and much to draw them together, but it all resulted in constraint. Fitz Hugh lifted his hat to Maynard, then advanced, and put out his hand. Neither seemed to think of appropriate words of greeting, and there was a few moments of silence, which was broken by Maynard referring to his mission.

"Colonel," he said, "I am the bearer of a letter for Corporal Ratigan—though the superscription gives a different title than corporal—the man who assisted me on the mission which you doubtless well remember. I saw Ratigan fall from his horse and suppose that he is dead. Am I right?"

"No, sir. Corporal Ratigan lives. He was severely wounded by a shot from your men. He managed to keep his saddle till his work was accomplished, when he fainted through loss of blood. For a time his life hung in the balance. We now hope for his recovery."

"I am rejoiced to hear it. Perhaps this letter is for him. Will you attend to its delivery?"

"If you will ride with me to Ringold, where he lies, you can deliver it in person."

"That would indeed be a pleasure. Can you get permission to take me so far within your lines?"

"I can try."

"In that case I may look, by the way, for the home of this little girl. I rescued her from the battlefield, where she was lost."

A request was sent up to headquarters for permission to take Colonel Maynard and two children to Ringold and to visit the recent field of battle by the way. While the party were waiting for a reply Maynard was introduced to a number of Confederate officers, and the story getting round that he had saved the life of a Confederate emissary—the sister of Colonel Fitz Hugh—he soon found himself an object of interest. There was little disposition to inquire into the right or wrong of his act; the service was quite sufficient, and the deposed colonel was as highly

honored among the Confederates as he had been condemned by his comrades.

Permission came for Colonel Fitz Hugh to take the
party forward, leaving the escort at Rossville and taking Colonel Maynard's parole not to divulge anything
he might see to the Union commanders; a useless
provision, for there was nothing of importance by the
way for him to see.

It was a singular party that crisp October morning,
cantering down the Chattanooga and Lafayette road—
the recent bone of contention—toward the now deserted battlefield. Maynard and Fitz Hugh rode
together at the front. Then came Jakey and Jennie,
both mounted like the rest, while a troop of Confederate cavalry formed the escort. The two colonels
talked on everything except what was uppermost in
their minds. Fitz Hugh several times attempted to
guide the conversation upon Maynard's service to his
sister in order that he might make a proper acknowledgment, but Maynard, foreseeing his intention, always
made some remark by way of thwarting him.

" There are the heights from which you shelled the
reserve marching to our relief," said Maynard, glancing to the left.

" And here our men found themselves near this
coveted road, over which we are passing, when
the fog lifted on Sunday morning," replied the
other.

" Now we come to the 'horse-shoe' ridge. Let us
ride around its base. From what the little girl has
told me I fancy she lives on the road leading to
Reed's Bridge."

" My pop lives down thar," said the child, pointing to a cabin a mile below them.

Leaving the Chattanooga road they followed another leading around the ridge, soon striking a third leading to Reed's Bridge. When they came to the house pointed out by Jennie, a man was sitting on the fence —or one section of it which happened not to have been taken for fire-wood like the rest—whittling a stick. Catching sight of the child, as the party rode up, he went to her, and taking her in his arms, covered her with kisses. The mother, hearing the exclamations, rushed out and repeated the father's caresses.

The parents expressed as well as they were able, and in their humble way, their thanks to the rescuer of their child, and the party proceeded on their way.

" Good-by, Jennie," said her friend Jakey as he rode off.

" Good-by."

" Ef y'll write me a letter, I'll make y' a doll outen a corn-cob. I know how ter make 'm."

" I can't write."

" Wal, I'll do 't anyhow. Yer a purty nice young 'un ef y' air only a gal."

Riding over Reed's Bridge the party passed through the gap in the ridge beyond, and descending the east slope, soon struck a road leading to Ringold. They rode into the town about noon, and soon drew rein before the house where Corporal Ratigan lay wounded. Fitz Hugh and Maynard dismounted and entered together, Jakey bringing up the rear. In the hallway, her eyes large with astonishment at seeing her brother in company with Colonel Maynard, stood Caroline Fitz Hugh.

If the brother had failed in expressing his thanks to Maynard the sister succeeded, but not by words. She grasped Maynard's hand, when suddenly, for the first time since her escape, a full realizing sense of the terrible end she had so narrowly escaped swept over her. She was looking her gratitude, with all the intensity of her expressive eyes, when her formal brother said :

" Caroline, Colonel Maynard suffered disgrace on your account. It is proper you should know how much we owe him."

This information was too much for even the strong nature of so resolute a woman. She burst into a passionate flood of tears.

" For the first time since it occurred," said Maynard gently, " I am satisfied with my act. What is the opinion of men to me beside the consciousness of having served so admirable a woman."

Fitz Hugh threw open a door near by, and led the way through it into a room where Corporal Ratigan, his ruddy locks contrasting with his pale face and the whiteness of his pillow, looked at them with the same astonishment as Miss Fitz Hugh.

" Why, Colonel," he exclaimed, " are ye a prisoner ? "

" No. I came by the courtesy of Colonel Fitz Hugh to deliver this letter, which I think is for you. Are you Hugh Ratigan ? "

" Oi am."

" Sir Hugh Ratigan ? "

" No ; me father was Sir Thomas Ratigan, of County Cavan, Ireland."

" Perhaps there have been changes," and Maynard handed him the letter.

The corporal took it and looked first at the black seal, and then at the handwriting, which he recognized at once as his mother's, and read, " To Sir Hugh Ratigan, United States Army, Tennessee, U. S. A."

" Me brother is dead," he said solemnly, and then tore open the envelope.

The letter advised him, as he supposed, of the death of his older brother, and as the title and estates of the family descended to him, he was adjured to go home and attend to his affairs.

" Is it as we supposed ? " asked Maynard.

" It is. Oi'm Sir Hugh true enough ; me brother, God rest 'em, is gone."

" We sympathize with you at your brother's death, and rejoice with you at your own inheritance," said Fitz Hugh.

All in turn took the corporal by the hand.

" You must go home at once," said Maynard.

" How will Oi go home when Oi'm enlisted for three years or during the war ? "

" We'll have to get you out of that," said Maynard. " Your duties are more important in Ireland, than as a corporal in our service. We have more than a plenty of men."

" I wish we could say the same," observed Colonel Fitz Hugh.

The visiting party, expecting to return that afternoon, had but little time to converse upon anything except, Sir Hugh Ratigan's future, and this they considered fully. It was arranged that as soon as the baronet should be able to travel he was to go through the lines, apply for a discharge and go to Ireland. Colonel Fitz Hugh anticipated no difficulty in securing his permission to depart from the Confederacy, and as he was a British subject of rank it was not expected that he would be held to a strict accountability for the part he had taken in the escape of Caroline Fitz Hugh ; especially as that act had been largely lost sight of in an event of greater moment—the battle of Chickamauga. These matters once settled the party moved toward the door, where adieus were spoken ; then mounted and rode away.

XXVIII.

THE CHOICE OF A POST.

CAROLINE FITZ HUGH had watched over Corporal Ratigan every day since his wounding, and by careful nursing had doubtless saved his life. It was not for the corporal to fall in love with his nurse, for he had loved her ever since the day he first met her. When the visiting party had left the house she went back to her charge, and after a few words of sympathy at the loss of his brother, putting out her hand frankly, and with a smile :

" Arise, Sir Hugh," she said. " You have been on your back long enough. You must get used to sitting up and prepare to go to Ireland and to administer your estate."

" Darlin'," he said, looking up at her wistfully.

" It's time you were breaking yourself of calling me that ; you must forget the Confederate ' telegraph worker,' go home and marry one of the daughters of the neighboring gentry and settle down to become ' a fine old Irish gentleman, one of the rare old stock.' "

" That's a fine picture ye'r maken for me ; and what'll ye be doing meantime ? "

" Working for my country."

" And haven't ye promised ye would do no more telegraph working ? "

' Oh, that duty has come to an abrupt termination. I shall never attempt it again. How could I, after the sacrifice you and Colonel Maynard have made for me ; besides, if seen within the Federal lines I should be recognized, and I would then deserve my fate."

" And what d'ye mean by worken for ye'r country? What dy'e call ye'r country? "

" The South ; the Confederate States of America."

" It'll not be separated from the rest."

" Do you really think that Ra— I mean Sir Hugh ? "

" I do."

" Do you doubt the bravery, the resolution of our men ? " she flushed, almost angrily.

" Tut, darlin' ; that has nothing to do with it. Ye' haven't more than a third the people of ye'r enemy, and of that third a third are black and no use to ye'— only an encumbrance. Ye'r seaports are blockaded and ye' have no manufactures. Ye'r grain-raising territory is swept by enemies and it is useless for ye' to plant crops since the enemy is as likely to gather them as ye'rselves. Besides all this ye'r principles are badly mixed ; ye' say ye'r fighting for ye'r independence, ye'r liberty ; and the reason for that is that ye' may more firmly fasten the yoke on the black."

" Rats," she said earnestly, " if you were a Yankee I would not listen to you a moment. But as a native of another land I confess your words impress me. Indeed in my heart of hearts I have often thought as you think ; not about our lack of resources and all that, but I doubt the success of a cause in which our inheritance of negro slavery forms so large a part."

" Ye'd better abandon it."

" Never, so long as it is a cause ; so long as my brothers continue the struggle I will be with them."

" Then so long as the Union Army is fighten' ye' Oi'll be in its ranks."

" You'll do no such thing. You will go home, where your presence is more needed ; to your mother, to your tenants. Ireland needs all her land-owners, such as you, at home. That is your country ; you have no interest here."

" And the United States is your country ; you have no other."

" Rats ! "

" Darlin'."

There was a silence between them for some moments. Ratigan laid his hand on hers while she was looking, with a pained expression, out of the window. In her eyes was a far look. Her companion had strengthened certain doubts which had at times come up to trouble her, as to the ultimate success, the real motives which underlay her cause ; and with her intense, devoted nature, had led her to feel that all this vast effort put forth by her people might in the end avail nothing, or would only, if successful, per-petuate a wrong. Her lover saw her troubled expres-sion. He did not attempt to comfort her by recalling what he had said : he pushed on further.

" Darlin," he said. " Ye're right when ye say Oi'm needed in Oirland. Go with me, darlin'. Be me wife. Let all this intense effort, this sacrifice ye're putting into a cause, which I foresee is doomed, be given to me tenants. The estate is a large one, and there are hundreds of people for ye to befriend. There ye can work to a purpose. There ye'r efforts in behalf of a really down-trodden people will be for good."

"And leave my brothers in the midst of this horrid struggle? I will stay here till the last gun is fired, till the last blow of the hammer has riveted our chains."

"Chains?"

"Yes, chains. Will they not govern us, if they conquer us, as subject provinces?"

"Republicans can't hold subject provinces, darlin'. They'd have to become a monarchy to do that, and go back a hundred years."

"Rats," she exclaimed, in admiration of the depth of his reasoning, the plain, common-sense way he had of putting the case. "You must go back and stand for parliament; you're a natural statesman."

"Never."

"Why never?"

"The chains."

His hand was on hers; and an arm was stealing around her waist, as she stood beside him. There was a certain breaking, a yielding in her words, which he had never noticed there before, as she said:

"What chains, Rats?"

"The real chains ye flung around me when ye stood in yer old rattlen buggy and chaffed me, the chains that were tightened when I captured ye, the chains that have held me to ye ever since, that bind me to ye now, that will keep me in America so long as you are in America."

There was a silence in which her face showed plainly she was turning over what he had said in her mind. But it did not last long. She was used to thinking quickly.

"Rats," she said, "granting all you have said is true : granting that we are embarked in an error ; I can never leave our people, right or wrong, until the struggle is ended one way or the other."

"I can understand ye'r feelings, but it is wrong to indulge them."

"Why so ? " Again the troubled look.

"By working in the cause of error, error is fostered. If ye think ye'r field lies here, choose the right cause ; devote ye'rself to the ignorant black ; teach him ; encourage him ; befriend him ; help him. Work upon your people with all the magnetic influence you possess to make him a free man instead of a chattel."

" Become an abolitionist? " She seemed thunderstruck at the audacity of the proposition.

" We're all abolitionists on the other side of the ocean. Ye'r two hundred years behind the age."

There was another pause, while Miss Fitz Hugh thought. Born and bred in the South, she had never seen except with Southern eyes. Here was a man who was giving her views never before open to her. She had a mind capable of grasping them, and saw the strength, the solid sense, beneath them when properly presented.

"Darlin'," the young baronet added, by way of

closing the argument, "the world moves on quickly. If ye'r people succeed in this war, in less than a quarter of a century ye'll either free ye'r slaves or be a blot on the face of the earth."

"Oh, Rats," she exclaimed, "why did I ever meet you? You've sapped the strength I possessed for my work. I can never again do my duty as I have done it thus far."

"Darlin'," he said, drawing her nearer to him, "Oi'll replace what Oi've taken. Oi'll give ye other duties ; the duties that belong to the mistress of a fine estate, the duties of a woman of high degree in a country where birth is respected far more than here. With your vigor, your strong impulses——"

"Guided by your more steady light."

"Ye may become one of the most influential women in the three kingdoms."

In her eyes came that humorous twinkle he had once seen before, when she stood in her buggy in the road up in Tennessee and tantalized him for his stupidity in having been duped by her.

"It *would* be nice to be——"

"To be what, darlin'?"

"Lady Rats," and she hid her blushes in the pillow on which his head rested.

XXIX.

PUNISHMENT AND REWARD.

THE sun setting over Lookout Mountain shone directly in the faces of Maynard and his party as, returning from Ringold, they rode into Chattanooga. It was a glorious October evening, and the heights towering above them, covered by unseen Confederates, reposed about the town like huge lions watching a wounded animal, confident that at last it must fall into their power.

Dismounting before his tent, Maynard entered it, and there found a letter from his wife. She begged him to come to her if it were possible, and if not, to write to her. He read and re-read the letter again and again, and then made an attempt at a reply. After writing half a dozen, all of which he tore up, he abandoned the task in despair. His position was too uncertain. The sentence of the court-martial hung over him like a sullen cloud. What could he say to her to comfort her ? He well knew that the only comforting she needed was to know that he was not miserable ; and of that he could not assure her.

And so matters hung for a week. Having no duties to perform the time passed all the more slowly. The Confederates were sending occasional shells from Lookout Mountain, and as they were harmless the reports were something of a relief to Maynard, breaking the monotony of the silence. He spent much of the time thinking of what he would do in case the sentence of the court were approved and carried into effect. He formed many plans, which were all abandoned. At last he settled down to the resolve that he would go to the army in the East, enlist under an assumed name ; and await the coming of some missile to end his career, as he had intended at Chickamauga.

One morning an orderly rode up to him and handed him an order to report in person at General Thomas' headquarters. Calling for his horse and for his own orderly, Jakey, to follow, he mounted, and in a feverish mood darted away to obey the order.

What did the summons mean ? Something definite in his affairs had come about ; that he felt reasonably sure of. Perhaps the papers of the court in his case had been found. Perhaps they had been made out in duplicate. The latter supposition was the most likely. His offense could not be ignored : indeed, he could not afford to have it ignored. The sentence must be either set aside or carried into effect. Dismissal would be far more desirable than living in suspense.

All these matters rushed through his mind while he rode to respond to the summons. The nearer he drew to headquarters, the less hopeful he became. After all, was it not absurd to expect anything except that new papers had been made, the sentence for-warded "approved," and he was now to be informed that he was no longer in the army. General Thomas could do much for him, but there was not a general in the army who had a higher sense of a soldier's obligations than he. How was it possible that so great a leader, so rigid a disciplinarian, one with such high conceptions, could do aught in his case but approve the sentence! And now he was sending for him to inform him of his degradation.

Following this reasoning, by the time he arrived at headquarters his expectations were at the lowest ebb. He dismounted, and so preoccupied was he that he left his horse standing without fastening her; but Jakey rode forward and seized the rein. Maynard gave his name to an orderly, and in a few minutes stood before the man whose very presence was quite sufficient to strike terror into the heart of a delinquent.

But the first face on which Maynard's eyes rested was not that of the general. Another was there to greet him; one who, he knew, whether he were honored or disgraced, would never love him the less. It was his wife. The thought flashed through his brain: "She is here to comfort me when the blow falls." He wanted to fly to her embrace. The impulse was checked. He saw that she burned to fly to him; but she, too, restrained herself; for there, between them, towered the figure of the general. Maynard gave him a quick glance, but could discover nothing in his countenance to indicate what his fate would be. These glances, these surmises, lasted but for a moment, for the general spoke:

"I have sent for you to inform you of your status in the army."

Maynard bowed his head and waited.

"The offense for which you were tried," the gen-

eral spoke slowly and impressively, " was too grievous
to be overlooked.   It would have pleased me in the
case of so brave a man to set it aside ; but such a
course would have condoned that which, if it should
go unpunished, would strike at the very foundation of
military discipline.   In liberating a spy, entrusted to
your care, you violated a sacred trust, and assumed
an authority such as is not accorded to any one, save
the President of the United States."

Maynard did not raise his eyes from the ground.
He knew what was coming, and a shiver passed over
him.

" A new set of papers were prepared and sent to
me.   I forwarded them——"

Maynard's eyes were almost starting from their
sockets.

" With my approval."

" O General ! " gasped the stricken man, catching
at the tent-pole for a support.   Laura could with
difficulty keep her seat, so eager was she to fly to him.

" They have also been approved by the President,
and you have been dismissed from the service of the
United States, with forfeiture of all pay and emoluments."

Maynard tried to speak.   He wished to say that
he could not complain of the sentence—that, considering the offense, it was merciful—but his tongue
would not obey him.

" So much for your punishment," the general went
on, after a slight pause.   " There are other matters,
however, to be considered.   These are your youth,
the circumstances under which you were placed, the

voluntary sacrifice of yourself made to save another, and in obedience to your own interpretation of your duty in repaying a sacred obligation. While these considerations do not destroy the act or its pernicious effect as an example, they show conclusively that it did not spring from base motives, but rather in obedience to a strong sense of honor, which a soldier should hold in highest esteem."

When the general began to speak of these palliating circumstances Maynard did not hear him. As he proceeded, however, his attention was arrested.

"Furthermore, there are your brilliant services, both as a scout, and, more recently, in the battle through which we have just passed. I have taken pains to learn of your services in the ranks on the nineteenth of September, and was myself a witness to your gallantry on the ridge on the twentieth. I cannot find it in my heart to fail in my acknowledgments to any man, however he may have erred, who engaged in that desperate struggle, which was a turning point in our fortune, and may be said to have saved us all from rout or capture. Besides, for more than a year I have watched your career with interest. I am sure that you are possessed of undoubted military talents—perhaps of a high order. I believe it to be true wisdom on the part of the government to retain those talents for the country. Therefore, in the interest of the United States, and for gallant and meritorious conduct at the battle of Chickamauga, I have suggested your name to the President for the appointment of Brigadier-General of Volunteers. A batch of such appointments, including yours, was yesterday sent to the Senate, and I have a telegram announcing that they were all confirmed."

Suddenly it seemed as if there had been a loosening of invisible cords that had been holding husband and wife apart. In the fraction of a second they were locked in each other's arms. Tears, the usual mode of expression of deep feeling in woman, did not come, only to the wife. Yet in a measure the sexes were reversed. Laura was more smiles than tears ; Maynard only wept.

Soon remembering in whose presence he stood, Maynard disengaged himself. Turning to General Thomas :

"General," he said, in a broken voice, " I cannot— thanks are nothing—time must show how well I appreciate what you have done. Is there another man in the army who could afford to take so enlarged a view in such a case ? Is there one with so farseeing an eye, so keen a sense of a soldier's duty, tempered with so kind a heart ? "

Maynard paused for a moment ; then, with a sudden burst of enthusiasm :

" But who shall reward the man who on that terrible day held together the Army of the Cumberland ? Can the President bestow an adequate rank ? Would the title of full ' General ' avail ? No ! It is for the people to reward you with a title, not given by an individual, but by the common consent of vast masses—not only for a day, but so long as there shall be a history of this war—the ROCK OF CHICKAMAUGA,"

XXX.

LAURA MAYNARD, after a long period of solicitude as to her husband,—detained at home by a
temporary illness of her child,—had at last found it
possible to go and seek him. She had arrived on the
morning of the news of his appointment, and at once
sought General Thomas's headquarters. There she
had been informed of the status, and a messenger was
at once sent for her husband.

Leaving the tent, where Maynard had first been
plunged in despair only to be elevated to a condition
of mind bordering on ecstasy, the two sought a hotel
where Laura could be made comfortable till the next
day, and there passed the time in going over the period
since they had parted, and rejoicing at the outcome
of the singular complications which Fate had been
pleased to bring down upon the husband.

But all meetings must have an end, and at last the
husband departing, rode to his tent. There he found
a messenger waiting for him.

"'Flag of truce' wants to see you on the picket
line, sir."

Without dismounting, the newly created general
rode in the direction of Mission Ridge and met "the
flag" at its base. There stood a mounted party of
Confederates, one of them bearing a white flag, headed

by an officer—a son of the South who spoke every
word as though it were of momentous importance,
never omitting the word "sir."

" Are you Colonel Maynard, sir ? "

" I am, or at least I was.   I hardly know what I am
just now.   I should not be surprised to be informed that
I was to command all the armies of the United States."

The officer looked puzzled.

" I am the bearer, sir, of a message from Corporal
Sir Hugh Ratigan.   He is to be married at seven
o'clock this evening at General Bragg's headquarters
on Mission Ridge."

" The devil he is ! "

" That is his intention, sir ; he desires your presence."

" Whom does he marry ? "

" Miss Caroline Fitz Hugh."

" I have been more surprised at other announce-
ments, I confess.   I don't wonder he invites me to
his wedding, since I helped him to a wife."

" Shall I transmit your acceptance of the invitation,
sir ? "

" On one condition."

" Please name it, sir."

" I fear it will be unacceptable to Colonel Fitz
Hugh, who will doubtless be the host or one of the
hosts.   He will not likely yield in a matter of etiquette
which I must insist on."

" Colonel Fitz Hugh cannot be present, sir.   He is
now in your rear with our cavalry completing the starvation of your army in Chattanooga, by destroying
your lines of supply."

"H'm. I was not aware of any hunger in our ranks ; indeed, my request is, knowing that your own larder in the Confederacy is not exactly abundant— that the horn of plenty is not burying you like Herculaneum under the ashes of Vesuvius—that the blockade——"

"The blockade is not effective, sir," interrupted the officer, stiffly.

"Has somewhat reduced your wine cellars, my condition is, I say, that I may be permitted to bring half a dozen cases of champagne for the wedding feast."

"I assure you, sir, that it is not necessary. We are getting cargoes of wine from Havre by a regular line of steamers. It is your own mess tables at Chattanooga that are doubtless bereft of beverages, owing to the fact that our General Wheeler is circus-riding in Tennessee, leaving no road or railroad open to you."

"Do you consent that I shall bring the wine ? "

"I do, sir, but shall claim for the host, a general officer related to the bride, the privilege of supplying an equal number of cases."

"Agreed. I will meet you here at six o'clock this evening, when you can conduct me and my party to the place where the ceremony is to take place. You may say, if you please, that I shall consider the invitation extended to my wife, whom I will bring with me."

"We shall feel highly honored, sir, at Mrs. Maynard's presence. Am I to infer, sir, that your wife has been able to reach you over the burnt bridges and trestlework in your rear ? "

"She has found no difficulty whatever in joining me,"

Maynard failed to add that Laura had only come a few miles to meet him.

" Good day, sir," said the officer, raising his hat. " I shall expect you at six."

" Good day ; I will be on time."

And each rode away in the direction of their respective camps.

Maynard's offer of the wine had come about in this wise : Jakey, during the previous week, had been investigating such empty houses as he could find in Chattanooga and had loaded himself down with knick-knacks, such as china ornaments, pictures, crockery, cutlery, including even daguerreotypes. On one occasion he thought he had discovered a box of muskets. This he reported to Colonel Maynard, whom he persuaded to go with him to a cellar, near by, and make a search for concealed arms. The muskets were found, besides half a dozen cases of champagne, which had doubtless been there since the beginning of the war.

Upon leaving the picket line, Maynard rode to the house where he had seen the wine, and secured it for the evening, placing a guard over it. Then he went to the hotel and bade Laura get ready to attend a wedding.

There was consternation in the Confederate camp when the officer returned with the information that the Yankee had tried to bluff him by claiming the privilege of bringing champagne with him, and that he had claimed the right for the hosts to furnish an equal amount. The telegraph was set in motion at once, directing search to be made in all the neighboring towns for the required beverage. Dalton, Cleveland, and other points were ransacked without success. About two o'clock in the afternoon, as despair was settling on the Confederates, a telegram was received that some champagne had been found in Atlanta. The authorities there were directed to send it by special locomotive, marking it "*Ammunition. Forward with dispatch.*"

At seven o'clock Maynard, accompanied by Laura, and Jakey who was always with him, besides a wagon containing the cases of wine, were at the appointed place on the picket line, where they were met by the Confederate "flag." Transferring the wine to the backs of pack-mules, all started up the side of Mission Ridge to General Bragg's headquarters.

As they approached the crest a body of Confederate officers, a gay cavalcade in gray and gold lace, rode out to meet them. They were received by the relative of the bride—an uncle—referred to by the officer who brought the invitation. He was an elderly man, of a dignified and serious mien. The party were conducted to a large marquee set up for the wedding feast. There they alighted and the wine was unloaded and carried inside.

A few minutes before seven o'clock the guests were conducted to a knoll, on the summit of which had been erected a canopy of flowers, and where stood a group of Confederates of high rank. On the eastern horizon stood the full moon ; below to the east was the battlefield of Chickamauga ; to the west, the Army of the Cumberland, besieged in Chattanooga, on half rations. As the guests approached, the groom still in his uniform of a corporal, attended by his best man—a Confederate non-commissioned officer of good family, detailed for the occasion, was seen moving from the north toward the knoll. At the same moment the bride—attired in a dress made of a coarse white stuff, manufactured in the Confederacy, and attended by several bridesmaids, who had come from a distance to officiate, approached from the south. The two met on the knoll under the canopy. An officer of high rank, who was also a bishop in the Church, stepped forward, and Corporal Sir Hugh Ratigan and Caroline Fitz Hugh were made one. The only lamp to light the nuptials was the round moon in the east. The only canopy, save that composed of flowers, was the broad heavens above, in which the stars had only just appeared for the night. The only wedding bells were occasional booms from guns on Lookout Mountain.

The ceremony over, the bride and groom repaired to the marquee, lighted with candles, where they took position to receive the congratulations of the company. All gave way to Colonel and Mrs. Maynard, who offered theirs first.

"We must give you up, I suppose," said Laura to the bride, " just as we would like to know you better. You go abroad, I suppose."

" No, I remain here."

" But Sir Hugh will go?"

"Yes, as soon as he can get his discharge. He goes to Virginia, from here, where he will pass through the lines to Washington, and will put his case in the hands of the British Minister. He anticipates no trouble in getting a discharge from the Federal Army, and hopes to sail within a month for Ireland."

" And you?" asked Laura, in some surprise that the bride could bear to part so soon with her husband.

" I ? I remain with my people till the last gun has been fired. We have argued that question, and such is my decision."

" Moi decisions," observed the groom, " are a thing of the past."

Leaving the newly married pair, Colonel Maynard approached the master of ceremonies, the bride's uncle.

" General," he said, " I esteem it a privilege that you have waived your right to furnish all the viands for the wedding feast, and have permitted me to contribute. " There," pointing to the boxes of wine he had brought, " are six cases of champagne, which I beg you to accept as a contribution from the army in Chattanooga."

At a signal from the officer addressed, a negro removed a blanket covering a dozen boxes in a corner of the tent, which had come a hundred miles and had not been in position ten minutes.

" I see your six cases, General, and go you six cases better."

" Having no further resources at hand," said Maynard, bowing, " I retire from the game."

" Hannibal," said the Confederate, " you may advance the force in the first box to a position in line on the table."

" Yes, sah," said the person addressed. And seizing a sabre standing in the corner, he unsheathed it with a flourish and pried open a box of the wine. In a moment a dozen bottles were standing on the table, like a platoon of soldiers.

"Now, Hannibal, you may fire the opening shot."

Hannibal broke the wires ; and a "pop," a far more welcome sound than those that had been so recently and frequently heard by all present, announced that the feast was not only set but begun.

"I must apologize for our glassware," said the master of ceremonies, "our champagne glasses were all shattered by the concussions at Chickamauga."

And well he might. The array consisted of tin cups, wooden cups, glass cups, and tumblers, all either cracked, broken, or dinted. And as a circle was formed to pledge the bride and groom, one Confederate screened himself behind his comrades to avoid being seen drinking from a gourd.

When the contents of eighteen cases—a regiment of "dead soldiers"—lay on the table, the guests prepared to depart. The last words had been spoken by General and Mrs. Maynard, and by Sir Hugh and Lady Ratigan. Jakey, who had thus far wandered about unobserved, though not unobserving, stepped up to the bride and groom. Though he had not tasted the wine, his eyes glistened with intoxication at the union of his two friends, whose attachment he had noticed from the first.

"Miss Baggs, air you'uns 'n Sir Rats goen ter ride roun' Tennessee some more in the Chicken Coop?"

There was a burst of laughter from the party, and Lady Ratigan, with a blush, informed Jakey that the Chicken Coop was broken in pieces.

"I didn't know nuthin' 'bout that. Reckon Sir Rats 'd find 't handy in Ireland. 'T's kind o' funny you 'uns starten out way up by the mountings, 'n fetchen up down hyar, nigh onter th' Georgy line." And Jakey surprised the company by giving the only " ha, ha," that had to this moment ever been heard to issue from his serious lips.

As the guests descended the side of the mountain, a cheer was heard in the direction of Chattanooga. They stopped and listened. A man rode out from the Union picket line to meet them.

" What's that cheering ? " asked General Maynard.

" Ole Pap's in command of the Army of the Cumberland."

THE END.

A MODERN KNIGHT.

ORMSBY MACKNIGHT MITCHEL,

ASTRONOMER AND GENERAL.

A Biographical Narrative by his Son, F. A. MITCHEL,
With Steel Portrait. Crown 8vo, gilt top, $2.00.

www.ingramcontent.com/pod-product-compliance
Lightning Source LLC
Chambersburg PA
CBHW020844020726
47497CB00005B/1250

* 9 7 8 3 3 3 7 3 4 7 9 0 1 *